喚醒你的英文語感！

Get a Feel for English !

喚醒你的英文語感 ！

Get a Feel for English !

BIZ English

搞定

總編審⊙王復國
作　者⊙Brian Foden

出差 英文

Biz Trip

溝通，往往是海外出差最大的壓力來源。一旦克服語言隔閡，就能回復搜尋資訊的本能，讓異地形同在地，出差任務圓滿達成。

16個出差最常見情境

36個擬真對話範例

256個出差任務達成好用句

240個異地溝通無礙加分詞彙

貝塔語言出版
Beta Multimedia Publishing

附1片實戰MP3

Preface

There is a very famous saying that goes, "No man is an island." It means that people are very dependent on others—they are not isolated. One person's actions influence another's. In today's interconnected world, I think I'd like to update that expression to read, "No country is an island." Of course, places such as Taiwan are indeed geographically islands. But with increased globalization, improved telecommunications, and the Internet, Taiwan is not just an isolated part of the Asian economy. Regional politics aside, it is very much a member of the "global village" and the world economy.

It is my hope that the phrases and vocabulary in this book will serve as a useful resource for you as you do business—and especially make business trips—on the stage of global commerce. There are chapters on contacting suppliers and clients, making travel arrangements, dealing with customs officials, giving presentations, socializing, and attending trade shows. In addition to being a book you can study at home, it is a guide you can take with you on trips abroad to English-speaking countries.

As a learning resource, the book provides you with 256 "Need-to-Know" phrases that will come in handy when you want to talk about specific issues and make various arrangements. You will also find 128 "Nice-to-Know" phrases that target other challenges of any business trip. The "Show Time" sections show you how the expressions can be used naturally in context. And to help you reinforce your learning and remember the vocabulary and phrases, there is an exercise section at the end of each chapter.

Lastly, I wish you all the best and much success in your journey of learning. Acquiring fluency and expertise in any language is difficult and requires good study habits and plenty of sustained motivation. It is a long, and sometimes frustrating process, but the more effort you put into it, the greater the results will be. Don't be disappointed by how long it takes and the mistakes you make, just keep your eye on the progress you achieve, no matter how slow it may be. Remember, as the proverb goes, "Rome wasn't built in a day."

Yours truly,

Brian Foden

Hsintien August 2007

作者序

　　有句眾所皆知的諺語是這麼說的：「無人是孤島。」這句話的意思是：人們彼此相互依賴——每個人都不是孤立的。一個人的行為會影響另一個人的行為。在現今互相緊密連結的世界裡，我想把那個說法更新為：「沒有國家是孤島。」當然，像台灣這樣的地方在地理上的確是獨立的島嶼。可是，隨著全球化、電訊傳播的改良和網路的誕生，台灣不只是亞洲經濟體裡一個孤立的部份。把區域的政治擺一邊，台灣毫無疑問是「地球村」與世界經濟體的一員。

　　當你在全球商務的舞台上大展身手——特別是出差時，我希望本書的片語和字彙能作為你有用的資源。書中章節包括了如何聯絡供應商與客戶、安排商務旅行、與海關人員交手、做簡報、社交以及參加商展等。本書除可供在家自修之外，也是你到英語系國家出差時能隨身攜帶的指南。

　　做為學習的資源，本書提供你256個「Biz必通句型」，當你想談某些特定的議題以及做各式各樣的安排時，這些句型就能隨時派上用場。你也會讀到128個「Biz加分句型」，這部份則是針對商務旅行的其他挑戰而設計。「實戰會話」的部份教你如何在情境中自然地運用這些詞語。為了幫助你強化學習並且牢記單字與片語，在每章章尾都有一個練習的部份。

　　最後，我要祝讀者在學習的過程中一切順利。要能夠流暢地運用並專精任何一個語言皆非易事。你需要的是良好的讀書習慣，以及充分且持續不懈的努力。這是個長久而且時而充滿挫折感和犯錯的過程，可是你投注的心力愈大，成果也會更出色。不要因為耗時甚久而氣餒。不論你的進步速度有多緩慢，應該注意的是你學到了什麼。記住，俗話說得好：「羅馬不是一天造成的。」

布萊恩・佛登敬上

新店

2007年八月

CONTENTS

第二部份 Section Two
行程相關用語 Travel-related English

第 五 章　啓程和抵達 Departure and Arrival

第 六 章　搭計程車和其他交通工具
Taking Taxis and Other Transportation

第 九 章　處理特殊情況 Dealing with Special Situations

第三部份 Section Three
洽談生意 Doing Business

第 十 章　高效率使用電話 Using the Telephone Effectively

Section One

行前準備要點
Pre-trip Preparation

From:	Jason Roth
To:	Mel Barnes; Daphne Chiang; Tony Potter; Cindy Kent
Subject:	Biz Trip Planning Meeting

Dear Friends,

As you know, we have to decide on a location for our convention in November. There is a lot of planning involved, so I suggest we get started soon. I'd like to have a videoconference call this month. Please tell me when you are available during the next few weeks.

Best regards,
Jason

親愛的朋友們：

如你們所知，我們需要為十一月的大會決定地點。因為牽涉到諸多的籌備計劃，所以我建議我們盡快開始。這個月我想要辦一場視訊會議。請告訴我，你們在接下來的幾個星期裡何時會有空。

傑森敬上

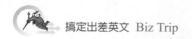
1 Biz 必通句型 Need-to-Know Phrases

1.1 ▶▶ 詢問問題 Questions to Ask

 track 02

---

❶ **What are the costs involved in (Ving)?**

（做……）需要哪些花費？

例 What are the costs involved in <u>holding</u> our <u>convention</u> in Los Angeles?

我們在洛杉磯舉行會議需要哪些花費？

---

❷ **What <u>factors</u> do we need to consider when (Ving)?**

當我們（做……）時，需要考量哪些因素？

例 What factors do we need to consider when choosing a location?

我們選擇地點時，需要考量哪些因素？

---

❸ **Is (place) conveniently <u>located</u>?**

（地方）的地點方便嗎？

例 Is the hotel conveniently located?

那家旅館的地點方便嗎？

---

❹ **Is (sth.) in a central location?**

（某事物）位於中心位置嗎？

例 Is the convention center in a central location?

那個會議中心位於中心位置嗎？

Ⓦord List

....

hold [hold] *v.* 舉行

convention [kən`vɛnʃən] *n.* 集會、會議

factor [`fæktɚ] *n.* 因素

locate [lo`ket] *v.* 使……坐落於（用被動式）

❺ What is the <u>transportation</u> system like in (place)?

（地方）的交通運輸系統如何？

例 What is the transportation system like in Bangkok?

曼谷的交通運輸系統如何？

❻ What are the <u>facilities</u> like in (place)?

（地方）的設施如何？

例 What are the facilities like in the downtown area?

市區的設施如何？

❼ Is (place) safe?

（地方）治安好嗎？

例 Is Boston safe?

波士頓治安好嗎？

❽ What's the (weather/climate) like in (place)?

（地方）的（天氣／氣候）如何？

例 What's the weather like in Vancouver this time of year?

每年這時候溫哥華的天氣如何？

ord List ·

transportation [ˌtrænspəˋteʃən] *n.* 運輸；交通工具

facilities [fəˋsɪlətɪz] *n.*（複數形）設施

1.2 ▸▸ 同意或反對某項決定 Agreeing or Disagreeing with a Choice

❶ I think (place) is <u>ideal</u>（for sth.）.
我認為在（地方）做（某事）很理想。
例 I think Singapore is ideal for our <u>annual</u> meeting.
　　我認為在新加坡舉行我們的年度會議很理想。

❷ I believe (place) is a great choice to (do sth.).
我相信在（地方）（做某事）是很棒的選擇。
例 I believe London is a great choice to hold our trade show.
　　我相信在倫敦辦我們的商展是很棒的選擇。

❸ (Place) is a good location because (reason).
（地方）是個好地點，因為（理由）。
例 Yes, Chicago is a good location because the prices are <u>reasonable</u>.
　　是的，芝加哥是個好地點，因為價格公道。

❹ (Place) is quite (adj.).
（地方）相當的（形容詞）。
例 In my opinion, the Royal Hotel is quite <u>suitable</u>.
　　依我看，皇家飯店相當合適。

Word List

ideal [aɪˋdiəl] *adj.* 理想的
annual [ˋænjʊəl] *adj.* 年度的
reasonable [ˋriznəbl] *adj.* 合理的
suitable [ˋsutəbl] *adj.* 合適的

❺ (Place) is not the best choice.

（地方）並非最佳選擇。

例 Jakarta? No, it's not the best choice.

雅加達？不，它並非最佳選擇。

❻ I think there are better (sth.) available.

我認為還有更好的（某事物）可以選擇。

例 I think there are better <u>venues</u> available than Shanghai.

我認為還有比上海更好的集會地點可以選擇。

❼ It's not <u>cost-effective</u> to (do sth.).

（做某事）不符合成本效益。

例 It's not cost-effective to have the hotel provide meals for <u>participants</u>.

要旅館供餐給與會者，並不符合成本效益。

❽ We don't have the <u>budget</u> to (do sth.).

我們沒有（做某事）的預算。

例 We don't have the budget to give everyone at the conference an expensive gift.

我們並沒有給參與大會的每一個人一份昂貴禮品的預算。

Ｗord List

venue [`vɛnju] *n.* 集合場所

cost-effective [`kɔst ɪ`fɛktɪv] *adj.* 符合成本效益的

participant [pɑr`tɪsəpənt] *n.* 參與者

budge [`bʌdʒɪt] *n.* 預算

2 實戰會話 Show Time

2.1 ▸▸ Deciding on a Good Location I

 track 03

In order to decide upon a good location for the next annual convention, a videoconference is being held among the five members of the organizing committee—each of whom lives in a different city. The meeting is being chaired by Jason Roth, who lives in New York.

Jason: Hi everyone. Thanks for making yourselves available this morning. I'd like to get your <u>opinion</u> of where we should hold the November convention. What factors do we need to consider this year?

Daphne: Last year, we held it in San Francisco, so I think it should be outside of the United States this time. What about somewhere in Europe? I suggest Switzerland; it's a beautiful country.

Mel: What are the costs involved in holding the convention in Switzerland? I think it's a very expensive country. Also, what's the weather like there in November? I think it's pretty cold. Switzerland's not the best choice.

Cindy: Right. It's not cost-effective to pick Switzerland. We don't have the budget to pay for all those extra costs involved. Why don't we choose a place like the <u>Czech Republic</u>? <u>Prague</u> is a great city, and it's not too expensive.

Jason: I think Prague is quite suitable. It's a good location. What about flights? How are the flight schedules?

Cindy: I'm not sure about that. I'll look into the flight schedules. But I do know of a good place for a convention: the European Star Hotel. I stayed there a few years ago. I'll have to find out about the price of rooms.

Jason: OK. Thanks, Cindy. Let's have another conference call on Monday to discuss this <u>further</u>.

譯文 決定一個好地點（一）

為了要替下一場年度大會決定一個好地點，籌備委員會的五名成員——每個人都住不同的城市，正在進行視訊會議。會議由住在紐約的傑森‧羅斯主持。

傑　森：大家好。感謝你們今天早晨撥冗出席。我們十一月的大會該在哪裡舉行，我想要聽聽你們的意見。今年我們該考慮哪些要素？

戴芬妮：去年我們在舊金山舉行會議，所以我想這次應該在美國境外。要不要在歐洲的某處呢？我提議瑞士；瑞士是個美麗的國家。

梅　爾：在瑞士舉辦會議需要哪些花費？我認為那國家的消費很貴。還有，那裡十一月的天氣如何？我想非常寒冷吧。瑞士不是最好的選擇。

辛　蒂：對。選瑞士不符合成本效益。我們沒有預算來給付那些額外的花費。我們何不選個像是捷克共和國的地方呢？布拉格是個很棒的城市，而且不會太貴。

傑　森：我想布拉格蠻合適的。地點不錯。那航班呢？航班時間如何？

辛　蒂：這點我不確定。我會查查班機時刻表。不過我倒知道有個開會的好地點：歐洲星辰飯店。我幾年前住過那裡。我得查一下房間的價錢。

傑　森：好。辛蒂，謝謝妳。星期一我們再辦一場視訊會議，以便進一步討論。

Ｗord List

opinion [ə`pɪnjən] *n.* 意見
Czech Republic [`tʃɛk rɪ`pʌblɪk] *n.* 捷克共和國
Prague [prɑg] *n.* 布拉格
further [`fɝðə] *adv.* 進一步地；深一層地

2.2 ▸ Deciding on a Good Location II

After doing some checking about flights and hotels, Cindy has some important news to tell the group during the second video-conference call.

Cindy: Well, I checked the flights and hotel information. Regarding flights—it's not a problem at all. However, we need to take another look at the hotel. I checked the Internet about the European Star Hotel. There was a fire at the hotel about six months ago, and I don't think it's been fully <u>repaired</u> and <u>renovated</u> yet.

Jason: Actually, I've changed my mind about Prague. I think we should reconsider our choice. The Czech Republic will be cold in November as well. I think a Mediterranean country like Spain would be better. What about Madrid?

Daphne: I think Madrid is ideal. It's a good location.

Mel: I agree. I think it's a great choice. It's <u>economical</u> and convenient.

Cindy: Is it safe? I've never been to Spain.

Mel: Of course; It's a great city.

Jason: What about convention facilities? We need to find something that suits our needs.

Mel: Let me check on that. I know some Spanish as well, so that will make it easier for me. I've stayed at the Ponderosa Madrid Hotel before and it's quite comfortable.

Daphne: Is it in a central location? What is the transportation system like?

Mel: It's actually pretty good. There shouldn't be any problems getting around Madrid.

Daphne: What are the costs involved in holding a convention there?

Mel: I'll have to find out those costs later today or tomorrow.

Jason: OK, please do that, Mel. Let's meet again on Friday.

譯文 決定一個好地點（二）

辛蒂查了班機與旅館後，在第二次的視訊會議時，她有些重要消息要跟那個小組的人說。

辛　蒂：嗯，我查過班機以及旅館的資料。關於班機──絕對沒問題。不過，我們得再評估一下那家飯店。我上網查了一下歐洲星辰飯店。大約六個月前這家飯店曾經失過火，我想它的修繕與整修還不完全。

傑　森：事實上，關於去布拉格，我已經改變了主意。我想我們應該重新考量我們的選擇。捷克在十一月也會很冷。我認為在地中海的國家，像是西班牙，應該會好一些。馬德里如何？

戴芬妮：我覺得馬德里很理想。地點挺好的。

梅　爾：我同意。我想這是個好選擇，經濟實惠又便利。

辛　蒂：馬德里治安好嗎？我沒去過西班牙。

梅　爾：當然。那是個很棒的城市。

傑　森：那會議設施方面呢？我們需要找到符合我們需求的地方。

梅　爾：那個我來查。我也懂一些西班牙文，查起來會輕鬆一些。我以前住過龐德羅沙馬德里飯店，十分舒適。

戴芬妮：飯店在中心位置嗎？交通運輸系統如何呢？

梅　爾：運輸系統事實上相當好。要在馬德里來來去去應該不成問題。

戴芬妮：在那邊舉辦會議需要哪些花費呢？

梅　爾：我今天稍晚或明天得把那些費用查明。

傑　森：好，那件事就麻煩你了，梅爾。我們星期五再見。

 ord List
....

repair [rɪ`pɛr] *v.* 修理　　　　　　　　economical [ˌikə`nɑmɪkl] *adj.* 經濟的

renovate [`rɛnəˌvet] *v.* 改善

3 Biz 加分句型 Nice-to-Know Phrases

3.1 ▸▸ 表達不確定性 Expressing Uncertainty track 04

❶ I'm not sure about (sth.).
我不確定（某事物）。
例 I'm not sure about the price of the hotel.
我不確定旅館的價格。

❷ I'll have to find out (sth.).
我得查明（某事物）。
例 I'll have to find out how often the flights <u>depart</u>.
我得查明多久發一次班機。

❸ Let me check on (sth.).
讓我查一下（某事物）。
例 Let me check on the time the trains run.
讓我查一下火車行駛的時間。

❹ I'll <u>look into</u> (sth.).
我會調查（某事物）。
例 I'll look into the cost of renting the <u>banquet</u> room.
我會調查租用宴會廳的花費。

Ｗord List

depart [dɪˋpɑrt] *v.* 出發；離開
look into 研究調查
banquet [ˋbæŋkwɪt] *n.* 宴會

3.2 ▸▸ 改變看法 Changing Your Opinion

❶ I think we should reconsider (sth.).

我認為我們應該重新考量（某事物）。

例 I think we should reconsider our decision in choosing Hong Kong as a <u>destination</u>.

我認為我們應該重新考量選擇香港為目的地的決定。

❷ We need to take another look at (sth.).

我們需要再評估（某事物）。

例 We need to take another look at our <u>key speakers</u>.

我們要再評估一下我們的主講者。

❸ I've changed my mind about (sth.).

關於（某事物）我已經改變了主意。

例 I've changed my mind about the hotel—I think we should choose a different one.

關於選哪家旅館，我已經改變了主意——我想我們應該選別家。

❹ I think we've made a mistake regarding (sth.).

關於（某事物），我想我們弄錯了。

例 I think we've made a mistake regarding the menu.

關於菜單的事，我想我們弄錯了。

ord List

destination [ˌdɛstəˈneʃən] *n.* 目的地
key speaker [ˈki ˈspikə] *n.* 主講人

4 Biz 加分詞彙 Nice-to-Know Words & Phrases

 track 05

① cost of living [ˋkɔst͵əvˋlɪvɪŋ] *n.* 生活費用

② convention center [kənˋvɛnʃən ͵sɛntə] *n.* 會議中心

③ exchange rate [ɪksˋtʃəndʒ ͵ret] *n.* 匯率

④ expense account [ɪkˋspɛns əˋkaunt] *n.* 公款支付帳戶

⑤ important considerations [ɪmˋpɔrtn̩t kənsɪdəˋreʃəns]
  n. 重要考量

⑥ overbudget [ˋovəˋbʌdʒɪt] *adj.* 超出預算的

⑦ miscellaneous expenses [͵mɪsəˋlenjəs ɪkˋspɛnsɪz]
  n. 雜項支出

⑧ precipitation [prɪ͵sɪpɪˋteʃən] *n.* 倉促；輕率

⑨ sound decision [ˋsaund dɪˋsɪʒən] *n.* 妥當的決定

⑩ subway system [ˋsʌb͵we ͵sɪstəm] *n.* 地下鐵系統

⑪ logistics [loˋdʒɪstɪks] *n.* 物流；統籌

⑫ managing director [ˋmænɪdʒɪŋ dəˋrɛktə] *n.* 總監

⑬ complimentary [͵kɑmpləˋmɛntərɪ] *adj.* 贈送的

⑭ handful [ˋhændful] *n.* 棘手的人事物

⑮ videoconference [ˋvɪdɪ͵o͵kɑnfərəns] *n.* 視訊會議

:::::::: 小心陷阱 ::::::::

☹ 錯誤用法

It's not cost-effective to **have** the hotel **to provide** meals for participants. 要旅館供餐給與會者，並不符合成本效益。

☺ 正確用法

It's not cost-effective to **have** the hotel **provide** meals for participants. 要旅館供餐給與會者，並不符合成本效益。

:::::::: Biz 一點通 ::::::::

There are a great many factors to take into consideration when choosing the right place for a convention, training session, or other event. Obviously, cost is a major factor, but there are also other considerations as well. The Economist magazine has put together a very useful guide to help you decide where to hold an event. You can find this guide at http://www. economist.com /theworldin/business/displayStory.cfm?story_id=5149435.

It lists Vancouver, Canada as the best location. Meanwhile, of the 127 countries it ranks, it puts Port Moresby, in the country of Papua New Guinea, as the worst. The Economist lists Taipei in the middle, at number 67.

要選擇適切的地點來舉行會議、培訓課程或其他活動時，有諸多因素需要納入考量。很明顯地，花費就是一項主要因素，不過還有其他事項也得考慮進去。《經濟學人》整合了一份非常有用的指引，幫助你決定在什麼地點舉辦活動。這份指引的網址如下：http://www.economist.com/theworldin/business/displayStory.cfm?story_id=5149435。

這份指引將加拿大的溫哥華列為最佳地點。同時，在 127 個國家的評比中，將巴布亞紐幾內亞的莫士比港市列為最差的地點。《經濟學人》將台北排在中間，名列第 67。

ord List

··

obviously [ˋɑbvɪəslɪ] *adv.* 明顯地　　　　rank [ræŋk] *v.* 排列

meanwhile [ˋmin͵hwaɪl] *adv.* 這時

5 實戰演練 Practice Exercises

I 請為下列三個畫底線的字選出最適合本章的中文譯義。

❶ What <u>factors</u> do we need to consider?

我們需要考慮什麼 (A) 工廠 (B) 因素 (C) 事實？

❷ It's <u>ideal</u>.

它很 (A) 有點子 (B) 理想 (C) 偶像。

❸ I think we should <u>reconsider</u>.

我認為我們應該 (A) 再協調 (B) 再磋商 (C) 再考量。

II 你會如何回答下面這兩句話？

❶ I think there are better venues available.

(A) You're right—it's the best choice.

(B) You're right—it's in a bad location.

(C) I agree—it's ideal.

❷ Is it in a central location?

(A) Yes, it's near the mountains.

(B) Yes, it's difficult to get to.

(C) Yes, it's in downtown.

III 請利用下列詞句寫一篇簡短的對話：

What are the costs involved   It's quite suitable

What are the facilities like   I'll look into it

I've changed my mind   It's (not) cost-effective

＊解答請見 246 頁

From:	Mel Barnes
To:	Juana Estevez, Prime Supply Inc.
Subject:	Spain in November

Dear Juana,

How are you? I'm traveling to Spain in November and I am wondering if you will be available to meet sometime between Nov. 10 and 16. Please let me know when is a good time for you.

Yours truly,
Mel

親愛的華娜：

你好嗎？我十一月要去西班牙，我想知道你在十一月十號到十六號之間是否有空見面。請讓我知道你何時方便。

梅爾敬上

1 Biz 必通句型 Need-to-Know Phrases

1.1 ▸▸ 安排會面時間 <u>Arranging</u> a Meeting Time **track 06**

❶ I'm traveling to (place) in (month).
我在（月份）要去（地方）。
例 Bill, I'm traveling to Chicago in August. When can we meet?
比爾，我八月要去芝加哥。我們什麼時候可以碰面？

❷ What day is convenient for you to (do sth.)?
你哪一天方便（做某事）？
例 What day is convenient for you to meet?
你哪一天方便見面？

❸ What's your schedule like (on day) / (in month)?
你（日子）／（月份）的行程如何？
例 What's your schedule like on Tuesday?
你週二的行程如何？
例 What's your schedule like in May?
你五月的行程如何？

❹ When is a good time for you to (do sth.)?
你什麼時候方便（做某事）？
例 When is a good time for you to <u>drop by</u> the office?
你什麼時候方便過來辦公室一趟？

Ⓦord List

arrange [əˋrendʒ] *v.* 安排
drop by 順道拜訪

❺ Are you <u>available</u> (on day) / (at time), (name)?

（名字），你（日子）／（時間）有空嗎？

例 Are you available on Friday, Sherry?

雪莉，你星期五有空嗎？

❻ Is (day) at (time) all right?

（日子）（時間）可以嗎？

例 Is Tuesday at 2:30 p.m. all right?

星期二下午兩點半可以嗎？

❼ Let's make it (day + day section), then.

那麼，我們就訂在（日子＋時段）吧。

例 Let's make it Monday afternoon, then.

那麼，我們就訂在週一下午吧。

❽ How about (day + day section / day section of date)?

（日子＋時段／日期的時段）如何？

例 How about Wednesday afternoon?

星期三下午如何？

例 How about the morning of the 15th?

十五號早上如何？

 ord List

available [ə`veləbl] *adj.* 有空的

1.2 ▶▶ 接受或拒絕對方提議的時間
Accepting or Rejecting a Suggested Time

❶ **Yes. (Day/time/date/month) is fine with me.**
好。（日子／時間／日期／月份）我沒問題。
例 Yes. Next Thursday is fine with me.
好。下星期四我沒問題。
例 Yes. The 4th is fine with me.
好。四號我沒問題。

❷ **I'm free (on day / at time).**
（日子／時間）我有空。
例 I'm free on Tuesday morning at 10:00. We can meet then.
星期二早上十點我有空。我們到時候見。

❸ **(Day/time) is a convenient time for me.**
（日子／時間）我比較方便。
例 Tomorrow afternoon is a convenient time for me.
明天下午我比較方便。

❹ **(Repeat time)? Sure. No problem.**
（複述時間）？當然。沒問題。
例 Next Thursday at 3:00 p.m.? Sure. No problem.
下星期四下午三點？當然。沒問題。

ord List

accept [ək`sɛpt] v. 接受
reject [rɪ`dʒɛkt] v. 拒絕

❺ I'm afraid (time) is not a good time (for me).

（時間）我恐怕不方便。

例 I'm afraid 9:00 a.m. is not a good time for me. Can we meet at another time?

早上九點我恐怕不方便。我們能不能約別的時間碰面？

❻ Actually, I'm <u>tied up</u> (on day) / (with sth.).

事實上，我（日子）／（有某事）走不開。

例 Actually, I'm tied up on Friday all day.

事實上，我星期五整天都走不開。

例 Actually, I'm tied up with a meeting.

事實上，我有個會議走不開。

❼ I'm sorry, we need to choose another time. I (reason/ excuse).

抱歉，我們得找別的時間。我（理由／藉口）。

例 I'm sorry, we need to choose another time. I'm busy on Thursday morning.

抱歉，我們得找別的時間。我星期四早上很忙。

❽ Sorry, but (day) (time) won't <u>work</u> for me.

抱歉，我（日子）（時間）不行。

例 Sorry, but Wednesday at 2:00 p.m. won't work for me.

抱歉，我星期三下午兩點不行。

ord List

tied up 忙得不可開交；忙得脫不了身

work [wɜk] v. 進行；運作；有效

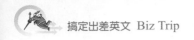
2 實戰會話 Show Time

2.1 ▸ Arranging a Meeting

 track 07

After <u>receiving</u> Mel's email, Juana calls to discuss the meeting <u>directly</u> with Mel.

Mel: Hello, Mel speaking.

Juana: Hi Mel, this is Juana calling from Madrid. I got your email and wanted to ask you about your trip. What is your schedule like while you're in Spain?

Mel: I'm arriving in Spain on November 10 and staying until the 16th. I'll be attending a two-day conference on November 11 and 12. Are you available on the morning of the 13th?

Juana: I'm afraid the 13th is not a good time for me. I have to meet a customer at that time, and it would be <u>extremely</u> difficult to change that appointment. Is the 14th at 1:30 p.m. all right? I'm free all afternoon on that day.

Mel: Actually, I'm tied up with other business at that time. How about November 15 in the morning?

Juana: Sorry, but that won't work for me, either. I've got another visitor coming on that day and I've <u>organized</u> a company tour at 10:00 a.m. for him. However, after 3:00 p.m. on that day is a convenient time for me.

Mel: That time is fine with me, too. Let's make it 4:00 p.m. on the 15th.

譯文 安排會面

收到梅爾的電子郵件後，華娜打電話直接跟梅爾討論會面事宜。

梅爾：喂，我是梅爾。

華娜：嗨，梅爾。我是華娜，從馬德里打過來的。我收到你的郵件了，想跟你談談你出差的事。你在西班牙的行程如何安排？

梅爾：我十一月十日抵達西班牙，會一直待到十六號。我十一月十一和十二日要參加一場為期兩天的會議。你十三日早上有空嗎？

華娜：十三號我恐怕不方便。那個時間我得跟一位客戶見面，要改約很難。十四號下午一點半行嗎？我那天整個下午都有空。

梅爾：事實上我那個時間要忙別的事走不開。十一月十五號早上如何？

華娜：真抱歉，那個時間我也不行。那天我有另一位訪客要來，我已經安排早上十點帶他參觀公司。不過，那天下午三點以後我沒問題。

梅爾：那個時間我也可以。我們就訂在十五號下午四點吧。

ord List

....

receive [rɪ`siv] *v.* 收到
directly [də`rɛktlɪ] *adv.* 直接地
extremely [ɪk`strimlɪ] *adv.* 非常地；極端地
organize [`ɔrgə͵naɪz] *v.* 安排；組織

2.2 ▸▸ <u>Setting up</u> a Meeting

Daphne's company also does business with Spanish companies. She has decided to set up a meeting with one of the companies that she <u>imports</u> from. Right now, she is on the phone with Don Ricardo, who <u>runs</u> a trading company near Madrid.

Daphne: Hello Don, this is Daphne Chiang calling from Taiwan. How are you?

Don: Fine, thank you. How are things with you?

Daphne: Very good, thanks. Don, the reason I'm calling is I'm taking a trip to Madrid in November. While I'm there, I'd like to talk to you about importing some more of your products.

Don: Wonderful. Would you like me to pick you up at the airport, Daphne? It would be no problem at all.

Daphne: No, don't worry about it, Don. I'll be meeting some people at the airport and we plan to make other arrangements to get to our hotel. But thank you very much for the offer. Do you want me to bring you anything from Taiwan?

Don: Some of those delicious pineapple cakes that you always bring would be nice.

Daphne: Of course! Is it OK if I visit your office on Wednesday, November 13?

Don: I'm sorry. We need to choose another time. I won't be in the office that day.

Daphne: OK. How about the 14th or 15th? What day is convenient for you?

Don: Either day is a convenient time for me.

Daphne: Great. Let's make it November 14 at 2:00 p.m.

Don: November 14 at 2:00 p.m.? Sure. No problem. I look forward to seeing you then.

譯文 籌劃會議

戴芬妮的公司也和西班牙的公司作生意。她決定要和她的進口公司之一安排一個會議。此刻她正和唐·里卡多在電話線上，唐·里卡多經營的貿易公司就在馬德里市附近。

戴芬妮：喂，唐，我是戴芬妮·江，從台灣打來的。你好嗎？

唐：　　很好，謝謝妳。妳那邊怎麼樣？

戴芬妮：很好，謝謝。唐，我打電話來是因為我十一月要去一趟馬德里。我在馬德里的時候，想跟你談一下再多進口一些你們產品的事。

唐：　　太好了。要我去機場接你嗎，戴芬妮？絕對不成問題的。

戴芬妮：不用，不用操心，唐。我在機場會跟一些人碰面，我們打算安排別的方法到飯店。不過很感謝你的提議。你要不要我從台灣帶什麼東西給你？

唐：　　帶些妳每次都會帶的那種鳳梨酥應該蠻不錯的。

戴芬妮：沒問題！我十一月十三號星期三到你的辦公室，可以嗎？

唐：　　真抱歉，我們得挑別的時間。我那天不在辦公室。

戴芬妮：好。那十四號或十五號呢？你哪天方便？

唐：　　我兩天都方便。

戴芬妮：太好了。我們就訂十一月十四號下午兩點吧。

唐：　　十一月十四號下午兩點？當然。沒問題。期待到時候和妳見面。

Word List

set up 安排；籌劃
import [ɪmˋport] *v.* 進口
run [rʌn] *v.* 經營

3 Biz 加分句型 Nice-to-Know Phrases

3.1 ▸▸ 解釋會面的原因
Explaining the Reasons for Meeting

---

❶ **The reason I'm (Ving) is to (do sth.).**

我（做⋯⋯）是因為（做某事）。

例 The reason I'm writing is to <u>confirm</u> our meeting next week.

我寫信來是因為要確認我們下週的會面。

---

❷ **I'd like to talk to you about (sth.).**

我想跟你談談（某事物）。

例 I'd like to talk to you about ordering some more parts.

我想跟你談談再多訂購一些零件的事。

---

❸ **I need to discuss (sth.) (with you today).**

（今天）我需要（跟你）討論一下（某事物）。

例 I need to discuss the project with you today.

今天我需要跟你討論一下那項計畫。

---

❹ **I want to <u>go over</u> (sth.) (with you).**

我想（跟你）詳盡討論（某事物）。

例 I want to go over some details with you.

我想跟你詳盡討論一些細目。

Ⓦord List

confirm [kən`fɜm] v. 確認

go over 仔細檢查

40

3.2 ▸ 提議與要求 Making Offers and Requests

❶ Would you like me to (do sth.)?

你要不要我（做某事）？

例 Hi Jim. Would you like me to send you a <u>brochure</u>?

嗨，吉姆。你要不要我寄一份小冊子給你？

❷ Do you want me to (do sth.)?

你要我（做某事）嗎？

例 Do you want me to deliver the items to you?

你要我把這幾樣東西送過去給你嗎？

❸ Would you mind (Ving)?

你介不介意（動名詞）？

例 Would you mind coming over to our office?

你介不介意過來到我們公司？

❹ Is it OK if (situation)?

（情況），可以嗎？

例 Is it OK if I stop by your office tomorrow morning?

我明天早上到你的辦公室一趟，可以嗎？

Word List

....

brochure [bro`ʃʊr] *n.* （說明書之類的）小冊子

4 Biz 加分詞彙 Nice-to-Know Words & Phrases

 track 09

❶ daily calendar [ˋdelɪ ˋkæləndə] *n.* 行事曆

❷ face-to-face [ˋfestəˋfes] *adj./adv.* 面對面

❸ get in touch [ˋgɛt ɪn ˋtʌtʃ] *v.* 聯絡

❹ no-can-do [ˋnoˏkænˋdu] *n.* 行不通;不行

❺ off-site location [ˋɔfˋsaɪt loˋkeʃən] *n.* 遠離(特定)活動的地點

❻ out of the question [ˋaut ʌv ðə ˋkwɛstʃən]
adj. 不可能的;絕對不行的

❼ prior engagement [ˋpraɪə ɪnˋgedʒmənt] *n.* 先前安排的約定

❽ scheduling conflict [ˋskɛdʒulɪŋ ˏkɑnflɪkt]
n. 撞期(時間安排有所衝突)

❾ touch base (with sb.) [ˋtʌtʃ ˋbes] *v.* 將事況告知(某人)

❿ working-lunch [ˋwɝkɪŋ ˏlʌntʃ] *n.*(午)餐敘

⓫ acquaintance [əˋkwentəns] *n.* 相識的人

⓬ at all costs [æt ɔl kɔst] *adv.* 無論如何

⓭ Chief Executive Officer [ˋtʃif ɪgˋzɛkjutɪv ˋɔfəsə]
n. (=CEO) 執行長

⓮ developer [dɪˋvɛləpə] *n.* 開發人員;研發員

⓯ organizer [ˋɔrgəˏnaɪzə] *n.* 萬用記事本

::::::: 小心陷阱 :::::::

☹ 錯誤用法

Would you **mind to come** over to our office?

你介不介意過來到我們公司？

☺ 正確用法

Would you **mind coming** over to our office?

你介不介意過來到我們公司？

::::::: **Biz 一點通** :::::::

Maintaining good customer relationships is essential to the development of a business. Regular contact is needed to ensure the customer feels appreciated and to make sure there are no outstanding issues to settle or problems to solve. There are a number of websites you can visit that give tips on establishing and maintaining customer relations. One very useful URL is: www.ecustomerserviceworld.com. This website offers a lot of valuable, free information on a large variety of topics.

維持良好的客戶關係對拓展生意來說至關緊要。要確保客戶覺得倍受重視，並確定沒有懸而待決的議題或問題，定期聯絡是必要的。有幾個網站可供瀏覽，這些網站會提供你跟客戶建立關係以及維持關係的竅門。其中一個很實用的網址是：www.ecustomerserviceworld.com。這個網址針對各式各樣的主題，提供了許多實用的免費資訊。

Ⓦord List

maintain [men`ten] *v.* 維持；保持

essential [ɪ`sɛnʃəl] *adj.* 必要的

ensure [ɪn`ʃʊr] *v.* 確保

appreciate [ə`priʃɪ͵et] *v.* 重視

5 實戰演練 Practice Exercises

I 請為下列三個畫底線的字或句子選出最適合本章的中文譯義。

❶ I'm sorry, we need to choose another time. <u>I have a scheduling conflict.</u>
很抱歉，我們需要另挑時間。

(A) 我的時間安排有所衝突。

(B) 我有時間衝突要安排。

(C) 我有一場衝突要安排時間。

❷ <u>I'm afraid next Thursday is not a good time.</u>

(A) 我害怕下個星期四不是個好時間。

(B) 下週四我恐怕不方便。

(C) 恐怕時間不是下週四。

❸ Actually, I'm <u>tied up</u> tomorrow afternoon.
事實上，明天下午我會 (A) 被綁起來。 (B) 走不開。 (C) 被追成平手。

II 你會如何回答下面這兩句話？

❶ I'm tied up at that time.

(A) Good, let's meet then.

(B) That is a nice tie, too.

(C) OK, let's meet at a different time.

❷ Wednesday at 4:30 p.m. is convenient for me.

(A) That's fine with me, too.

(B) OK, let's choose a different time, then.

(C) That's not good for me, either.

III 請利用下列詞句寫一篇簡短的對話：

When is a good time for you?   Let's make it

I'd like to talk to you about   is convenient

Are you available   Won't work for me

＊解答請見 247 頁

From:	Jason Roth
To:	Mel Barnes; Daphne Chiang; Tony Potter; Cindy Kent
Subject:	Biz Trip Arrangements

Dear all,

This email is to let you know that I have talked to Cindy about the arrangements we need to make in terms of booking rooms and equipment for the convention. Thanks a lot, Cindy!

Yours truly,
Mel

大家好：

這封郵件是要通知你們，我已經跟辛蒂談過關於大會我們需要安排預訂房間與設備的事。多謝了，辛蒂！

梅爾敬上

1 Biz 必通句型 Need-to-Know Phrases

1.1 ▸▸ 妥善辦理預約 Making the <u>Proper</u> <u>Bookings</u> **track 10**

❶ I'd like to <u>inquire</u> about (sth.).
我想詢問（某事物）。
例 Excuse me. I'd like to inquire about finding some chairs I can rent.
對不起，我想詢問哪裡能找到出租的椅子。

❷ I'd like to <u>book</u> (sth.) (on date).
我想在（日期）預約（某事物）。
例 I'd like to book your largest conference room on Sunday, September 12.
我想在九月十二日星期天預約你們最大的會議室。

❸ I wish to <u>reserve</u> (sth.) (on date) (for length of time).
我想在（日期）（時間長短）預訂（某事物）。
例 I wish to reserve two <u>minivans</u> on Tuesday the twelfth for the whole day.
我想在十二號星期二整天預訂兩輛小型廂型車。

❹ Could you <u>put</u> (sth.) <u>on hold</u> for me (date(s))?
你能不能在（日期）幫我保留（某事物）？
例 Could you put the main conference room on hold for me December 19 and 20?
你能不能在十二月十九和二十號時幫我保留主會議廳？

Ｗord List

proper ['prɑpə] *adj.* 合適的
booking ['bʊkɪŋ] *n.* 預約
inquire [ɪn'kwaɪr] *v.* 詢問
book [bʊk] *v.* 預約

reserve [rɪ'zɜv] *v.* 預訂
minivan ['mini͵væn] *n.* 小型廂型車
put (sth.) on hold 保留（某物）

❺ Do you rent (sth.)?

你們出租（某事物）嗎？

例 Do you rent <u>peripherals</u> for notebook computers?

你們有沒有出租手提電腦的周邊器材？

❻ Could you tell me the <u>availability</u> of (sth.) (on date/day)?

你能不能告訴我在（日期／日子）有沒有（某事物）可用？

例 Could you tell me the availability of moving vans on March 24?

你能不能告訴我三月二十四號有沒有搬家貨車可租用？

❼ Can you supply me with (sth.)?

你能不能提供我（某事物）？

例 Can you supply me with one hundred fifty folding tables and ten tents?

你能不能提供我一百五十張折疊桌和十個帳棚？

❽ What types of <u>amenities</u> does (place) have?

（地方）有哪些類型的設施？

例 What types of amenities does the <u>recreation</u> center have?

這座休閒中心有哪些類型的設施？

Ｗord List

peripheral [pə`rɪfərəl] *n.* （電腦）周邊設備

availability [ə،velə`bɪlətɪ] *n.* 可利用；可獲得

amenity [ə`minətɪ] *n.* （娛樂或便利之）設施 （常用複數）

recreation [،rɛkrɪ`eʃən] *n.* 娛樂

1.2 ▸▸ 預訂房間 Reserving Rooms

❶ I want to make a <u>reservation</u> for a (single/double/ non-smoking) room (on date/day) for (length of time).

我想在（日期／日子）預訂一間（單人／雙人／禁煙）房，住（時間長短）。

例 I want to make a reservation for a double room on January 2 for three nights.

我想在一月二號預訂一間雙人房，住三晚。

❷ I'd like to book a room (on day + date) for (length of time).

我想訂一間房間，（日子＋日期）住（時間長短）。

例 Hi. I'd like to book a room on Saturday, March 15 for one night.

嗨，我想訂一間房間，三月十五號星期六住一晚。

❸ Do you have any <u>vacancies</u> (on day / from date to date)?

（日子／從日期到日期）你們有沒有空房？

例 Excuse me. Do you have any vacancies from November 1 to November 4?

對不起，請問你們十一月一號到四號有沒有空房？

❹ What is the (check-in/checkout) time?

（入住／退房）的時間是幾點？

例 What is the checkout time at your hotel? Would it be possible to check-in early?

你們旅館的退房時間是幾點？有可能早一點入住嗎？

Word List

reservation [ˌrɛzəˈveʃən] *n.* 預約
vacancy [ˈvekənsɪ] *n.* 空位；空缺

❺ Could you please tell me the room <u>rates</u> for (type of room)?

可不可以請你告訴我（房間類型）的房間價錢？

例 Could you please tell me the room rates for a non-smoking suite?

可不可以請你告訴我禁煙套房的房間價錢？

❻ What are your (<u>corporate</u>) rates (in month)?

（月份）的（公司團體）房間價錢是多少？

例 What are your corporate rates in December?

十二月的公司團體房間價錢是多少？

❼ Can you tell me about the hotel <u>features</u>? Is there (sth.)?

你能不能告訴我旅館有什麼特色？有沒有（某物）？

例 Can you tell me about the hotel features? Is there wireless Internet? Is there a swimming pool?

你能不能告訴我旅館有什麼特色？有沒有無線網路？有沒有游泳池？

❽ Are the rooms very (<u>spacious</u>/large/clean/modern)?

房間很（寬敞／大／乾淨／現代化）嗎？

例 Are the rooms very spacious? Are the rooms very modern?

房間很寬敞嗎？房間設備很現代化嗎？

ord List

rate [ret] *n.* 費用

corporate [`kɔrpərɪt] *adj.* 公司的；團體的

feature [`fitʃə] *n.* 特點；特色

spacious [`speʃəs] *adj.* 寬敞的

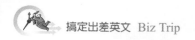

2 實戰會話 Show Time

2.1 ▸ Booking for the Convention I

 track 11

Cindy is on the phone with the manager of the Ponderosa Madrid Hotel making arrangements.

Cindy: Hello, I'd like to inquire about your convention facilities. <u>Specifically</u>, could you tell me the availability of your convention rooms for November 10 and 11?

Manager: Yes, we can <u>accommodate</u> you at that time. Would you like to make a reservation now?

Cindy: Yes, I'd like to book the largest room you have on November 10 and 11. Could you put the room on hold for me on those days?

Manager: Certainly. Are there any special arrangements you need?

Cindy: Do you rent <u>projectors</u> and screens?

Manager: Yes, we do. We have projectors that work with any IBM-<u>compatible</u> computer.

Cindy: Unfortunately, that won't <u>do</u>. I have an Apple notebook. Can you <u>supply</u> me with a projector that is Mac compatible?

Manager: I'm very sorry, we don't have that available. However, I can give you the number of a <u>rental</u> agency in Madrid.

Cindy: Thank you very much. <u>Regarding</u> the screen, I wish to reserve that on November 10 and 11 for eight hours each day.

Manager: I will place a hold on the screen for you. Anything else?

Cindy: What types of amenities does the convention room have?

Manager: It has wireless Internet <u>connectivity</u>, a large screen LCD monitor, controllable climate control, and numerous electrical outlets.

譯文 為大會做預約（一）

辛蒂在電話中與龐德羅沙馬德里飯店的經理安排會議事宜。

辛蒂：你好，我想要詢問一下有關你們的會議設備。明確地說，你能不能告訴我十一月十號和十一號你們的會議室是否可供使用？

經理：可以，我們那個時段可以提供您使用。您要不要現在預約呢？

辛蒂：好。我想要在十一月十號和十一號訂你們最大的會議室。那幾天你能不能幫我保留那個房間？

經理：當然可以。您需要做什麼特別的安排嗎？

辛蒂：你們有投影機和螢幕出租嗎？

經理：是的，我們有。我們有和任何一種 IBM 電腦都相容的投影機。

辛蒂：真不巧，那樣不行。我用的是蘋果筆記型電腦。你能不能提供跟 Mac 電腦相容的投影機？

經理：非常抱歉，我們沒有那種的可以使用。不過，我能給您馬德里一家出租公司的電話。

辛蒂：非常謝謝你。至於螢幕，我希望能在十一月十號和十一號兩天各預約八個小時。

經理：我會為您保留螢幕的。還需要什麼嗎？

辛蒂：會議室裡有什麼樣的設施呢？

經理：有無線上網、一座大型的液晶螢幕顯示器、室溫調控，及許多電源插座。

Word List

specifically [spɪˋsɪfɪk]ɪ] *adv.* 特別地

accommodate [əˋkɑmə,det] *v.* 供應；順應；通融

projector [prəˋdʒɛktə] *n.* 投影機

compatible [kəmˋpætəb]] *adj.* 相容的

do [du] *v.* 足夠；合適；行

supply [səˋplaɪ] *v.* 供給

rental [ˋrɛnt]] *adj.* 出租的

regarding [rɪˋgɑrdɪŋ] *prep.* 關於

connectivity [,kɑnɛkˋtɪvətɪ] *n.* （電腦）連線

2.2 ▸▸ Booking for the Convention II

Cindy continues her conversation with the hotel manager.

Cindy: Do you have any vacancies from November 10 to November 16? I want to make a reservation for those dates if I can.

Manager: How many rooms?

Cindy: I'd like to book three double rooms and two single rooms for five days. Could you tell me your room rates?

Manager: The singles are €125 per night; doubles are €160.

Cindy: What are your corporate rates?

Manager: We give a ten percent discount.

Cindy: Are the rooms very spacious?

Manager: Yes, they are quite large. They <u>feature</u> a seating area and <u>beverage</u> bar that includes a <u>refrigerator</u>.

Cindy: Can you tell me about the hotel features?

Manager: We have a swimming pool, a business center, a four-star restaurant, a café, and a <u>lounge</u>.

Cindy books the rooms and calls the rental agency next.

Cindy: What do you have regarding projectors for a notebook for rent?

Rental Agency: We have several IBM-compatible models.

Cindy: I'm afraid IBM-compatible models are not acceptable. I have an Apple notebook.

Rental Agency: We have one Apple model that is €65 per day.

Cindy: Is there anything else available?

Rental Agency: Sorry, no.

Cindy: OK. Is there a charge for delivery?

Rental Agency: No.

Cindy: Great. Please send it to the Ponderosa Madrid Hotel on November 10 at 8:00 a.m.

譯文　為大會做預約（二）

辛蒂繼續跟飯店經理商談。

辛蒂：十一月十號到十六號你們有沒有空房？如果可以的話，我想要預訂那幾天的房間。

經理：幾個房間呢？

辛蒂：我想訂三間雙人房和兩間單人房，住五天。你可不可以告訴我房間的價錢？

經理：單人房一晚 125 歐元；雙人房 160 歐元。

辛蒂：你們的公司團體優惠價是多少？

經理：我們打九折。

辛蒂：房間很寬敞嗎？

經理：是的，房間相當大。特別設有座位區，還有附冰箱的飲料吧。

辛蒂：你可不可以告訴我旅館的特色是什麼？

經理：我們有游泳池、商務中心、四星級餐廳、咖啡廳和休息室。

辛蒂訂了房間，接下來打電話給出租公司。

辛蒂：　　　你們有哪種能跟手提電腦搭配的投影機出租？

出租公司：我們有幾款能跟 IBM 相容的機型。

辛蒂：　　　與 IBM 相容的機型恐怕不行。我用的是蘋果筆記型電腦。

出租公司：我們有一台機型是蘋果牌的，一天租金 65 歐元。

辛蒂：　　　還有沒有什麼別的可以租用的呢？

出租公司：抱歉，沒有。

辛蒂：　　　好吧。運送要付費嗎？

出租公司：不必。

辛蒂：　　　好極了。請你在十一月十日早上八點送到龐德羅沙馬德里飯店。

Word List

feature [ˈfitʃə] *v.* 以……為特色；以……為號召
beverage [ˈbɛvərɪdʒ] *n.* 飲料
refrigerator [rɪˈfrɪdʒə.retə] *n.* 冰箱
lounge [laʊndʒ] *n.* 休息室；娛樂廳

3 Biz 加分句型 Nice-to-Know Phrases

3.1 ▸▸ 排除不適當的情況
Rejecting Unsuitable Conditions

 track 12

❶ I'm afraid (sth.) is not acceptable.
（某事物）我恐怕無法接受。
例 I'm afraid this room is not acceptable.
　　這房間我恐怕無法接受。

❷ Unfortunately, (sth.) won't do—(reason).
很遺憾，（某事物）不適用——（理由）。
例 Unfortunately, the <u>equipment</u> won't do—it's too old.
　　很遺憾，這個設備不適用——太老舊了。

❸ Is there anything else available (for sth.)?
還有沒有什麼別的可以（做某事）的嗎？
例 Is there anything else available for rent?
　　還有沒有什麼別的可以出租的嗎？

❹ What (else) do you have regarding (sth.) for rent?
你們有（別種的）（某事物）可出租嗎？
例 What else do you have regarding <u>PA systems</u> for rent?
　　你們有什麼別種的擴音裝置可出租嗎？

Ⓦord List

equipment [ɪˋkwɪpmənt] *n.* 設備
PA system 擴音系統（PA = public address）

3.2 ▸▸ 自行領取和派人遞送物品
Picking Up Things and Having Things Delivered

❶ When can you deliver (sth.)?

你們何時可以把（某事物）送過來？

例 When can you deliver the tables and chairs?

你們何時可以把桌椅送過來？

例 When can you deliver the coffee and donuts?

你們何時可以把咖啡和甜甜圈送過來？

❷ Please send (sth.) to (address).

請將（某事物）送至（地址）。

例 Please send the product samples to 4398 Bayview West Road.

請將產品樣品送至灣景西路 4398 號。

❸ Is there a charge for delivery?

運送需要付費嗎？

例 Is there a charge for delivery? How much?

運送需要付費嗎？要多少錢？

❹ I can pick (sth.) up (on day + at time).

我可以在（日子＋時間）來取（某事物）。

例 Yes, I can pick the car up on Friday at 2:00 p.m.

可以，我可以在星期五下午兩點來取車。

4 Biz 加分詞彙 Nice-to-Know Words & Phrases

 track 13

① booked solid [ˋbʊkt ˋsɑlɪd] *adj.* 全訂滿了

② cash deposit [ˋkæʃ dɪˋpɑzɪt] *n.* 現金押金

③ deadline for return [ˋdɛd͵laɪn fɔr rɪˋtɜn] *n.* 歸還的截止日期

④ down payment [ˋdaʊn ˋpemənt] *n.* 頭期款

⑤ late charge [ˋlet ͵tʃɑrdʒ] *n.* 逾期手續費

⑥ minimum charge [ˋmɪnəməm ˋtʃɑrdʒ] *n.* 最低收費

⑦ non-refundable [͵nɑnrɪˋfʌndəbl̩] *adj.* 無法退費的

⑧ out of stock [ˋaʊt əv ˋstɑk] *adj.* 缺貨

⑨ rain check [ˋren ͵tʃɛk] *n.* （保持以後索取權力的）暫時拒絕

⑩ shuttle bus [ˋʃʌtl̩ ͵bʌs] *n.* 接駁巴士

⑪ attendee [ətɛnˋdi] *n.* 出席者（= attendant）

⑫ big name [bɪg nem] *n.* 名人；重要人物

⑬ layover [ˋle͵ovə] *n.* 中途停留

⑭ wireless Internet access [ˋwaɪrlɪs ˋɪntɜnɛt ͵æksɛs]
　　n. 無線上網

⑮ electrical cord [ɪˋlɛktrɪkl̩ ˋkɔrd] *n.* 電線

::::::::: **小心陷阱** :::::::::

☹ 錯誤用法：

Do you have any **empty rooms**?

你們有沒有空房？

☺ 正確用法：

Do you have any **vacancies**?

你們有沒有空房？

::::::::: **Biz 一點通** :::::::::

There are a lot of factors to consider when making arrangements and booking all the necessary things involved in a convention or trade show. For instance, you need to make sure the space is <u>adequate</u> for the number of people who will be attending. Do the facilities allow for easy access by <u>disabled</u> people? Will there be <u>audio-visual</u> equipment at the convention center, or do you have to make your own arrangements? For a very good checklist of things to think about when planning and booking, check out the website by the US-based Society for Human Resource Management: https://www.shrm.org/chapters/resources/successconf.asp/.

為舉行會議或參加商展做安排和預訂種種相關事物時，有許多因素得納入考量。譬如說，你要確定那個空間是不是夠容納參與的人數。相關設備是否方便殘障人士使用？會議中心會有視聽設備嗎？或者你得要自行安排？做籌畫和預訂時所要衡量的重要事物表單，可參閱設於美國的人力資源管理協會的網站：https://www.shrm.org/chapters/resources/successconf.asp/。

Word List

adequate [ˋædəkwɪt] *adj.* 足夠的；適當的

disabled [dɪsˋeb!d] *adj.* 殘障的

audio-visual [ˋɔdɪˏoˋvɪʒuəl] *adj.* 視聽的

5 實戰演練 Practice Exercises

I 請為下列三個問題選出最適合本章的中文譯義。

❶ What types of amenities does it have?

(A) 它有哪些類型的設施？

(B) 它有哪些典型的禮節？

(C) 它有哪些象徵的優雅？

❷ Unfortunately, the equipment won't do.

(A) 很不幸，這個設備不行做。

(B) 很遺憾，這個設備不適用。

(C) 很可惜，這個設備不會做。

❸ Is there a charge for delivery?

(A) 貨物要充電嗎？　(B) 運送需要付費嗎？　(C) 分娩要收費嗎？

II 你會如何回答下面這兩句話？

❶ Could you put that on hold for me?

(A) Where should I put it?

(B) Sure, I'll reserve it for you.

(C) Yes, I can wait.

❷ Are the rooms very spacious?

(A) Yes, they are very large.

(B) Yes, they are very clean.

(C) Yes, they are very beautiful.

III 請利用下列詞句寫一篇簡短的對話：

I'd like to inquire	I'd like to book
Do you have any vacancies	That won't do
Is there anything else available	Could you tell me the room rates?

＊解答請見 248 頁

From:	Daphne
To:	Sandra
Subject:	My Trip to Madrid

Dear Sandra,

Could you please look into booking a ticket for me to Madrid to attend the conference in November? Also, I'd like a stopover in London for two days.

Thank you,
Daphne

親愛的珊德拉：

妳能不能處理一下我十一月到馬德里參加會議訂機票的事？還有，我想中途在倫敦停留兩天。

謝謝妳。

戴芬妮

1 Biz 必通句型 Need-to-Know Phrases

1.1 ▶ 安排班機 Arranging Flights

 track 14

❶ **I'd like to book a (direct/non-stop) flight to (location) on (date), please.**
我想訂（日期）飛往（地點）的（直飛／直航）班機，麻煩你。
例 Hello. I'd like to book a direct flight to New York on February 12, please.
你好，我想訂二月十二號飛往紐約的直飛班機，麻煩你。

❷ **(Sb.) wish to have a <u>stopover</u> in (location) for (number of days)**
（某人）希望中途能在（地點）停留（天數）。
例 Also, I wish to have a stopover in Bangkok for three days.
還有，我希望中途能在曼谷停留三天。

❸ **What is the (<u>departure</u>/arrival) time for (airline name + flight number)?**
（航空公司名稱＋班機號碼）的（起飛／抵達）時間是幾點？
例 Excuse me, what is the departure time for United Airlines flight number UA032?
對不起，請問聯合航空 UA032 號班機的起飛時間是幾點？

❹ **(Sb.) would like a(n) (aisle/window) seat.**
（某人）想要（走道／靠窗）的座位。
例 I'd like an aisle seat with a lot of <u>legroom</u>.
我想要伸腳空間很大的走道座位。
例 I'd like a window seat near the <u>lavatory</u>.
我想要接近盥洗室的靠窗座位。

❺ How much <u>carry-on</u> luggage can I take onboard?

我可以帶多少件隨身行李上飛機？

例 How much carry-on luggage can I take onboard the plane?

　　我想了解一下：我可以帶多少件隨身行李上飛機？

❻ At which (<u>terminal</u>/gate) do I catch the flight?

我要在哪個（航廈／登機門）搭機？

例 At which terminal do I catch the flight?

　　我要在哪個航廈搭機？

❼ (Sb.) have a(n) (air-miles/<u>frequent</u> flyer) card.

（某人）有（累積哩程數／飛行常客）卡。

例 I have a frequent flyer card. Can you make sure my miles are <u>calculated</u>?

　　我有飛行常客卡。你能不能確認一下我的哩程數有算進去？

❽ Can (sb.) get an e-ticket?

（某人）能不能拿電子機票？

例 Can I get an e-ticket for the flight? Is this flight ticketless?

　　我能不能拿這個班機的電子機票？這是無票班機嗎？

Ⓦord List

....

stopover [ˋstɑpˏovɚ] v. 中途停留

departure [dɪˋpɑrtʃɚ] n. 出發

legroom [ˋlɛgˏrum] n. 伸腳空間

lavatory [ˋlævəˏtorɪ] n. 盥洗室

carry-on [ˋkærɪˏɑn] adj. 可隨身帶進機艙內的

terminal [ˋtɝmənl] n. 航站

frequent [ˋfrikwənt] adj. 時常的

calculate [ˋkælkjəˏlet] v. 計算

1.2 ▸▸ 辦理簽證和護照
Taking Care of Visa and Passport Requirements

❶ **My (passport/visa) is <u>valid</u> until (date).**
我的（護照／簽證）一直到（日期）都有效。
例 My passport is valid until March 1, 2010.
我的護照一直到 2010 年三月一日都有效。

❷ **I want to apply for a visa to (country).**
我想申請（國家）的簽證。
例 Hi, I want to apply for a visa to Vietnam, please.
你好，我想申請越南的簽證，麻煩你。

❸ **I would like a (single/multiple) entry visa for (country).**
我想辦（國家）的（單次／多次）入境簽證。
例 I would like a single <u>entry</u> visa for China. How much does it cost?
我想辦中國的單次入境簽證。要多少錢？

❹ **I have all the proper travel documents.**
我所有的旅行證件都齊備。
例 Yes, I have all the proper travel documents, including stamped copies.
是的，我所有的旅行證件都齊備加蓋官印的影本。

Word List

valid [ˋvælɪd] *adj.* 有效的
entry [ˋɛntrɪ] *n.* 進入

❺ Where do I get the form (for sth.) to fill out?

我要去哪裡拿（某種用途）要填的表格？

例 Pardon me. Where do I get the form for a visa <u>application</u> to <u>fill out</u>?

對不起。請問我要去哪裡拿申請簽證要填的表格？

❻ My <u>country of origin</u> is (country).

我的國籍地是（國家）。

例 My country of origin is Taiwan.

我的國籍地是台灣。

❼ My length of stay is (number) days.

我停留的期間是（數目）天。

例 My length of stay is ten days.

我停留的期間是十天。

❽ How do I get a visa extension?

我要如何辦理延期簽證？

例 How do I get a visa extension if I need to?

如果需要的話，我要如何辦理延期簽證？

 ord List

application [͵æpləˋkeʃən] *n.* 申請書

fill out 填寫

country of origin [ˋɔrədʒɪn] *n.* 國籍地；原產國

2 實戰會話 Show Time

2.1 ▸▸ Calling the Travel Agent

track 15

Daphne Chiang's secretary, Sandra, is on the phone to a travel agent to arrange her boss's trip to Madrid.

Travel Agent: Global Travel Agents. Daniel speaking.

Sandra: I'd like to book a flight to Madrid on November 7 for Daphne Chiang. Also, she wishes to have a stopover in London for two days.

Travel Agent: Let me see. Yes, there're seats available on that <u>route</u>.

Sandra: Daphne would like a window seat. What is the departure time?

Travel Agent: The flight leaves at 11:00 a.m.

Sandra: She has air-miles as well. Can she get an e-ticket?

Travel Agent: Yes, she can. No problem.

Sandra: How much carry-on luggage can she take on the plane?

Travel Agent: Two pieces. And they must be able to fit in the overhead <u>bin</u> or under the seat.

Sandra: OK, thank you. Goodbye.

A few days later, Sandra calls the travel agency again.

Sandra: I'm sorry, I need to change Daphne's travel plans. My boss says that 11:00 a.m. is too early for her on November 7. Is there a charge for changing the flight time?

Travel Agent: No, there isn't.

Sandra: Great. I'd like to change the departure time from November 7 to November 8, with only a one-day stopover in London.

Travel Agent: Of course. No problem. Is there anything else?

Sandra: Does she need any <u>immunizations</u> to go to Spain?

Travel Agent: Let me check. No, she doesn't.

Sandra: She wants to buy several thousand US dollars in

<u>traveler's checks</u>, and exchange some NT dollars for euros. Can she do that at the airport?

Travel Agent: Of course.

譯文 致電旅行社

戴芬妮‧江的秘書珊德拉正在電話上和旅行社人員安排她老闆的馬德里之行。

旅行社人員：寰宇旅行社您好。我是丹尼爾。

珊德拉：　　我想幫戴芬妮‧江訂十一月七號到馬德里的班機。還有，她希望中途能在倫敦停留兩天。

旅行社人員：我看看。是的，那條航線還有位子。

珊德拉：　　戴芬妮想要靠窗的位子。起飛時間是幾點呢？

旅行社人員：這個班機早上十一點離開。

珊德拉：　　她也有累積哩程。她能不能拿電子機票呢？

旅行社人員：是的，可以。沒問題。

珊德拉：　　她能帶多少件隨身行李上飛機呢？

旅行社人員：兩件。而且要能放進座位上方的置物櫃或是座位底下的空間。

珊德拉：　　好。謝謝你，再見。

幾天之後，珊德拉再次致電旅行社。

珊德拉：　　很抱歉，我需要改變戴芬妮的行程計畫。我老闆說十一月七號早上十一點對她來說太早了。改班機時間要手續費嗎？

旅行社人員：不，不用。

珊德拉：　　太好了。我想把啟程時間從十一月七號改到十一月八號，中途只在倫敦停一天。

旅行社人員：好的，沒問題。還有別的事情嗎？

珊德拉：　　她去西班牙，需要打預防針嗎？

旅行社人員：我查一下。不，不用。

珊德拉：　　她想要買幾千美元的旅行支票，也要把台幣換成歐元。她能在機場辦嗎？

旅行社人員：當然可以。

Word List

route [rut] *n.* 航線；路程

bin [bɪn] *n.* 箱；倉

immunization [ˌɪmjənəˋzeʃən] *n.* 免疫

traveler's check　旅行支票

2.2 ▸▸ Applying for the Visa

Daphne is at the Spanish trade office in Taiwan applying for a visa to Spain.

Daphne: I want to apply for a visa to Spain. Where do I get the form for a visa application to fill out?

Clerk: Over there on the counter to your right.

Daphne fills out the form and <u>hands</u> it to the clerk.

Daphne: How long will it take to get the visa? What is the cost?

Clerk: It usually takes two or three working days, as long as you have <u>provided</u> all the proper documents. The cost is NT$2,000.

Daphne: OK, thank you. Is there anything else I need to give you?

Clerk: Do you have a valid passport? You need a passport with <u>at least</u> six months of <u>validity</u> left. <u>Otherwise</u>, you will have to apply for a new one.

Daphne: That's not a problem—my passport is valid until December 2009. Here it is. I also have two passport photos as well.

Clerk: What type of visa are you applying for?

Daphne: I would like a single-entry, tourist visa.

Clerk: And how long will you be staying in Spain?

Daphne: My length of stay is five days.

Clerk: Your country of origin is Taiwan?

Daphne: Yes. I also need to buy some travel <u>insurance</u> before I go as well. Where can I buy travel insurance around here?

Clerk: There is an agency that sells travel insurance on Dunhua North Road. It's about five minutes from here.

譯文 申辦簽證

戴芬妮到西班牙的駐台貿易代表處申請西班牙簽證。

戴芬妮：我想要申請到西班牙的簽證。我要到哪裡拿申請簽證要填的表格？

辦事員：妳右手邊的櫃台那裡。

戴芬妮填好表格並遞給辦事員。

戴芬妮：要多久能拿到簽證？費用多少？

辦事員：只要妳備妥所有的證件，通常要兩到三個工作天。費用是台幣兩千元。

戴芬妮：好，謝謝你。我還需要給你別的東西嗎？

辦事員：妳的護照還有效嗎？護照有效期至少要有六個月。否則，妳得申請一本新護照。

戴芬妮：那沒問題——我的護照一直到 2009 年十二月都有效。在這兒。我也有兩張護照用的大頭照。

辦事員：妳要申請哪種簽證？

戴芬妮：我想辦單次入境的觀光簽證。

辦事員：妳要在西班牙待多久？

戴芬妮：我會待五天。

辦事員：妳的國籍地是台灣嗎？

戴芬妮：是的。我出發前也需要買旅遊保險。這附近哪裡可以買旅遊保險？

辦事員：敦化北路有一家公司賣旅遊保險。離這裡大概五分鐘。

Ｗord List

hand [hænd] *v.* 遞給
provide [prə`vaɪd] *v.* 提供
at least 至少

validity [və`lɪdətɪ] *n.* 有效性
otherwise [`ʌðə͵waɪz] *adv.* 否則
insurance [ɪn`ʃʊrəns] *n.* 保險

3 Biz 加分句型 Nice-to-Know Phrases

3.1 ▸▸ 更動計畫 Changing Plans

 track 16

❶ I'd like to change (sb.'s) date of departure time from (date/time) to (date/time).

我想將（某人的）啟程時間從（日期／時間）改成（日期／時間）。

例 I'd like to change my departure time from August 27 at 10:00 a.m. to August 29 at 8:00 a.m.

我想將我的啟程時間從 8 月 27 日早上 10 點改成 8 月 29 日早上 8 點。

❷ Is there any (charge/<u>penalty</u>) for changing (sb.'s) flight time?

更改（某人的）航班時間要付（手續費／罰款）嗎？

例 Hello. Is there any charge for changing my flight time to another date?

你好，把我的航班時間改成別的日期要付手續費嗎？

❸ Is it possible to make a change to (sb.'s) <u>itinerary</u>?

有沒有可能變更（某人的）行程？

例 Is it possible to make a change to my itinerary? I have a scheduling problem.

有沒有可能變更我的行程？我有時間安排上的問題。

❹ I need to change (sth.).

我需要改變（某事物）。

例 I need to change my plans because something <u>unexpected</u> has <u>come up</u>.

我需要改變我的計畫，因為突然有事發生。

Ⓦord List
....

penalty [ˈpɛnltɪ] *n.* 罰款
itinerary [aɪˈtɪnəˌrɛrɪ] *n.* 旅程

unexpected [ˌʌnɪkˈspɛktɪd] *adj.* 意外的
come up 發生

3.2 ▸▸ 其他考量 Other Considerations

❶ Where can I buy travel insurance?
我可以在哪裡買旅遊保險呢？

例 Excuse me. Where can I buy travel insurance at this airport?
對不起，請問我可以在這機場的哪裡買旅遊保險？

❷ I'd like to exchange some (currency a) for (currency b).
我想把一些（甲貨幣）換成（乙貨幣）。

例 Hi. I'd like to exchange some NT dollars for Thai baht.
你好，我想把一些台幣換成泰銖。

❸ I want to buy (monetary amount) in traveller's checks.
我想買（幣值）的旅行支票。

例 I want to buy €5,000 in traveller's checks.
我想買五千歐元的旅行支票。

❹ What immunizations do I need to go to (country)?
我去（國家）需要打什麼預防針？

例 What immunizations do I need to go to Cambodia?
我去柬埔寨需要打什麼預防針？

 ord List

currency [ˋkɝənsɪ] *n.* 貨幣
baht [bɑt] *n.* 銖（泰國貨幣單位）

monetary [ˋmʌnə͵tɛrɪ] *adj.* 貨幣的
Cambodia [kæmˋbodjə] *n.* 柬埔寨

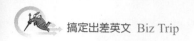
4 Biz 加分詞彙 Nice-to-Know Words & Phrases

 track 17

❶ baggage carousel [ˋbægɪdʒ͵kærʊˋzɛl] *n.* 行李轉盤

❷ confirm your flight 確認你的班機

❸ consulate [ˋkɑnsͺlɪt] *n.* 領事館

❹ customs [ˋkʌstəmz] *n.* 海關

❺ duty free 免稅

❻ embassy [ˋɛmbəsɪ] *n.* 大使館

❼ expiry date 到期日

❽ extend my visa 延長我的簽證

❾ original copy [əˋrɪdʒənl ˋkɑpɪ] *n.* 原始文件

❿ turbulence [ˋtɝbjələns] *n.* 亂流

⓫ valise [vəˋlis] *n.* 旅行用手提包

⓬ spirit [ˋspɪrɪt] *n.* 烈酒

⓭ quarantine [ˋkwɔrənͺtin] *n./v.* 隔離；檢疫

⓮ liable [ˋlaɪəbl̩] *adj.* 應負責的；有責任的

⓯ smuggle [ˋsmʌgl̩] *v.* 夾帶；私運

:::::::: 小心陷阱 ::::::::

☹ 錯誤用法：

I want to buy €5,000 **travel checks**.

我想買五千歐元的旅行支票。

☺ 正確用法：

I want to buy €5,000 **in traveler's checks**.

我想買五千歐元的旅行支票。

:::::::: **Biz** 一點通 ::::::::

Visa requirements for different countries <u>vary</u>, so it's best to make sure whether or not you will require a visa to travel to a certain country well <u>in advance</u>. If you are traveling to the United States, you can check out the U.S. State Department's site (www.state. gov). For Canada, you can visit that government's site at www.cic.gc.ca. <u>In addition</u>, Delta Airlines has a very useful indicator in its "plan a flight" section (under "International Travel Information") that allows you to choose <u>virtually</u> any country in the world to see if you require a visa to enter it. You can access the Delta site at www.delta.com. And don't forget to make sure you have enough time left on your passport <u>as well</u>.

因為不同的國家對簽證有不同的要求，所以你最好事先確定走訪某個國家到底需不需要簽證。如果你要去美國，可以上美國國務院的網站（www. state.gov）查一查。如果是去加拿大，可以上官方的網站 www.cic.gc. ca 看一下。除此之外，達美航空公司在它的「計劃搭機旅行」區裡有個相當實用的指引（列於「國際資訊」之下），可以讓你選擇世界上任何一個國家，查看該國是否需要簽證才能入境。達美航空的網址是：www.delta. com。別忘了也要確定自己護照上的有效期夠長。

Ⓦord List

vary [ˈvɛrɪ] v. 不同

in advance 事先

in addition 除此之外

virtually [ˈvɝtʃʊəlɪ] adv. 實際上

as well 也

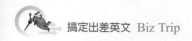

5 實戰演練 Practice Exercises

I 請為下列三句話選出最適合本章的中文譯義。

❶ I would like a multiple-entry visa.

(A) 我想辦單次入境簽證。

(B) 我想辦多次入境簽證。

(C) 我想辦永久入境簽證。

❷ I would like to exchange some Taiwanese currency.

(A) 我想交換一些台幣。　(B) 我想調換一些台幣。　(C) 我想兌換一些台幣。

❸ What immunizations do I need?

(A) 我需要具有什麼免疫力？

(B) 我需要具備什麼豁免權？

(C) 我需要打什麼預防針？

II 你會如何回應下面這兩句話？

❶ Your passport is not valid.

(A) You're right. I lost it.

(B) You're right. It has expired.

(C) You're right. It is not mine.

❷ What is your country of origin?

(A) I live in Taiwan.

(B) I'm going to Canada.

(C) Right now, I'm visiting your country.

III 請利用下列詞句寫一篇簡短對話：

| I'd like to book a flight | I'd like a window seat | apply for a visa |
| multiple-entry visa | I have a frequent flyer card | length of stay |

＊解答請見 249 頁

Section Two

行程相關用語
Travel-related English

第 **5** 章 | 啓程和抵達
Departure and Arrival

From:	Jason Roth
To:	Mel Barnes; Daphne Chiang; Tony Potter; Cindy Kent
Subject:	Bon Voyage!

Dear Friends,

It's amazing how time flies. Our big convention is only a few days away now. I'm looking forward to seeing you all again and having a very good meeting. I'll see you after we check in at the Ponderosa Madrid Hotel. See you soon!

Best regards,
Jason

親愛的朋友們：

時光飛逝，真是不可思議！我們的大會離現在只剩幾天了。我很期待與你們所有人再見面，也期待會議成功。在龐德羅沙馬德里飯店辦好住宿手續之後就可以與各位碰面。不久見！

傑森敬上

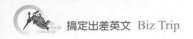
1 Biz 必通句型 Need-to-Know Phrases

1.1 ▸▸ 在登機櫃台與飛機上
At the Check-in Counter and On Board

 track 18

❶ **I have (number) suitcases to check in.**

我有（數量）個行李箱要托運。

例 Hello, I have three suitcases to check in today.

你好，我今天有三個行李箱要托運。

❷ **I have (number) piece(s) of carry-on luggage.**

我有（數量）件隨身行李。

例 I have two pieces of carry-on luggage. Is that OK?

我有兩件隨身行李。可以嗎？

❸ **I want to check my baggage to (place).**

我要把行李托運到（地方）。

例 I want to check my baggage all the way to Denver, please.

我要把行李直接托運到丹佛，麻煩你。

❹ **Do I need to (claim my baggage / check in again) in (place) when I (change planes / transfer)?**

我在（地方）轉機時，需要（提領行李／再報到一次）嗎？

例 Do I need to claim my baggage in Los Angeles when I change planes?

我在洛杉磯轉機時，需要提領行李嗎？

例 Do I need to check in again in Hong Kong when I transfer?

我在香港轉機時，需要再報到一次嗎？

Ⓦord List

check-in counter 辦理登機手續的櫃台

on board 在飛機、船或火車上

luggage [ˋlʌgɪdʒ] *n.* 行李

baggage [ˋbægɪdʒ] *n.* 行李

claim [klem] *v.* 認領

❺ The overhead baggage <u>compartment</u> is full.

座位上方的行李櫃滿了。

例 The overhead baggage compartment is full. Where can I put my bags?

座位上方的行李櫃滿了。我的袋子可以放在哪裡呢？

❻ I think I'll have the/a (food/drink choice).

我想要（食物／飲品的選項）。

例 I think I'll have the chicken, thank you.

我想要雞肉，謝謝。

❼ May I have (a/the/another/some) (noun)?

我可不可以要（一個／那個／再一個／一些）（名詞）呢？

例 May I have another bag of peanuts, please?

我可不可以再要一包花生，麻煩你？

例 May I have some hot water, please?

我可不可以要些熱水，麻煩你？

❽ Excuse me. (Sth.) (isn't/aren't) <u>working</u>.

對不起。（某事物）不管用／無法運作。

例 Excuse me. My headphones aren't working. Could I have a new pair?

對不起。我的耳機不管用。我能不能要一副新的？

例 Excuse me. The entertainment system isn't working. Could you help me with it?

對不起。娛樂系統無法運作。你能不能幫我弄一下？

Ⓦord List

compartment [kəm`pɑrtmənt] *n.* 隔間（overhead compartment 指飛機座位上方之行李櫃）

work [wɜk] *v.* 運轉；運作

1.2 ›› 抵達、通關和入境檢查
Arrival, Customs, and Immigration

❶ What is your <u>destination</u>?
你的目的地是什麼地方？
例 What is your destination on this trip?
你此行的目的地是什麼地方？

❷ May I see your (sth.) and (sth.)?
我可以看一下你的（某事物）和（某事物）嗎？
例 Good morning, sir, may I see your passport and <u>disembarkation</u> card, please?
先生，早安，我可以看一下你的護照和入境卡嗎？

❸ What is the <u>purpose</u> of your visit to (place)?
你到（地方）來的目的是什麼？
例 What is the purpose of your visit to Mexico?
你到墨西哥來的目的是什麼？

❹ I'm here on (business/pleasure).
我來此（出差／旅遊）。
例 I'm here on business. I work for IBM.
我來這裡出差。我為 IBM 工作。

Ⓦord List
....

destination [ˌdɛstəˈneʃən] *n.* 目的地
disembarkation [ˌdɪsɛmbɑrˈkeʃən] *n.* 登陸（disembarkation card 指入境卡）
purpose [ˈpɜpəs] *n.* 意圖

❺ Do you have anything to <u>declare</u>?

你有什麼東西要申報嗎？

例 Do you have anything to declare today?

你今天有什麼東西要申報嗎？

❻ I have (nothing / these items) to declare.

我（沒有／有這幾樣東西）要申報。

例 No, I have nothing to declare at all.

沒有，我沒有任何東西要申報。

❼ (These things / This stuff)? (They are / It's some) (sth.).

（這些東西／這個東西）嗎？（它們是／這是一些）（某事物）。

例 These things? They are duty-free items.

這些東西嗎？這些是免稅商品。

例 This stuff? It's some gifts for my clients.

這個東西嗎？這是一些給我客戶的禮物。

❽ You are over the limit on (<u>alcohol</u>/cigarettes).

你買的（酒／菸）超過規定限額。

例 You are over the limit on alcohol. You must pay duty on these.

你買的酒超過規定限額。這些你必須付稅。

Ｗord List

declare [dɪˋklɛr] *v.* 申報

alcohol [ˋælkəˌhɔl] *n.* 酒

2 實戰會話 Show Time

2.1 ▸▸ Setting off for the Trip

 track 19

After making all the necessary arrangements for traveling, Mel asks his wife to drop him off at the airport and he checks in at the airline counter.

Clerk: Good afternoon, sir. How many bags are you checking in today?

Mel: I have two suitcases to check in and I also have three pieces of carry-on luggage. I want to check my baggage to Madrid.

Clerk: I'm sorry, sir, your luggage <u>exceeds</u> the <u>weight</u> limit, and we only allow two pieces of carry-on luggage on board.

Mel: What? What kind of <u>policy</u> is that? Well, OK, I'll <u>stuff</u> one of my carry-on bags into a suitcase and I'll pay the difference concerning the weight limit.

Clerk: Thank you, sir. Here is your boarding pass. I also must <u>apologize</u> because the plane has been delayed by two hours. Sorry for the inconvenience.

Mel: What?! This is terrible. Oh, I almost forgot. I want to upgrade my ticket to first class.

Clerk: I'm sorry again, sir, but first class is full.

A little upset, Mel boards the plane.

Mel: What?! The overhead compartment is full!

Flight attendant: Let me help you. The compartment over there still has some room.

Mel: Thank you.

Later on during the flight.

Flight attendant: Excuse me, sir, we are serving dinner now. We have fish, chicken, or beef.

Mel: I think I'll have the fish, please.

Flight attendant: Here you are, sir.

Mel: May I have another orange juice?

Flight attendant: Certainly.

| Mel: | And one more thing. My headphones aren't working. Could I have a new pair? |
| Flight attendant: | Of course. |

譯文 啟程出發

在安排好旅程所需的一切後，梅爾請太太載他到機場去。他到航空公司的櫃臺辦理登機。

地勤： 先生午安。您今天要拖運幾件行李？

梅爾： 我有兩件行李要托運，還有三件隨身行李。我要把行李托運到馬德里。

地勤： 先生，真抱歉。您的行李超重，而且我們只能允許兩件隨身行李上機。

梅爾： 什麼？這是什麼規定嘛？唉，好吧，我會把其中一個隨身行李塞進行李箱裡，超重的部分我會付錢。

地勤： 謝謝您，先生。這是您的登機證。我也要跟您致歉，因為飛機誤點了兩個鐘頭。很抱歉造成您的不便。

梅爾： 什麼？真糟糕。噢，我差點忘了。我要把我的機票升等為頭等艙。

地勤： 先生，再次跟您道歉，頭等艙已經滿了。

梅爾登機的時候有點不高興。

梅爾： 什麼？！上面的行李櫃已經滿了！

空服員：我來幫您。那邊的行李櫃還有一些空間。

梅爾： 謝謝妳。

稍後在飛行的時候。

空服員：對不起，先生，我們現在要提供晚餐。有魚、雞或牛肉。

梅爾： 我想點魚，麻煩妳。

空服員：先生，這給您。

梅爾： 我可以多要一杯柳橙汁嗎？

空服員：當然可以。

梅爾： 還有一件事。我的耳機不管用。我能不能要一副新的？

空服員：當然可以。

Word List

exceed [ɪkˋsid] *v.* 超過

weight [wet] *n.* 重量

policy [ˋpɑləsɪ] *n.* 政策

stuff [stʌf] *v.* 塞進

apologize [əˋpɑləˏdʒaɪz] *v.* 道歉

2.2 ▸ Arriving at the Destination

Mel's plane lands in London, where he must catch a <u>connecting</u> flight to Madrid.

Mel: Hi. Where do I go to transfer planes?

Clerk: What is your destination?

Mel: Madrid.

Clerk: Just follow this hallway until you get to a large doorway on your right and then you'll see the area.

Mel transfers planes and then arrives later in Madrid.

Customs officer: May I see your passport and return ticket?

Mel: Sure.

Customs officer: What is the purpose of your visit to Spain?

Mel: I'm here on business. I'm <u>attending</u> a convention.

Customs officer: Do you have anything to declare?

Mel: No, I have nothing to declare.

Customs officer: What's in those <u>plastic</u> bags?

Mel: This stuff? It's some duty-free items.

Customs officer: But I see you have five <u>liters</u> of spirits. You are over the limit on alcohol. You must pay a duty on some of that. You will have to fill out this form and then pay the fee.

Mel fills out the form and pays the money. Afterwards, he passes through customs.

Mel: Excuse me, can you tell me where the baggage carousel is?

Clerk: Yes, it's on the lower floor. You can take the <u>escalator</u> over there.

Mel finds the baggage carousel and waits for his luggage, but it doesn't arrive.

Mel: What?! My luggage is lost. What do I do now?

Clerk: Please fill in this form, and we will do our best to <u>trace</u> it. We will contact you at your hotel when we locate your suitcases.

譯 文　抵達目的地

梅爾的飛機在倫敦降落，他得轉機去馬德里。

梅爾：你好，請問我要到哪裡轉機呢？

地勤：您的目的地是什麼地方？

梅爾：馬德里。

地勤：只要沿著走廊下去，在你的右手邊會有個大入口，你就會看見轉乘區了。

梅爾轉搭飛機，然後抵達馬德里。

海關官員：我可以看一下你的護照和回程機票嗎？

梅爾：　　沒問題。

海關官員：你到西班牙來的目的是什麼？

梅爾：　　出差。我要參加一場會議。

海關官員：你有沒有東西要申報？

梅爾：　　沒有，我沒有東西要申報。

海關官員：那些塑膠袋裡面裝的是什麼東西？

梅爾：　　這個東西嗎？是一些免稅商品。

海關官員：可是我看到你帶了五公升的烈酒。你超過酒類的購買限額。有些你　　　　　得要付稅。你要先填這張表，然後繳費。

梅爾填好表，然後付了錢。隨後他通過海關。

梅爾：　　對不起，能不能請你告訴我行李轉盤在哪裡？

機場人員：好的，在下層樓。你可以搭那邊的手扶梯。

梅爾找到行李轉盤，然後等他的行李，可是行李竟然沒到。

梅爾：　　什麼？！我的行李丟了。我現在要怎麼辦？

機場人員：請填好這張表格，我們會盡力追蹤您的行李。找到您的行李箱之　　　　　後，我們會致電旅館與您聯繫。

Word List

connect [kə`nɛkt] *v.* 連結

attend [ə`tɛnd] *v.* 參加

plastic [`plæstɪk] *adj.* 塑膠的

liter [`litɚ] *n.* 公升

escalator [`ɛskə.letɚ] *n.* 電扶梯

trace [tres] *v.* 追蹤

3 Biz 加分句型 Nice-to-Know Phrases

3.1 ▸▸ 處理行李問題
Dealing with Luggage Problems

❶ Your (luggage/baggage) exceeds the (weight/size) limit.
你的（行李）超過（重量／大小）限制。
例 I'm very sorry, but your luggage exceeds the weight limit.
非常抱歉，您的行李超過重量限制。

❷ I will pay the difference.
我會付超重的部份。
例 That's OK. I will pay the difference. How much is it?
沒關係。我會付超重的部份。多少錢？

❸ Which is the baggage carousel for flight (number)?
班機（號碼）的行李轉盤是哪一個？
例 Excuse me, which is the baggage carousel for EVA flight BR2127? I can't find it.
對不起，請問長榮航空 BR2127 號班機的行李轉盤是哪一個？我找不到。

❹ My (sth.) is (lost/missing).
我的（某事物）（遺失／不見）了。
例 Can you help me? My luggage is lost.
你能幫我嗎？我的行李丟了。

3.2 ▸▸ 處理雜項事宜
Dealing with Miscellaneous Matters

❶ May I upgrade my ticket to (business/first) class?

我能不能把機票升等到（商務／頭等）艙？

例 Hello, may I upgrade my ticket to business class on this flight?

你好，我能不能把我這班飛機的機票升等到商務艙？

❷ Where do I go to transfer planes to (place)?

去（地方），要到哪裡轉機？

例 Excuse me—where do I go to transfer planes to Chicago?

對不起，請問去芝加哥要到哪裡轉機？

❸ The plane has been delayed for (length of time).

這班飛機已經誤點（時間長度）了。

例 The plane has been delayed for three hours.

這班飛機已經誤點三個鐘頭了。

❹ There was a lot of <u>turbulence</u>.

有好多亂流。

例 There was a lot of turbulence. We had a scary landing.

有好多亂流。 我們降落的時候很嚇人。

Ⓦord List

turbulence [ˋtɝbjələns] *n.* 亂流

4 Biz 加分詞彙 Nice-to-Know Words & Phrases

 track 21

❶ baggage claim ticket [`bægɪdʒ ,klem ,tɪkɪt] *n.* 行李號碼牌

❷ clear customs 通關

❸ customs officer [`kʌstəmz ,ɔfəsɚ] *n.* 海關官員

❹ disembark [,dɪsɪm`bark] *v.* 下機

❺ dutiable item [`djutɪəbl̩ `aɪtəm] *n.* 應稅物品

❻ immigration official [,ɪmə`greʃən ə,fɪʃəl] *n.* 入境檢查官

❼ in-flight magazine [`ɪn,flaɪt ,mægə`zin] *n.* 機上雜誌

❽ moving sidewalk [`muvɪŋ `saɪd,wɔk] *n.* 行動步道／電動走道

❾ point of (dis)embarkation [`pɔɪnt əv ,(dɪs),ɛmbar`keʃən]
  n. 下機／登機點

❿ prohibited item [prə`hɪbɪtɪd `aɪtəm] *n.* 違禁品

⓫ quarantine [`kwɔrən,tin] *n./v.* 檢疫

⓬ security check [sɪ`kjʊrətɪ ,tʃɛk] *n.* 安全檢查

⓭ tax-exempt [`tæks ɪg ,zɛmpt] *adj.* 免稅的

⓮ vegetarian meal [,vɛdʒə`tɛrɪən mil] *n.* 素食餐

⓯ X-ray machine [`ɛks`re mə,ʃin] *n.* X 光機

:::::::: **小心陷阱** ::::::::

☹ 錯誤用法：

You are over the limit **in** alcohol. You must pay duty **for** these.
你買的酒超過規定限額。這些你必須付稅。

☺ 正確用法：

You are over the limit **on** alcohol. You must pay duty **on** these.
你買的酒超過規定限額。這些你必須付稅。

:::::::: **Biz 一點通** ::::::::

If you are traveling with a lot of luggage, since regulations for international and domestic flights are different and always <u>subject</u> to change, it's a good idea to check with the airline concerning the weight limitations and number of carry-on items <u>permitted</u> onboard the aircraft. <u>Conversely</u>, you could consider "traveling light," and taking only carry-on luggage—this way you can simply avoid the bother of checking in suitcases, waiting at the baggage claim, and <u>lugging</u> around heavy bags, not to mention the headaches of lost or stolen luggage. Just make sure your carry-on bags are the proper size to fit in overhead bins and go through X-ray machines. And remember, always <u>comply</u> with customs regulations, and never mention bombs, guns, or other weapons. Language like this can land you in court, instead of your destination!

因為國際航班與國內航班不同，也常有變動，所以你如果帶很多行李旅行的話，最好先跟航空公司查一下重量的限制以及上機隨身行李的件數。反過來說，你可以考慮「輕裝便行」，只帶隨身行李上機——這樣一來你就能避免托運行李、等候提領以及拖著笨重行李袋來來去去的麻煩，更別提弄丟行李或行李被竊的頭痛事。只要確定你的隨身行李袋能放得進座位上方的置物櫃也能通過 X 光檢查機就行了。而且要記得，一定要遵守海關的規定，絕對不要提到炸彈、槍枝或其他武器的事情。提這些事只會害你上法院，而不能把你平安送往旅行目的地。

Word List

subject [ˈsʌbdʒɪkt] *adj*. 受制於……的
permit [pəˋmɪt] *v*. 允許
conversely [kənˋvɝslɪ] *adv*. 相反地

lug [lʌg] *v*. 用力拖
comply [kəmˋplaɪ] *v*. 遵從（後接 with）

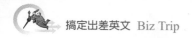

5 實戰演練 Practice Exercises

I 請為下列三句話選出最適合本章的中文譯義。

❶ Do you have anything to declare?

(A) 你有什麼東西要宣佈嗎？

(B) 你有什麼東西要聲明嗎？

(C) 你有什麼東西要申報嗎？

❷ You are over the limit.

(A) 你超過規定限額了。

(B) 你超過界線了。

(C) 你太過份了。

❸ May I see your passport and boarding pass?

(A) 我可以看見你的護照和居留證嗎？

(B) 我可以看見你的護照和通行證嗎？

(C) 我可以看一下你的護照和登機證嗎？

II 你會如何回答下面這兩個問題？

❶ What is your destination?

(A) I'm going to New York.

(B) I am from Taipei.

(C) I am a student.

❷ What is the purpose of your visit?

(A) I am staying two weeks.

(B) I am traveling on business.

(C) I have nothing to declare.

III 請利用下列詞句寫一篇簡短對話：

| check in | boarding pass | duty-free item |
| nothing to declare | destination | baggage carousel |

＊解答請見 250 頁

From:	Cindy Kent
To:	Mel Barnes
Subject:	Arrival in Madrid

Dear Mel,

Hi. I hope you get this email before you arrive in Madrid. Anyway, I remember that our planes are arriving at about the same time. I hope we see each other at the airport. Maybe we can share a cab to the hotel.

Yours truly,
Cindy

親愛的梅爾：

嗨。我希望你在抵達馬德里之前能收得到這封電子郵件。總之，我記得我們的飛機會在差不多同一時間抵達。我希望我們能在機場碰頭。也許我們可以一起搭計程車去飯店。

辛蒂敬上

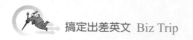
1 Biz 必通句型 Need-to-Know Phrases

1.1 ▸▸ 搭乘計程車或接駁巴士
Taking a Taxi or Shuttle Bus

 track 22

❶ Where can I catch a (taxi / shuttle bus) to (place)?
我可以在哪裡搭（計程車／接駁巴士）去（地方）呢？
例 Hi. Where can I catch a taxi to <u>downtown</u> Los Angeles?
你好。請問我可以在哪裡搭計程車到洛杉磯市中心呢？

❷ Where is the (taxi / shuttle bus) <u>stand</u>?
（計程車／接駁巴士）招呼站在哪裡？
例 Sorry to bother you, but where is the taxi stand?
抱歉打擾你，請問計程車招呼站在哪裡？

❸ Could you please call me a (taxi/car/<u>limousine</u>) to go to (place)?
可以麻煩你幫我叫一輛（計程車／小客車／豪華轎車）到（地方）嗎？
例 Hello. Could you please call me a taxi to go to the airport?
你好。可以麻煩你幫我叫一輛計程車到機場嗎？

❹ Is there a shuttle bus to (hotel/place)?
有沒有接駁巴士到（旅館／地方）？
例 May I ask you a question? Is there a shuttle bus to the Royal Hotel?
我可不可以問你一個問題？有沒有接駁巴士到皇家旅館？

Ｗord List

downtown [ˋdaʊnˋtaʊn] *n.* 市中心
stand [stænd] *n.* 停車處；招呼站

limousine [ˋlɪməˌzin] *n.* 豪華轎車

❺ Is this a <u>metered</u> taxi, or do you charge a <u>flat</u> rate?

這輛計程車會照表收費,還是你收均一費用?

例 Excuse me, driver. Is this a metered taxi, or do you charge a flat rate?

對不起,司機先生。請問你這輛計程車照表收費,還是收均一費用?

❻ I'd like to go to (place), please. / Please take me to (place).

我想到(地方),麻煩你。/請你載我到(地方)。

例 I'd like to go to the Metropolitan Museum, please.

我想到大都會博物館,麻煩你。

例 Please take me to the convention center.

請你載我到會議中心。

❼ It's on the corner of (street name) and (street name).

那個地方在(街名)與(街名)之間的轉角上。

例 It's on the corner of Main Street and Broadway.

那個地方在緬因街與百老匯街的轉角上。

❽ How much is the fare (going to be)?

車資是多少?

例 How much is the fare for the <u>ride</u>?

搭這一趟車資是多少?

例 How much is the fare going to be to the airport?

去機場車資是多少?

Ⓦord List

meter [ˋmitɚ] v. 以表測量　　　　ride [raɪd] n. 搭乘

flat [flæt] adj. 均一的

1.2 ▶▶ 租交通工具 Renting a Vehicle

❶ I'd like to rent a (compact/mid-size/large/luxury/ sports/two-door/four-door) car.

我想要租一輛（小型／中型／大型／豪華／跑／雙門／四門）車。

例 Hello, I'd like to rent a mid-size car. What do you have available?

你好，我想要租一輛中型車。你們有哪些車可租用？

❷ Do you have any other models? Can I get a (type)?

你們有其他的車型嗎？我能不能租一輛（款型）車嗎？

例 Do you have any other models besides subcompact? Can I get a minivan or SUV?

除了超小型車之外，你們有其他車型嗎？我能不能租一輛小型廂型車或是休旅車？

❸ Is there a charge for (kilometers/miles)?

（里／哩程數）要另行計費嗎？

例 Is there a charge for kilometers, or are they included in the price?

里程數要另行計費嗎？還是含在租車費裡？

❹ What does the insurance cover?

保險涵蓋哪些項目？

例 What does the insurance cover? What about collision insurance?

保險涵蓋哪些項目？包不包括碰撞險？

ⓦord List

....

compact [kəm`pækt] *adj.* 小型的

subcompact [.sʌb`kɑmpækt] *n.* 超小型汽車

SUV = sport-utility vehicle 休旅車；多功 能運動休閒車

cover [`kʌvə] *v.* 涵蓋

collision [kə`lıʒən] *n.* 碰撞

❺ **How much <u>coverage</u> does the insurance provide?**
這份保險所提供的項目有哪些？
例 Excuse me, how much coverage does the insurance provide?
對不起，請問這份保險所提供的項目有哪些？

❻ **(What / How much) is the (<u>deductible</u>/<u>premium</u>)?**
（保險扣除額／保險費）是多少呢？
例 What is the deductible? How much is the premium?
保險扣除額是多少？保險費是多少？

❼ **You need to leave a <u>deposit</u> of (amount).**
你得留（數額）的押金。
例 You need to leave a deposit of US$200 on this car.
這輛車你得留兩百美元的押金。

❽ **(Bring it back / Return the car) with a full tank of gas.**
（車子開回來／歸還車子）的時候要把油加滿。
例 We ask that you bring it back with a full tank of gas, please.
我們要求車子開回來的時候要把油加滿，麻煩你。

 Word List

coverage [`kʌvərɪdʒ] *n.* 保險項目
deductible [dɪ`dʌktəbl] *n.* 扣除額

premium [`primɪəm] *n.* 保險費
deposit [dɪ`pɑzɪt] *n.* 押金

2 實戰會話 Show Time

2.1 ▸▸ Taking a Taxi to the Hotel

 track 23

Cindy arrives in Madrid about two hours before Mel's plane lands. She waits for a while, but finally decides to just go on ahead to the hotel by herself.

Cindy: Hi. Excuse me. Is there a shuttle bus to the Ponderosa hotel?

Clerk: Yes, there is, but I'm afraid you just missed it. You'll have to wait another hour to catch the next one.

Cindy: I don't really want to wait that long. Where can I catch a taxi to the Ponderosa Hotel? Could you please call me a taxi?

Clerk: No, I'm sorry. You'll have to go to the taxi stand and find a taxi.

Cindy: Where is the taxi stand?

Clerk: Outside, to your left.

Cindy: Thank you.

Cindy finds a taxi.

Cindy: Hello. Is this a metered taxi, or do you charge a flat rate?

Taxi Driver: It is metered. Where do you want to go?

Cindy: I'd like to go to the Ponderosa Hotel. <u>According to</u> the map, the hotel is on the corner of Cordero Drive and Mesina Street.

Taxi Driver: Yes. I know that hotel very well. It will only take about 20 or 25 minutes to get there. <u>Hop in</u>.

Cindy: Thanks.

About 20 minutes later, the taxi arrives at the Ponderosa Hotel.

Taxi Driver: Here we are. The Ponderosa Hotel.

Cindy: How much is the fare?

Taxi Driver: Twenty euros.

Cindy: OK. Here you go. Thank you.

譯文 搭計程車到飯店

在梅爾的飛機降落前兩個小時，辛蒂就抵達馬德里了。她等了一陣子，最後決定自己先到旅館去。

辛蒂：	嗨。對不起，請問有沒有接駁巴士去龐德羅沙飯店？
服務人員：	是，有的，不過你恐怕剛錯過一班。妳得再等一個鐘頭才能搭到下一班。
辛蒂：	我實在不想等那麼久。我可以在哪裡搭計程車去龐德羅沙飯店呢？你能幫我叫一輛計程車嗎？
服務人員：	抱歉，我沒辦法。你必須到計程車招呼站去找一輛。
辛蒂：	計程車招呼站在哪裡？
服務人員：	在外面，妳的左手邊。
辛蒂：	謝謝你。

辛蒂找到一輛計程車。

辛蒂：	你好。這輛計程車照表收費，還是收均一費用？
計程車司機：	照表。妳要去哪裡？
辛蒂：	我想去龐德羅沙飯店。從地圖上看來，飯店在柯德羅道和美西納街的轉角上。
計程車司機：	沒錯。那家飯店我很熟。只要二十到二十五分鐘就可以到那裡。上來吧。
辛蒂：	謝謝。

二十分鐘過後，計程車抵達龐德羅沙飯店。

計程車司機：	我們到了。龐德羅沙飯店。
辛蒂：	車資多少？
計程車司機：	二十歐元。
辛蒂：	好。錢在這。謝謝你。

Word List

according to　根據

Hop in.（口語）上來吧（指坐進車裡）。

2.2 ▸ Renting a Car

After passing through customs, Mel waits in the airport, trying to find Cindy. After half an hour, Mel <u>gives up</u> and decides to rent a car because he will use it later to visit his <u>supplier</u> in Madrid.

Mel: Hello. I'd like to rent a mid-size car. What do you have available?

Clerk: We have a few Fords and Chryslers.

Mel: Do you have any other models?

Clerk: Yes, we have some nice European cars as well.

Mel: Is there a charge for kilometers?

Clerk: No, you get unlimited kilometers. We charge by the day.

Mel: How about insurance? What does the insurance cover?

Clerk: Our <u>comprehensive</u> <u>policy</u> covers everything. Please leave a deposit of €300. Also, please return the car back with a full tank of gas.

Mel: Where can I get a map of Madrid?

Clerk: Here is a free one. Have a great stay in Madrid.

After showing his international <u>driver's license</u> and signing the documents, Mel drives away in the rental car, but soon he gets lost.

Mel: Excuse me. I'm not sure where I am. Can you tell me how to get to the Ponderosa Hotel?

Pedestrian: Yes. You need to follow this road for two kilometers and then turn left and drive for about five minutes.

Mel: Thanks for your help.

A few minutes later, another car hits Mel's car.

Mel: What?! Hey, why did you hit my car?

Driver: It wasn't my <u>fault</u>.

Mel: Yes, it was. Let's exchange information. Are you insured?

Driver: Of course. The <u>accident</u> was your fault.

Mel: What?! Are you crazy? You were definitely to blame. I think we should call the police to <u>settle</u> this problem.

譯文 租車

通過海關後，梅爾在機場等候，想要找辛蒂。半個鐘頭之後梅爾就放棄了，並決定租一輛車來用，因為他之後還得去拜訪馬德里的供應商。

梅爾：哈囉，我想租一輛中型車。你們有哪些車款可租用？

職員：我們有幾輛福特和克萊斯勒。

梅爾：你們還有其他車型嗎？

職員：有，我們也有一些不錯的歐洲車。

梅爾：里程數要另外計費嗎？

職員：不用，里程數不限。我們以天數來計費。

梅爾：那保險呢？保險涵蓋哪些項目？

職員：我們保的全險涵蓋所有項目。請留下押金三百歐元。還有，請你在歸還車子的時候把油加滿。

梅爾：我可以在哪裡弄到一張馬德里的地圖？

職員：這裡有免費的。希望你在馬德里期間過得很愉快。

梅爾出示他的國際駕照並簽好文件後，就開著出租車離開，不過他很快就迷路了。

梅爾：對不起，我不確定自己在哪裡。你能不能告訴我龐德羅沙飯店要怎麼走？

路人：好。你必須沿著這條路開兩公里，然後左轉，再開五分鐘左右就到了。

梅爾：謝謝你的幫忙。

幾分鐘過後，有輛車撞上梅爾的車。

梅爾：什麼？！喂，你為什麼撞我的車？

駕駛：又不是我的錯。

梅爾：當然是你的錯。我們交換一下資料。你有保險嗎？

駕駛：當然有。這起事故是你的錯。

梅爾：什麼？！你有毛病啊！明明就是你的錯。我想我們應該找警察來解決這個問題。

Ｗord List

give up 放棄
supplier [sə`plaɪə] *n.* 供應商
comprehensive [ˌkɑmprɪ`hɛnsɪv] *adj.* 全面的
policy [`pɑləsɪ] *n.* 保險（單）

driver's license 駕駛執照
fault [fɔlt] *n.* 錯誤
accident [`æksədənt] *n.* 事故
settle [`sɛtl] *v.* 解決（問題）

3 Biz 加分句型 Nice-to-Know Phrases

3.1 ▸▸ 找路 Finding Your Way

 track 24

❶ **Where can I get a map of (city)?**

我在哪裡可以弄到一張（城市）的地圖？

例 Hello. Do you know where I can get a map of London?

你好。你知道我在哪裡可以弄到一張倫敦的地圖嗎？

❷ **Can you tell me how to get to (place)?**

你能不能告訴我要怎麼到（地方）嗎？

例 Hi. Can you please tell me how to get to the nearest subway station?

嗨。你能不能告訴我要怎麼到最近的地鐵站？

❸ **Am I (near / far from) the (place)?**

我離（地方）（近／遠）嗎？

例 I'm not sure where I am. Am I near the Regent Hotel?

我不確定自己在哪裡。我離麗晶酒店近嗎？

❹ **I'm lost. / I've lost my way.**

我迷路了。／我找不到路。

例 I'm lost—can you help me?

我迷路了──你能幫我嗎？

3.2 ▸▸ 處理一樁事故 Handling an Accident

❶ **(Let's / We'd better) exchange information.**
（我們來／我們最好）交換一下資料。
例 Let's exchange information. Here's my driver's licence number and <u>contact</u> info.
我們交換一下資料。這是我的駕駛執照號碼和連絡資料。

❷ **Are you insured? / Do you have insurance?**
你有保險嗎？／你有沒有保險？
例 Are you insured? May I have your insurance policy number?
你有保險嗎？可不可以把你的保險號碼給我？

❸ **It wasn't my fault. / It was your fault.**
那不是我的錯。／那是你的錯。
例 It wasn't my fault that you hit my car.
你撞上我的車，並不是我的錯。

❹ **I think we should call the (police/<u>authorities</u>).**
我想我們應該叫（警察／有關當局）來。
例 I think we should call the police to help us settle this problem.
我想我們應該叫警察來幫我們解決這個問題。

Ⓦord List
....
contact [ˋkɑntækt] *n.* 聯絡
authorities [əˋθɔrətɪz] *n.* （複數型）當局；管理機構

4 Biz 加分詞彙 Nice-to-Know Words & Phrases

 track 25

❶ a crack in the windshield 擋風玻璃上的一道裂痕

❷ cab [kæb] *n.* 計程車

❸ fender bender [ˋfɛndɚ ˏbɛndɚ] *n.* 小交通事故

❹ sideswipe [ˋsaɪdˏswaɪp] *v.* 擦撞

❺ file an accident claim 申報意外賠償

❻ flat tire [ˋflæt ˋtaɪr] *n.* 爆胎

❼ keep going straight 繼續直行

❽ lane [len] *n.* 車道

❾ radar [ˋredɑr] *n.* 雷達

❿ service station [ˋsɝvɪs ˏsteʃən] *n.* 維修站；加油站

⓫ slow down 放慢速度

⓬ speed up 加速

⓭ speeding ticket [ˋspidɪŋ ˏtɪkɪt] *n.* 超速罰單

⓮ trunk [trʌŋk] *n.* 後行李廂

⓯ up ahead 在前面

:::::::: 小心陷阱 ::::::::

☹ 錯誤用法：

Here's my **driving license** number and contact info.

這是我的駕駛執照號碼和聯絡資料。

☺ 正確用法：

Here's my **driver's license** number and contact info.

這是我的駕駛執照號碼和聯絡資料。

:::::::: **Biz 一點通** ::::::::

Depending on the country, riding in taxis can be convenient, safe, and inexpensive, or using them for <u>transportation</u> can be expensive, difficult, and perhaps even dangerous. There are <u>numerous</u> websites that offer useful information about taxi service in various countries. For example, for advice on taking taxis in New York City, you can visit http://www.nycabbie.com/taxitips.html. Consult similar URLs for other cities. As you'll find, taxi regulations and fares can vary dramatically from city to city. For example, in Singapore, the industry is <u>deregulated</u>, so prices can be very different from one company to another. There are also certain <u>surcharges</u> you may need to be aware of depending on the time of day and the section of the city you are traveling through.

每個國家的情況不同，在有些地方搭計程車方便安全又實惠，有的地方則所費不貲，車又不好叫，或許還很危險。有幾個網站提供了各個國家計程車服務的實用資訊。比如，要看看在紐約市搭計程車有什麼要注意的，可以上 http://www.nycabbie.com/taxitips.html 查詢。其他城市的狀況則可以參考其他類似的網站。你會發現，在計程車法規與車資方面，城市與城市之間的差異很大。譬如說在新加坡，計程車工業早已解除管制，因此計程車公司之間的價差很大。你可能也需要留意，因搭乘時間以及路經城市某一地段而衍生出的額外費用。

ord List

transportation [ˌtrænspɚˋteʃən] *n.* 交通工具

numerous [ˋnjumərəs] *adj.* 許多的

deregulate [diˋrɛgjʊˌlet] *v.* 解除管制

surcharge [ˋsɝˌtʃɑrdʒ] *n.* 額外費

5 實戰演練 Practice Exercises

I 請為下列三句話選出最適合本章的中文譯義。

❶ How much coverage does the insurance provide?

(A) 這份保險所提供的賠償有多少？

(B) 這份保險所提供的項目有哪些？

(C) 這份保單所提供的投保年齡是多少？

❷ Please leave a deposit.

(A) 請留下存款。

(B) 請留下存摺。

(C) 請留下押金。

❸ It wasn't my fault. You ran into me.

(A) 不是我的責任，是你遇到我的。

(B) 不是我的毛病，是你碰到我的。

(C) 不是我的錯，是你撞到我的。

II 你會如何回答下面這兩個問題？

❶ Is this a metered taxi?

(A) Yes, I charge $100 for each trip.

(B) Yes, I have a license.

(C) Yes, I charge $2.00 for each kilometer.

❷ How much is the fare?

(A) Yes, it is a fair price.

(B) I owe you $20.00.

(C) It is $20.00.

III 請利用下列詞句寫一篇簡短的對話：

catch a taxi	taxi stand	flat rate
I'd like to go to	I'm lost	fare

＊解答請見 251 頁

第 **7** 章 | 入住旅館
Lodging in a Hotel

From:	Tony Potter
To:	Madrid Hilton Hotel
Subject:	My Reservation

To Whom It May Concern:

I have a reservation (confirmation number: 1108DRTP) for a standard double room from November 10 to 17. Would it be possible to upgrade to the "business package?"

Kind regards,

Tony Potter

敬啓者：

我預訂了一間標準雙人房，從十一月十日到十七日（確認編號：1108DRTP）。有沒有可能升等為「商務套裝住宿」？

東尼・波特敬上

1 Biz 必通句型 Need-to-Know Phrases

1.1 ▸▸ 入住房間 Getting to the Room

track 26

❶ **I have a reservation for (name) for (number) nights.**

我用（名字）預約了（數量）個晚上。

例 I have a reservation for Peggy Liu for six nights.

我用佩琪・劉的名字預約了六個晚上。

❷ **Could you please have someone show me (sth.)?**

可不可以請你們找人帶我參觀（某事物）？

例 Could you please have someone show me the business center?

可不可以請你們找人帶我參觀商務中心？

❸ **Can you tell me if the room has (sth.)?**

你能不能告訴我房裡是否有（某事物）？

例 Can you tell me if the room has wireless Internet?

你能不能告訴我房裡是否有無線網路？

❹ **How much does (sth.) cost?**

（某事物）要多少錢？

例 How much does <u>laundry</u> service cost? How long does it take?

衣物送洗服務要多少錢？要多久時間？

Ⓦord List

laundry [ˋlɔndrɪ] *n.* 送洗的衣物

❺ Do you provide (sth.)?

你們有沒有提供（某事物）？

例 Do you provide <u>massage</u> service? I'd like one this evening.

你們有沒有提供按摩服務？我今天晚上想要按摩一下。

❻ I'd like to be able to sign for (sth.).

我希望能夠把（某事物）簽在帳上。

例 I'd like to be able to sign for my meals. Can I charge them to my room?

我希望我的餐點能夠簽帳。我能不能把帳記在我房間的費用上？

❼ Where is (place) and what time does it (open/close)?

（地方）在哪裡？幾點（營業／打烊）？

例 Where is the restaurant and what time does it close?

那家餐廳在哪呢？幾點打烊？

❽ I'd like (sb.) to help me (with sth.).

我想找（某人）幫我（處理某事物）。

例 I'd like a clerk to help me with my bags.

我想找個服務人員幫我提行李袋。

Ⓦord List

massage [mə`sɑʒ] *n.* 按摩

1.2 ▸▸ 在房間裡 In the Room

❶ **This bed is too (hard/soft), is it possible to change it or (solution)?**
這張床太（硬／軟）了，有沒有可能換掉或是（解決辦法）？
例 This bed is too hard, is it possible to change it or can I move to another room?
這張床太硬了，有沒有可能換掉或是讓我搬到別的房間？

❷ **The (sth.) in my room isn't working properly—can you (solution)?**
我房間的（某事物）無法正常運作──你能不能（解決辦法）？
例 The television in my room isn't working properly—can you send someone to fix it, please?
我房間的電視無法正常運作──請問你能不能派個人來修理？

❸ **I like to order room service. This is room (number). I'd like ....**
我想叫客房服務。這是（數字）號房。我要……。
例 I like to order room service. This is room 2418. I'd like bacon and eggs, <u>eggs over easy</u>, toast, orange juice, and coffee.
我想叫客房服務。這是 2418 號房。我要培根和蛋，蛋要雙面煎的荷包蛋、蛋黃半熟就好，還要烤麵包、柳橙汁和咖啡。

❹ **Is it possible that you could send someone up to room (number) to (do sth.)?**
你可以派個人來（數字）號房（做某事）嗎？
例 Is it possible that you could send someone up to room 359 to pick up my laundry?
你可以派個人來 359 號房拿我要送洗的衣物嗎？

Ⓦord List

eggs over easy 雙面煎、蛋黃未全熟的荷包蛋

❺ This is room (number). I'd like a <u>wake-up call</u> for (time).

這是（數字）號房。我（時間）的時候想要起床電話服務。

例 This is room 760. I'd like a wake-up call for 6:30 a.m.

這是 760 號房。我早上六點半的時候想要起床電話服務。

❻ I'm not happy with my room—I like to move to (place).

我對我的房間不滿意──我想搬到（地方）。

例 I'm not happy with my room—I'd like to move to a larger room.

我對我的房間不滿意──我想搬到比較大的房間。

❼ Is it possible that you can upgrade my room? This room doesn't have (sth.).

你們有沒有可能幫我把房間升等？這個房間沒有（某事物）。

例 Is it possible that you can upgrade my room? This room doesn't have a balcony.

你們有沒有可能幫我把房間升等？這個房間沒有陽台。

❽ How much would it cost to upgrade (sth.)? This (sth.) is not <u>up to my standards</u>.

把（某事物）升等要多少錢？這（某事物）不合我的要求。

例 How much would it cost to upgrade my room? This view is not up to my standards.

把我的房間升等要多少錢？這房間的視野不合我的要求。

 ord List

wake-up call 起床電話

up to one's standards 達某人的標準

2 實戰會話 Show Time

2.1 ▸▸ Checking In

track 27

Tony arrives at the hotel. He wants to learn more about the hotel's services, so he doesn't <u>hesitate</u> to ask lots of questions.

Front Desk: Welcome to the Madrid Hilton. How may I help you?

Tony: I have reservation for Tony Potter for seven nights.

Front Desk: May I have your passport and credit card, please?

Tony: Here you are. Where is the restaurant and what time does it close?

Front Desk: You'll find it on the second floor across from the elevators. It's open twenty-four hours, sir.

Tony: Great. I'd like to be able to sign for everything at the hotel.

Front Desk: That won't be a problem, sir. You have the upgraded double room, with a queen-size bed. Is that correct?

Tony: Yes. Can you tell me if the room has <u>Internet access</u>?

Front Desk: Yes, it does, sir. That's included in the business package.

Tony: I know. I just wanted to make sure. But how does it work? Can I <u>plug</u> my laptop <u>into</u> the network?

Front Desk: Yes. There is an <u>Ethernet</u> cable in the room for that. You can also check out a wireless mouse and keyboard if you'd like and use the TV as a monitor.

Tony: OK. Also, could you please have someone show me the business center?

Front Desk: Perhaps you'd like to settle in your room first, Mr. Potter. We'd be happy to give you a tour of the business facility after that.

Tony: That's a good idea. I'd like a clerk to help us with our bags.

Front Desk: Certainly, sir. The <u>porter</u> will be right with you.

譯 文　辦理入住登記

東尼抵達飯店。他想多了解飯店所提供的各項服務，所以直接問了很多問題。

櫃臺人員：歡迎光臨馬德里希爾頓。有什麼能為您效勞的嗎？

東尼：　　我用東尼‧波特的名字預訂了房間，總共七個晚上。

櫃臺人員：我能看一下您的護照和信用卡嗎，麻煩您？

東尼：　　在這兒。請問餐廳在哪裡？幾點打烊？

櫃臺人員：就在二樓電梯的對面。餐廳二十四小時營業，先生。

東尼：　　好極了。我希望飯店裡的所有消費我都能簽帳。

櫃臺人員：那沒問題，先生。您訂的是升過等的雙人房，大號床。這樣對嗎？

東尼：　　對。你能不能告訴我房間裡可不可以上網？

櫃臺人員：可以的，先生。那包含在商務套裝住宿裡。

東尼：　　我知道。我只是想確認一下。可是要怎麼用呢？我插上手提電腦的線就能連上網嗎？

櫃臺人員：是的。房間裡有乙太網路連接線可用。如果您想要，也可以借用無線滑鼠和鍵盤，然後用電視當螢幕。

東尼：　　好的。還有，可以麻煩你找個人帶我去商務中心看看嗎？

櫃臺人員：或許您想先去房間安頓一下，波特先生。您安頓好之後我們很樂意帶您參觀我們的商務設施。

東尼：　　好主意。我想找個服務人員幫我們提行李袋。

櫃臺人員：沒問題，先生。行李服務員會馬上過來您這邊。

Ｗord List

hesitate [ˈhɛzə‚tet] *v.* 猶豫不決

Internet access（連線）上網

plug into 將插頭插上以連結

Ethernet [ˈiθə‚nɛt] *n.* 乙太網路

porter [ˈportə] *n.*（在飯店幫客人搬行李的）服務生

2.2 ▸▸ Asking for Service

Daphne is very <u>particular</u> about the rooms she stays in. If there is a problem, she doesn't hesitate to call the front desk. She also loves to <u>take advantage of</u> hotel service, especially when the company is paying the bill!

Front Desk: Front desk. Can I help you?

Daphne: Hi. This is Daphne Chiang in room 420. The shower in my room isn't working properly—can you send someone to fix it, please? There isn't enough water pressure.

Front Desk: Yes, I'm very sorry. I'll send someone up to your room right away. Is that all?

Daphne: I'd like to order some room service.

Front Desk: Let me transfer you to the restaurant. One moment, please.

Daphne listens to the on-hold music.

Restaurant: Good afternoon. This is the restaurant. How may I help you?

Daphne: Hi. This is room 420. I'd like to order room service. I'd like a cheeseburger, chocolate milkshake, and French fries.

Restaurant: Is that all, ma'am?

Daphne: I'd also like a wake-up call.

Restaurant: OK. Let me transfer you back to the front desk.

Daphne: Thank you.

Daphne hums along to the on-hold music.

Front Desk: Front desk. How can I be of service?

Daphne: Hi, this is room 420 again. I'd like a wake-up call for 6:30 a.m.

Front Desk: Not a problem, Ms. Chiang. One wake-up call for tomorrow morning at 6:30. Is there anything else I can assist you with?

Daphne: Yes, actually. I have some <u>garments</u> I'd like to have <u>dry-cleaned</u>....

譯文 要求提供服務

戴芬妮對自己住的房間非常講究。一有問題，她會毫不遲疑地馬上打電話給櫃臺人員。她也喜歡享受旅館的服務，尤其是公司出錢的時候。

櫃臺人員：這裡是櫃臺。有什麼需要幫忙的嗎？

戴芬妮： 嗨，我是 420 號房的戴芬妮・江。我房間的淋浴設備無法正常使用——可以請你派個人來修一下嗎？水壓不夠。

櫃臺人員：好的，非常抱歉。我會馬上派人到您的房間。還有別的需要嗎？

戴芬妮： 我想叫客房服務。

櫃臺人員：我幫你轉給餐廳。請等一下。

戴分妮聽者等待的音樂聲。

餐廳： 午安。這裡是餐廳。有什麼能為您效勞的嗎？

戴芬妮： 嗨。這裡是 420 號房。我想要客房服務。我要一個起司漢堡、巧克力奶昔和薯條。

餐廳： 就這樣嗎，小姐？

戴芬妮： 我也想要起床電話服務。

餐廳： 好的。我幫您轉回櫃臺。

戴芬妮： 謝謝你。

戴芬妮隨著等待的音樂哼著歌。

櫃臺人員：這是櫃臺。需要什麼服務嗎？

戴芬妮： 嗨，又是 420 號房。我早上六點半想要起床電話服務。

櫃臺人員：沒問題，江小姐。明天早上六點半起床電話服務。您還有別的事情需要我幫忙嗎？

戴芬妮： 事實上是有的。我有些衣物想要乾洗……

Word List

particular [pəˋtɪkjələ] *adj.* 講究的；挑剔的

take advantage of 利用

garment [ˋgɑrmənt] *n.* 衣服

dry-clean [ˋdraɪ ˋklin] *v.* 乾洗

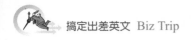
3 Biz 加分句型 Nice-to-Know Phrases

3.1 ▸▸ 尋求其他服務 Finding Other Services **track 28**

❶ Since I'll be staying for (number) nights, can I have a discount?

既然我要住上（數量）個晚上，能不能給我一個折扣？

例 Since I'll be staying for six nights, can I have a discount or room upgrade?

既然我要住上六個晚上，能不能給我一個折扣或是把房間升等？

❷ Do you have (sth.) that I can (book/reserve) for (amount of time)?

你們有沒有（某事物）可以讓我（預訂／預約）（多少時間）？

例 Do you have a conference room that I can book for a couple of hours?

你們有沒有會議室可以讓我預訂幾個小時？

❸ I'd like to reserve (sth.).

我想要預約（某事物）。

例 I'd like to reserve a table for six for dinner at 8:15 p.m.

我想預約一張六人桌，以便八點十五分的時候用晚餐。

❹ I'm having trouble (Ving).

我沒辦法順利（做……）。

例 I'm having trouble making a long distance phone call. I think I need some <u>assistance</u>.

我沒辦法順利撥長途電話。我想我需要協助。

Ⓦord List

assistance [ə`sɪstəns] *n.* 協助

3.2 ▸▸ 在房間裡 In the Room

❶ This room is (problem). Can you do something about it?

這個房間（問題）。你能不能處理一下？

例 This room is very noisy. Can you do something about it? I need to get some sleep.

這個房間很吵。你能不能處理一下？我需要睡一覺。

❷ I'm having trouble sleeping—the (room/people) (location) are too noisy.

我沒辦法入睡——（地點）的（房間／人）太吵了。

例 I'm having trouble sleeping—the people across the hall are too noisy. Can you ask them to quiet down?

我沒辦法入睡——走廊對面的人太吵了。你能不能叫他們小聲一點？

❸ Does this hotel have (sth.)? I'm not feeling well.

這飯店有（某事物）嗎？我覺得不舒服。

例 Does this hotel have a doctor? I'm not feeling well.

這飯店有醫生嗎？我覺得不舒服。

❹ Is there a <u>pharmacy</u> in the hotel or can someone...?

飯店裡有藥房嗎？或者是不是有人能⋯⋯嗎？

例 Is there a pharmacy in the hotel or can someone go to the pharmacy for me?

飯店裡有藥房嗎？或者是不是有人能為我去一趟藥房？

Ⓦ ord List
⋯⋯⋯⋯⋯⋯⋯⋯⋯⋯⋯⋯⋯⋯⋯⋯⋯⋯⋯⋯⋯⋯⋯⋯⋯⋯⋯⋯⋯⋯⋯⋯⋯⋯

pharmacy [ˈfɑrməsɪ] *n.* 藥房

4 Biz 加分詞彙 Nice-to-Know Words & Phrases

track 29

① bellboy [ˈbɛlˌbɔɪ] *n.* 門房小弟

② bidet [bɪˈde] *n.* 潔便沖洗器

③ brunch [brʌntʃ] *n.* 早午餐

④ continental breakfast [ˌkɑntəˈnɛntḷ ˈbrɛkfəst] *n.* 歐式早餐

⑤ courtyard [ˈkortˌjɑrd] *n.* 庭院；中庭

⑥ drapery [ˈdrepərɪ] *n.* 厚窗簾

⑦ emergency exit [ɪˈmɝdʒənsɪ ˌɛksɪt] *n.* 緊急出口

⑧ fire extinguisher [ˈfaɪr ɪkˌstɪŋgwɪʃə] *n.* 滅火器

⑨ hallway [ˈhɔlˌwe] *n.* 走廊

⑩ hotel security [hoˈtɛl sɪˌkjʊrətɪ] *n.* 旅館保全

⑪ lobby [ˈlɑbɪ] *n.* 大廳

⑫ parking garage [ˈpɑrkɪŋ gəˌrɑʒ] *n.* 停車場

⑬ shuttle service [ˈʃʌtḷ ˌsɝvɪs] *n.* 接駁服務

⑭ suite [swit] *n.* 套房

⑮ presidential suite [ˌprɛzəˈdɛnʃəl ˌswit] *n.* 總統套房

小心陷阱

☹ 錯誤用法：
I'm having trouble **to make** a long distance phone call.
我沒辦法順利撥長途電話。

☺ 正確用法：
I'm having trouble **making** a long distance phone call.
我沒辦法順利撥長途電話。

Biz 一點通

A stay in a hotel is not without danger. Theft and emergencies—primarily fires and earthquakes—are always within the realm of possibility. As a pre-travel preparation, you should browse the Internet for content related to hotel safety. There are some things you can get in the habit of doing during your hotel stay to protect yourself. For example, while you check in, instruct the desk clerk to write your room number down rather than telling it to you. This will prevent strangers in the lobby from knowing where your room is. And keep in mind that you should never take an elevator during an emergency.

下榻旅館並不能保證安全。竊盜以及緊急事件——主要是火災和地震——總是可能會發生。做為出發前的準備，你應該上網瀏覽一下討論旅館安全的網站。你停留在旅館的期間，為了自保有些事要養成習慣。譬如說，當你辦理入住手續時，要指示櫃臺人員將你的房號寫下來而不是口頭告訴你，這樣才不會讓大廳裡的陌生人知道你的房間在哪裡。另外，謹記在緊急情況中絕對不能搭電梯。

Word List

theft [θɛft] *n.* 偷竊
emergency [ɪˋmɝdʒənsɪ] *n.* 緊急情況

earthquake [ˋɝθ͵kwek] *n.* 地震
realm [rɛlm] *n.* 範圍；領域

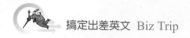

5 實戰演練 Practice Exercises

I 請為下列三句話選出最適合本章的中文譯義。

1 Would it be possible to change rooms?

(A) 有沒有可能可以換房間？

(B) 會不會是在裝修房間？

(C) 可不可以調換房間？

2 I'd like to charge the meal to my room.

(A) 我希望能夠把餐點送到我房間。

(B) 我希望能夠把餐點的帳記在我房間的費用上。

(C) 我希望能夠把房間的帳和餐點的一起算。

3 The guests next door are being too noisy. Can something be done?

(A) 隔壁的客人太吵了。能不能想點辦法？

(B) 對門的客人太吵了。能不能管一管？

(C) 旁邊的客人太吵了。能不能行行好？

II 你會如何回答下面這兩句話？

1 I'm sorry, but our Internet access is down right now.

(A) When will it be back up?

(B) When is it not going to come down?

(C) When is it going to be OK?

2 I'm sorry, but we don't have a comparable room available right now.

(A) Then when can I move?

(B) Then maybe I should check in.

(C) Then can you move me to a better room?

III 請利用下列詞句寫一篇簡短的對話：

I'm having trouble hooking up	I'd like to change rooms
wireless Internet	is not working properly
too far from the elevator	won't stop running

＊解答請見 252 頁

第 **8** 章 | 觀光與購物
Sightseeing and Shopping

Attention Visitors!

While in Madrid, there are many great attractions to see. Don't forget to sign up for some excellent tours of the city. Visit the museums and art galleries Madrid has to offer. A must-see is bullfighting, where you will experience the thrill of an exciting sport of man versus beast! You can also take excursions to nearby cities, such as Toledo. One thing is for sure—you'll never be bored in Madrid. As for shopping, you will find a large selection of stores, including everything from bargain stores to luxury shops.

旅客注意！

在馬德里有不少風光名勝供您遊覽。可別忘了報名參加一些精彩的市區遊覽。走一趟馬德里的博物館和藝廊。千萬不能錯過鬥牛，屆時您將能親身體驗到人獸對峙的驚險刺激！您也可以走訪鄰近的城市，比方像托雷多。有件事情無庸置疑——您在馬德里絕對不會無聊。至於購物，您可以找到各種類型的店家，從低價商店到精品店，一應俱全。

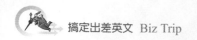
1 Biz 必通句型 Need-to-Know Phrases

1.1 ▶ 參觀景點 Enjoying the Sights

❶ What are the popular tourist <u>attractions</u> in (city/country)?

（城市／國家）有哪些熱門的觀光景點？

例 What are the popular tourist attractions in Los Angeles?

洛杉磯有哪些熱門的觀光景點？

❷ Where can I buy a <u>guidebook</u> for (city/country)?

我可以在哪裡買到（城市／國家）的導覽手冊？

例 Hello. Where can I buy a guidebook for Sydney?

你好。我可以在哪裡買到雪梨的導覽手冊？

❸ How long is the (tour/show/<u>event</u>)?

（遊覽／表演／活動）要多久？

例 Excuse me, how long is the riverboat tour?

對不起，請問遊一趟河船要多久？

❹ Where do I catch the (bus/boat)?

我要在哪裡搭乘（巴士／船）？

例 Where do I catch the bus for the tour?

我要在哪裡搭乘遊覽巴士？

Word List

attraction [ə`trækʃən] *n.* 觀光景點

guide book [`gaɪd͵bʊk] *n.* 導覽手冊；旅遊指南

event [ɪ`vɛnt] *n.* 活動

❺ What time will I be (picked up / dropped off)?

幾點會（來接我／讓我下車）？

例 What time will I be picked up for the <u>scuba</u> lesson tomorrow morning?

明天早上幾點會來接我去上水肺潛水課？

❻ Does (event) include (breakfast/lunch/dinner/meals)?

（活動）包含（早餐／午餐／晚餐／三餐）嗎？

例 Does the jungle <u>trek</u> include lunch, or should I bring my own food?

這趟叢林之旅包含午餐嗎？還是我得自己帶食物？

❼ What is the <u>admission</u> fee to (place)?

（地方）的入場費要多少？

例 Pardon me, what is the admission fee to the <u>amusement park</u>?

對不起，請問遊樂園的入場費要多少？

❽ When does (place) (open/close)?

（地方）幾點（營業／打烊）？

例 When does Disney World close today?

迪士尼世界今天幾點打烊？

Ⓦord List

scuba [ˋskubə] *n.* 水肺；自攜式潛水呼吸器

trek [trɛk] *n.* （長途而辛苦的）旅行

admission [ədˋmɪʃən] *n.* 入場費

amusement park [əˋmjuzmənt ˏpɑrk] *n.* 遊樂場

1.2 ▸▸ 去購物 Going Shopping

❶ **Is this (product) on sale?**

這（商品）在特價中嗎？

🔲 Hi. Is this jacket on sale?

嗨。這件夾克是不是在特價？

🔲 Excuse me. Is this box of candy on sale?

對不起，請問這盒糖果是不是在特價？

❷ **Is the price of this (product) <u>negotiable</u>?**

這（商品）的價格可以商量嗎？

🔲 Is the price of this necklace negotiable?

這條項鍊的價格可以商量嗎？

❸ **Can I get a <u>discount</u> on this (product)?**

這（商品）可以給我一個折扣嗎？

🔲 Can I get a discount on this suit?

這套西裝可以給我一個折扣嗎？

❹ **This (product) is (percentage) off.**

這（商品）打（百分比）折。

🔲 This dress is 30 percent off the regular price.

這件洋裝原價打七折。

Ⓦord List

negotiable [nɪˋgoʃɪəbl] *adj.* 可商議的

discount [ˋdɪskaʊnt] *n.* 折扣

❺ Does this (product) <u>come in</u> any other (colors/styles/ models)?

這（商品）有其他的（顏色／設計／款式）嗎？

例 Does this briefcase come in any other colors? I'm looking for something lighter.

這個公事包有其他的顏色嗎？我在找顏色淺一點的。

❻ Is this (product) <u>returnable</u>?

這（商品）可不可以退還？

例 Excuse me. Is this camera returnable if I have any problems with it?

對不起，請問如果我在使用時有問題，這台相機可不可以退還？

❼ Can I pay for this (product) with (payment method)?

這（商品）我可不可以用（付費方法）來支付？

例 Can I pay for these pants with a credit card?

這件褲子我可不可用信用卡來支付？

例 Can I pay for this with traveler's checks?

這個我可不可以用旅行支票來支付？

❽ I'd like to pay for this (product) with (payment method).

我想用（付費方法）支付這（商品）。

例 I'd like to pay for this ring with a credit card. Will that be OK?

我想用信用卡支付這只戒指。這樣可以嗎？

---

ord List

come in 有⋯⋯（款式花樣等）

returnable [rɪ`tɜnəbl] *adj.* 可退還的

2 實戰會話 Show Time

2.1 ▸ Sightseeing Plans

 track 31

The day after arriving in Madrid, Tony and Cindy decide they would like to do some sightseeing.

Cindy: Excuse me, what are the popular tourist attractions in Madrid?

Hotel Clerk: Well, there are many. This brochure is very good.

Cindy: Thank you. Where can we buy a guidebook for Madrid?

Hotel Clerk: The gift shop has a good one. Actually, I can <u>recommend</u> a tour of Madrid.

Cindy: Thank you. How long is the tour?

Hotel Clerk: It's about three and a half hours.

Cindy: Where do I catch the tour?

Hotel Clerk: Right here at the hotel.

Cindy: What time will I be picked up?

Hotel Clerk: At 8:00 a.m.

Cindy: Does the tour include lunch?

Hotel Clerk: No, it doesn't. But there are plenty of places to eat where they take you.

Cindy: How about the Prado Museum? What is the admission fee? When does it open?

Hotel Clerk: I'm not sure, but it isn't very much. It opens at 9:00 a.m.

Cindy: Oh, I forgot to ask about the nightlife. What are the popular bars in Madrid?

Hotel Clerk: Here, let me give you another brochure. But I will recommend the San Pedronas. It is very <u>lively</u>.

Cindy: Is there a <u>cover charge</u> to get in?

Hotel Clerk: No, there is no admission charge.

Cindy: Is there a <u>dress code</u>?

Hotel Clerk: Don't wear tennis shoes or shorts.

Cindy: Is the San Pedronas Bar very expensive?

Hotel Clerk: No, it is very <u>reasonable</u> for Madrid.

Cindy: Thank you for answering all my questions.

Hotel Clerk: My pleasure. I hope you have a wonderful time in our city.

譯文 觀光遊覽計畫

抵達馬德里的隔天，東尼和辛蒂決定要去觀光。

辛蒂： 對不起，請問馬德里熱門的觀光景點有哪些？
旅館人員：嗯，有很多。這本小冊子很好用。
辛蒂： 謝謝你。我們在哪裡可以買到馬德里的導覽手冊？
旅館人員：禮品店有一本很棒。實際上，我可以推薦你們參加馬德里的遊覽。
辛蒂： 謝謝。一趟要多久時間？
旅館人員：大概三個鐘頭半。
辛蒂： 我可以在哪裡參加這個遊覽？
旅館人員：就在旅館這裡。
辛蒂： 幾點會來接人呢？
旅館人員：早上八點。
辛蒂： 行程包括中餐嗎？
旅館人員：沒有，不包括中餐。不過他們帶你們去的地方有很多都可以用餐。
辛蒂： 那普拉多美術館呢？入場費是多少？幾點開放？
旅館人員：我不確定，可是不貴。早上九點開。
辛蒂： 噢，我忘了打聽一下夜生活的事。馬德里有哪些熱門的酒吧？
旅館人員：我這再給你另一本冊子。不過我推薦聖佩多那司，那裡很熱鬧。
辛蒂： 入場要基本費嗎？
旅館人員：不用，不需要付入場費。
辛蒂： 有服裝規定嗎？
旅館人員：別穿網球鞋或短褲就行了。
辛蒂： 聖佩多那司酒吧會不會很貴？
旅館人員：不會，就馬德里當地來說，價格很合理。
辛蒂： 謝謝你幫我解答了所有的問題。
旅館人員：是我的榮幸。希望妳在我們的城市玩得很開心。

Word List

recommend [ˌrɛkəˋmɛnd] *v.* 推薦
lively [ˋlaɪvlɪ] *adj.* 熱烈的
cover charge 基本費；入場費

dress code 服裝規定
reasonable [ˋriznəbl] *adj.* 合理的

2.2 ▸▸ Shopping in London

While the others have all landed in Madrid and checked into their hotel, Daphne is enjoying her short stopover in London. Right now, she's shopping.

Daphne: Pardon me, is this notebook computer on sale?

Clerk: I'm sorry, that's the regular price.

Daphne: Is the price negotiable? Can I get a discount?

Clerk: No, I'm sorry. But perhaps you'd like to consider this model. It is 20 percent off the regular price.

Daphne: Does it come in any other colors than black?

Clerk: Yes, we have that model in white.

Daphne: Can I pay for it with traveler's checks?

Clerk: No, I'm sorry, we don't accept them.

Daphne: OK, I'll pay by credit card, then.

Once back at her hotel, she has problems with the computer. She returns to the shop.

Daphne: Hello, do you remember me? I bought a notebook from you a few hours ago. Well, this notebook is <u>defective</u>. It doesn't work properly. I'd like to get a <u>refund</u> on it.

Clerk: I'm sorry, our store policy is no refunds. We do offer exchanges, though.

Daphne: <u>In that case</u>, I'd like to exchange this notebook for another one. Actually, this notebook is a little too large, so can I exchange it for a smaller one?

Clerk: Certainly. Let's just make sure this new one works well.

The sales clerk tries the other notebook, and it works fine.

Clerk: There you go. I'm sorry for the inconvenience.

Daphne: That's all right. Thanks for your assistance.

譯文 在倫敦購物

在其他人都已經抵達馬德里，也登記入住旅館之時，戴芬妮正享受在倫敦的短暫過境。此刻她正在逛街購物。

戴芬妮：請問一下，這台筆記型電腦是不是在特價？

店員： 抱歉，那是定價。

戴芬妮：價格可以商量嗎？能不能給我一個折扣？

店員： 不行，抱歉。不過也許妳想考慮一下這個機型，原價打八折。

戴芬妮：除了黑色以外，還有其他的顏色嗎？

店員： 有，那個機型我們有白色的。

戴芬妮：我可不可以用旅行支票付款？

店員： 不行，抱歉。我們不收旅行支票。

戴芬妮：好吧，那我用信用卡付好了。

一回到飯店，她的電腦就出了問題。她回到店裡。

戴芬妮：你好，還記得我嗎？我幾個小時前跟你買了一台筆記型電腦。嗯，這台電腦有瑕疵。無法正常使用。我想退款。

店員： 抱歉，我們店裡的政策是不退款。不過我們可以換貨。

戴芬妮：那樣的話，我想把這台換成另一台。事實上這台有點太大，所以我能不能換小一點的？

店員： 當然可以。我們來確定一下這台新的能夠使用。

銷售員測試了另一台筆記型電腦，它的運作狀況良好。

店員： 這是您的。造成您的不便我非常抱歉。

戴芬妮：沒關係。謝謝你的協助。

Word List

defective [dɪˋfɛktɪv] *adj.* 有瑕疵的

refund [ˋrɪˏfʌnd] *n.* 退款

In that case,... 那樣的話，……

3 Biz 加分句型 Nice-to-Know Phrases

3.1 ▸▸ 盡情享受夜生活 Enjoying the Nightlife track 32

❶ What are the popular (bars/nightclubs) in (city)?

（城市）有哪些熱門的（酒吧／夜店）？

例 What are the popular bars in Toronto?

多倫多有哪些熱門的酒吧？

❷ Is there a cover charge to get into (place)?

（地方）入場要基本費嗎？

例 Is there a cover charge to get into this nightclub?

這家夜店入場要基本費嗎？

❸ Is there a dress code for (place)?

（地方）有沒有服裝規定？

例 Is there a dress code for the Miramax Nightclub?

米拉美克斯夜店有沒有服裝規定？

❹ Is (name of establishment) very expensive?

（場所名稱）會不會很貴？

例 Is the Candlelight Restaurant very expensive?

燭光餐廳會不會很貴？

Ⓦord List

establishment [əs`tæblɪʃmənt] *n.* （為商業或其他目的而）建立的機構

3.2 ▸▸ 處理購物的問題 Dealing with Shopping Problems

❶ This (product) is too (large/small).
這（商品）太（大／小）了。
例 This sweater is too small.
這件毛衣太小了。

❷ This (product) (is defective / doesn't work).
這（商品）（有瑕疵／不能用）。
例 This camera is defective.
這台相機有瑕疵。
例 These batteries don't work.
這些電池不能用。

❸ I'd like to get a refund on this (product).
這（商品）我想要退款。
例 I'd like to get a refund on this MP3 player.
這台 MP3 我想要退款。

❹ I'd like to exchange this (product) for (another one / something else).
我想把這（商品）換成（另外一個／其他東西）。
例 I'd like to exchange these pants for another pair.
我想把這件褲子換成另外一件。

4 Biz 加分詞彙 Nice-to-Know Words & Phrases

 track 33

❶ admission ticket [əd`mɪʃən ˌtɪkɪt] *n.* 入場券

❷ city tour [`sɪtɪ ˌtur] *n.* 市區遊覽

❸ closed to the public 不對外開放

❹ discounted item [`dɪskauntɪd `aɪtəm] *n.* 打折商品

❺ GST (Goods and Services Tax) 商品暨服務稅

❻ guided tour [`gaɪdɪd `tur] *n.* 有導覽的旅程

❼ hours of operation [`aurz əv ˌɑpə`reʃən] *n.* 辦公時間

❽ lost and found [`lɔst ənd `faund] *n.* 失物招領處

❾ receipt [rɪ`sit] *n.* 收據

❿ proof of purchase [`pruf əv `pɜtʃəs] *n.* 購買證明

⓫ sale price [`sel ˌpraɪs] *n.* 售價

⓬ sales slip [`sels ˌslɪp] *n.* 銷貨單

⓭ souvenir shop [ˌsuvə`nɪr ˌʃɑp] *n.* 紀念品店

⓮ store directory [`stor də`rɛktərɪ] *n.* 店面簡介

⓯ VAT (Value Added Tax) 加值稅

::::::::: 小心陷阱 :::::::::

☹ 錯誤用法：

This dress is **70 percent discount of** the regular price.
這件洋裝原價打七折。

☺ 正確用法：

This dress is **30 percent off** the regular price.
這件洋裝原價打七折。

::::::::: **Biz 一點通** :::::::::

Traveling in a foreign country can be a wonderful experience, but there are also some things to be careful about. In addition to typical safety concerns, you should <u>be aware of</u> being <u>ripped off</u> by vendors who make a living from cheating customers—especially foreign ones. Some destinations with <u>tourist traps</u> increase prices <u>dramatically</u>, so it's in your best interest to bargain as much as you can in places such as Thailand, Indonesia, and Cambodia. There are several good websites that offer general travel tips. One is called www.1000tips4trips.com. The BBC has put together a pretty good site at http://www.bbc.co.uk/holiday/tips/general. shtml. For travel in Asia, this URL may <u>come in handy</u>: www. asiatraveltips.com.

在異國旅行的經驗可能多采多姿，不過有些事情也要當心。除了特定的安全考量之外，你也要小心別被那些靠欺騙顧客討生活的攤販敲了竹槓——特別是當顧客是外國人時。某些觀光景點會胡亂哄抬價格來坑觀光客，所以你在像是泰國、印尼和柬埔寨等地方時，最好盡全力殺價。有一些不錯的網站提供了概略的旅遊建議，其中一個叫 www.1000tips4trips.com。英國廣播公司 BBC 也整合了一個很好的網站在 http://www.bbc.co.uk/holiday/tips/general.shtml。在亞洲旅遊的話，下面這個網址可能派得上用場：www.asiatraveltips.com。

Ⓦord List
....
be aware of 小心
rip off 敲竹槓
tourist trap 坑觀光客的商家

dramatically [drə`mætɪk]ɪ] *adv.* 戲劇性地
come in handy 派上用場

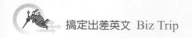

5 實戰演練 Practice Exercises

Ⅰ 請為下列三句話選出最適合本章的中文譯義。

❶ What is the admission fee?

(A) 入場費要多少？

(B) 許可費要多少？

(C) 會費要多少？

❷ Is there a cover charge?

(A) 被子要收費嗎？

(B) 有涵蓋保險費嗎？

(C) 要基本費嗎？

❸ I'd like to get a refund.

(A) 我想再次融資。

(B) 我想退款。

(C) 我想還錢。

Ⅱ 你會如何回應下面這兩句話？

❶ Is the price negotiable?

(A) Yes, it is a sale price.

(B) Yes, it is the lowest price.

(C) Yes, we can give you a discount.

❷ This product is defective.

(A) In that case, I'll give you a discount.

(B) In that case, I'll give you a refund.

(C) In that case, I'll pay for it by credit card.

Ⅲ 請利用下列詞句寫一篇簡短的對話：

a guidebook	tourist attraction	recommend
get a refund	pick up	defective

＊解答請見 253 頁

第 **9** 章 | 處理特殊情況
Dealing with Special Situations

From:	Jason Roth
To:	Madrid Property Management Co.
Subject:	Short-Term Rental Property

Dear Antonia,

As I mentioned earlier, I'm coming to Madrid soon. I would like to enquire about the cost of renting an apartment for six months. I will call you when I arrive.

Sincerely,

Jason Roth

親愛的安東妮雅：

如同我之前提到的,我就快來馬德里了。我想詢問一下租用六個月公寓的費用。我抵達的時候會打電話給妳。

傑森・羅斯敬上

1 Biz 必通句型 Need-to-Know Phrases

1.1 ▶▶ 安排長期住宿
Arranging Long-term Accommodations

 track 34

❶ **I'd like to rent a (fully/<u>partially</u> <u>furnished</u>) (apartment/house) in (city) for (length of time).**

我想在（城市）租一間（裝潢齊全／部份裝潢）的（公寓／房子），為期（時間長短）。

例 I'd like to rent a fully furnished apartment in Boston for three months.

我想在波士頓租一間裝潢齊全的公寓，為期三個月。

❷ **You need to sign a <u>lease</u> for (length of time).**

你必須簽（時間長短）的租約。

例 You need to sign a lease for at least two months.

你必須簽至少兩個月的租約。

❸ **A (long-term/short-term) lease of (length of time) is preferred.**

（時間長短）的（長期／短期）租約比較被接受。

例 A long-term stay of one year or more is preferred.

一年或更久的長期租約比較被接受。

❹ **The minimum stay is (number of days/months).**

最短要住（天數／月數）。

例 The minimum stay is (at least) ninety days.

最短要住（至少）九十天。

Ⓦord List

accommodation [əˌkɑmə`deʃən] *n.* 住宿
partially [`pɑrʃəlɪ] *adv.* 部分地

furnish [`fɜnɪʃ] *v.* 給房間配置家具設備
lease [lis] *n.* 租約

❺ The <u>utilities</u> are (not) included.

水電瓦斯（不）含在內。

例 I'm sorry, the utilities are not included in the price I quoted you.

抱歉，水電瓦斯不含在我報給你的價格內。

❻ How much is the <u>security deposit</u>?

保證金要多少錢？

例 I have a question—how much is the security deposit?

我有個問題——保證金要多錢？

❼ The kitchen is fully equipped.

廚房設備齊全。

例 The kitchen is fully equipped with everything you'll need.

廚房設備齊全，你需要的東西一應俱全。

❽ You must leave a security deposit of (amount of money).

你得留（錢數）的保證金。

例 You must leave a security deposit of US$1,000.

你得留一千美元的保證金。

ord List

utility [ju`tɪlətɪ] *n.* 水電等公用事業

security deposit [sɪ`kjʊrətɪ dɪ.pazɪt] *n.* 保證金

133

1.2 ▸ 處理病痛 Dealing with Illness

❶ **I feel (sick/<u>nauseous</u>/<u>dizzy</u>).**

我（不舒服／反胃／頭暈）。

例 I don't feel well; I feel dizzy.

我不舒服；我頭暈。

❷ **I have (a <u>fever</u> / a headache / the <u>flu</u> / a cold).**

我（發燒／頭痛／得流行性感冒／感冒）了。

例 I'm not feeling very well; I think I have a fever.

我不舒服；我想我發燒了。

❸ **There's something wrong with my (arm/leg/ankle/knee/neck/back).**

我的（手臂／腿／腳踝／膝蓋／脖子／背部）不大對勁。

例 There's something wrong with my ankle. I fell and <u>injured</u> it.

我的腳踝不大對勁。我跌倒時弄傷了。

❹ **I have (<u>symptom</u>). I need to see a doctor.**

我（症狀）。我需要看醫生。

例 I have a sore throat. I need to see a doctor.

我喉嚨痛。我需要看醫生。

例 I have <u>allergies</u>. I need to see a doctor.

我過敏。我需要看醫生。

Word List

nauseous [ˋnɔʒəs] *adj.* 反胃的；噁心的

dizzy [ˋdɪzɪ] *adj.* 頭暈的

fever [ˋfivə] *n.* 發燒

flu [flu] *n.* 流行性感冒

injure [ˋɪndʒə] *v.* 弄傷

symptom [ˋsɪmptəm] *n.* 症狀

allergy [ˋæləˌdʒɪ] *n.* 過敏

❺ Where is the nearest (medical/emergency/health) clinic?

離這裡最近的（醫療／緊急／保健）診所在哪裡？

例 Pardon me. Where is the nearest medical clinic?

對不起，請問離這裡最近的醫療診所在哪裡？

❻ I want some <u>over-the-counter</u> medication for (problem).

我要治（毛病）的成藥。

例 Hello. I want some over-the-counter medication for <u>motion sickness</u>.

你好。我要治暈車的成藥。

❼ Can you please fill this <u>prescription</u> for me?

能不能請你幫我配這張處方簽的藥？

例 Excuse me—can you please fill this prescription for me?

對不起──能不能請你幫我配這張處方簽的藥？

❽ What have you got for (<u>diarrhea</u>/allerigies/sunburns/ <u>rashes</u>/<u>insomnia</u>)?

你們有什麼治（腹瀉／過敏／曬傷／疹子／失眠）的藥？

例 What have you got for diarrhea?

你們有什麼治腹瀉的藥？

Word List

over-the-counter 無須醫師處方即可出售的

motion sickness 暈車、暈船、暈機

prescription [prɪ`skrɪpʃən] *n.* 處方簽（配藥動詞用 fill）

diarrhea [ˌdaɪə`riə] *n.* 腹瀉

rash [ræʃ] *n.* 疹子

insomnia [ɪn`sɑmnɪə] *n.* 失眠

2 實戰會話 Show Time

2.1 ▸ Renting an Apartment or House

 track 35

Following his arrival in Madrid, Jason checks into his hotel and later calls the <u>property</u> management company and talks to his agent, Antonia.

Jason: Hi, Antonia, I'm wondering if you could show me some apartments over the next few days? I'd like to rent a fully furnished apartment in Madrid for six months.

Antonia: Certainly. But that will limit your <u>options</u> a bit, because in many cases a long-term lease is preferred. Of course there are still many apartments that will allow a short-term lease. However, you will need to sign a lease for three months.

Jason: That's not a problem. The minimum stay will be at least three months.

Antonia: OK, good. I have several I can show you tomorrow, if you like. For example, there's a very nice apartment in downtown Madrid available for €700 per month. The utilities are not included in that price, though.

Jason: How much is the security deposit?

Antonia: You must leave a security deposit of €1,200.

Jason: Is the apartment fully furnished?

Antonia: Actually, it's only partially furnished. I think there is some furniture, such as a sofa and a bed, but you would need to buy some things, such as a coffee table and perhaps a few lamps. The kitchen is fully equipped, though.

Jason: That sounds pretty good. Maybe I can look at that one tomorrow along with a few other apartments as well.

Antonia: Good. I will pick you up at your hotel lobby at 9:00 a.m. tomorrow.

譯文 租公寓或房子

傑森抵達馬德里之後就在旅館辦好入住手續，稍後便打電話給房地產管理公司與他的仲介員安東妮雅談話。

傑森： 嗨，安東妮雅。我想知道妳接下來這幾天能不能帶我去看幾間公寓？我想在馬德里租一間設備齊全的公寓，為期六個月。

安東妮雅：當然可以。不過那樣你的選擇會有所限制，因為在大部分的情況下長期租約比較被接受。當然可以住短期的公寓還是很多，可是你得簽三個月的租約。

傑森： 那沒問題。我最少也要住三個月。

安東妮雅：好，那很好。如果你要的話，我有幾間公寓，我明天就可以帶你去看。譬如說，在馬德里市中心就有一間非常好的公寓可租，月租是七百歐元。不過，這個價錢並不包含水電瓦斯。

傑森： 保證金是多少呢？

安東妮雅：你得留一千兩百歐元的保證金。

傑森： 那間公寓設備齊全嗎？

安東妮雅：事實上只有部份裝潢。我想那裡有一些家具，像是沙發和床，不過你會需要買些東西，比如茶几和也許幾盞燈吧。不過，廚房倒是設備齊全。

傑森： 聽來很不錯。也許明天我可以去看看那間公寓，也可以看一下其他幾間。

安東妮雅：好。我明天早上九點會到你的旅館大廳接你。

ord List

property [ˈprɑpətɪ] *n.* 房地產
option [ˈɑpʃən] *n.* 選擇；選擇的自由

2.2 ▸▸ A Terrible Day

Tony had a good flight, but now that he's in Madrid, he doesn't feel very well. He decides to visit a pharmacy to get some medicine.

Tony: Hi. I feel sick. I think I have a fever.

Clerk: I can fill out a prescription for you if you have one.

Tony: No, I don't have a prescription. I want some over-the-counter medicine for the flu.

Clerk: Sure. Here you are. Is there anything else?

Tony: What have you got for diarrhea?

Clerk: Here, this will help. Just follow the directions and don't exceed the <u>dosage</u>.

Tony: Thanks a lot.

Tony leaves the drugstore. A short time later, a man with a knife <u>demands</u> that he give him his wallet. <u>Slightly</u> injured, and deeply upset, Tony goes to the police department.

Tony: I'd like to <u>report a crime</u>. I was robbed.

Policewoman: Are you OK? What did the robber take?

Tony: My wallet was stolen. I was also attacked. I need to see a doctor. Where is the nearest medical clinic?

Policewoman: I will call an <u>ambulance</u> for you.

Tony: No, it's not that serious. I can just go to the hospital myself.

Policewoman: In that case, I can arrange for an officer to drive you.

The policewoman drops Tony off at the hospital. At the hospital, Tony smells something strange.

Tony: Hey, I smell smoke. Yes, there's a fire!

Nurse: There's been an accident! Someone call the fire department right now! Everyone must get out of the hospital at once.

Tony: What a terrible day!

譯文　悲慘的一天

東尼搭機的時候狀況還不錯，不過一到了馬德里，他就覺得不舒服。他決定去藥局買藥。

東尼：你好。我覺得不舒服。我想我發燒了。

店員：如果你有處方簽，我可以幫你配藥。

東尼：沒有，我沒有處方簽。我要治流行性感冒的成藥。

店員：好。這給你。還要別的嗎？

東尼：你有什麼治腹瀉的藥？

店員：吶，這個會有幫助。只要照著用藥指示吃，別超過劑量。

東尼：多謝。

東尼離開藥局。過了一會兒，一名持刀男子命令東尼把皮夾給他。受了輕傷的東尼非常沮喪地去警察局。

東尼：我要報案。我被搶了。

女警：你還好嗎？搶匪搶走了什麼？

東尼：我的皮夾被拿走，我也受到攻擊。我需要看醫生。最近的診所在哪裡？

女警：我幫你叫救護車。

東尼：不用，沒那麼嚴重。我可以自己去醫院。

女警：那樣的話。我可以安排一個警員載你去。

女警讓東尼在醫院下車。在醫院裡，東尼聞到奇怪的味道。

東尼：嘿，我聞到煙味。沒錯，失火了！

護士：發生了意外事故！誰馬上打電話給消防隊！每個人都必須立刻離開醫院。

東尼：好慘的一天！

Ｗord List

dosage [ˋdosɪdʒ] *n.*（藥的）劑量
demand [dɪˋmænd] *v.* 命令；要求
slightly [ˋslaɪtlɪ] *adv.* 輕微地

report a crime　報案
ambulance [ˋæmbjələns] *n.* 救護車

139

3 Biz 加分句型 Nice-to-Know Phrases

3.1 ▸▸ 向警察通報事故
Reporting an Incident to the Police

track 36

❶ **I'd like to report (crime).**
我要報（罪行）。
例 I'd like to report a <u>theft</u>.
我要報竊案。

❷ **My (sth.) was stolen.**
我的（某事物）被偷了。
例 My wallet was stolen.
我的皮夾被偷了。

❸ **I was (robbed/<u>mugged</u>).**
我被（搶／搶劫）了。
例 I was robbed by two men who took my money.
我被兩個男人搶了，他們拿走了我的錢。

❹ **I have been (<u>assaulted</u>/attacked)!**
我遭到（襲擊／攻擊）了！
例 I have been attacked by a man outside my hotel!
我在旅館外遭到一名男子攻擊！

Ⓦord List

theft [θɛft] *n.* 偷竊
mug [mʌg] *v.* 襲擊搶劫
assault [əˋsɔlt] *v.* 襲擊

3.2 ▸▸ 處理緊急事件 Dealing with Emergencies

❶ Call (the police / an ambulance / the fire department)!
打電話叫（警察／救護車／消防隊）！
例 Call an ambulance! Someone is hurt!
　　快叫救護車！有人受傷了！

❷ There's been an accident.
發生了意外。
例 There's been an accident—please help me.
　　發生了意外──請幫幫我。

❸ I smell smoke / see <u>flames</u>.
我聞到煙味／看到火焰。
例 I smell smoke somewhere in the building.
　　我聞到這棟樓某處有煙味。

❹ There's (a fire / an earthquake)!
失火了！／地震了！
例 There's a fire! Get out of the hotel!
　　失火了！快離開旅館！

Word List
....
flame [flem] *n.* 火焰

4 Biz 加分詞彙 Nice-to-Know Words & Phrases

 track 37

① assailant [ə`selənt] *n.* 攻擊者

② blood type [`blʌd, taɪp] *n.* 血型

③ break a contract 違約

④ heart attack [`hɑrt ə, tæk] *n.* 心臟病發作

⑤ landlord [`lænd, lɔrd] *n.* 房東

⑥ minor/serious injury [`maɪnə/`sɪrɪəs `ɪndʒərɪ] *n.* 小傷／重傷

⑦ monthly rent [`mʌnθlɪ `rɛnt] *n.* 月租金

⑧ mugger [`mʌgə] *n.* 偷襲搶劫者

⑨ police report [pə`lis rɪ, port] *n.* 警方的報告

⑩ scene of the crime 犯罪現場

⑪ patrol car [pə`trol , kɑr] *n.* （警察的）巡邏車

⑫ stroke [strok] *n.* 中風

⑬ surgery [`sɝdʒərɪ] *n.* 外科手術

⑭ tenant [`tɛnənt] *n.* 房客

⑮ victim [`vɪktɪm] *n.* 受害者

::::::::: 小心陷阱 :::::::::

☹ 錯誤用法：

Can you please **make** this prescription for me?

能不能請你幫我配這張處方簽的藥？

☺ 正確用法：

Can you please **fill** this prescription for me?

能不能請你幫我配這張處方簽的藥？

::::::::: Biz 一點通 :::::::::

If you're traveling overseas, it's a good idea to buy travel insurance. Some people don't realize that their regular insurance won't cover them if they are in another country. Depending on the country, medical costs can be extremely expensive. Other things to consider are finding out if you need any specific <u>vaccinations</u>, or if you need to take any precautions against diseases such as <u>malaria</u> or <u>dengue fever</u>. A good website to consult is one hosted by the famous Mayo Clinic: www.mayoclinic.com. The U.S. Centers for Disease Control and Prevention (CDC) also has a useful site at www.cdc.gov/travel.

如果你要到海外旅行，最好要買旅遊平安險。有些人不知道他們的一般保險並不包括人在異國時的保險。依國家而定，有些地區的醫療費用可能極為昂貴。其他需要考慮到的事情是，查明自己是否需要打特定的預防針，或是需要特別留意預防一些疾病，比如瘧疾或是登革熱。美國梅約醫學中心設了一個不錯的網站可供查閱：www.mayoclinic.com。美國疾病管制預防中心的網站也相當管用：www.cdc.gov/travel。

Ⓦord List

vaccination [ˌvæksn̩ˈeʃən] *n.* 接種疫苗；預防注射

malaria [məˈlɛrɪə] *n.* 瘧疾

dengue fever [ˈdɛŋgɪ ˌfivɚ] *n.* 登革熱

5 | 實戰演練 Practice Exercises

I 請為下列三句話選出最適合本章的中文譯義。

❶ How much is the security deposit?

(A) 保護費要多少錢？

(B) 安全存款要多少錢？

(C) 保證金要多少錢？

❷ What have you got for nausea?

(A) 你們有什麼治反胃的藥？

(B) 你吐了些什麼？

(C) 你有什麼可以給我裝吐的東西？

❸ A long-term lease is preferred.

(A) 期限長的租賃物比較被喜歡。

(B) 條款長的租約比較好。

(C) 長期的租約比較被接受。

II 你會如何回答下面這兩句話？

❶ The minimum stay is three months.

(A) I'm planning to stay longer than three months.

(B) That's good, because I'm only staying one month.

(C) Sure, three months is long enough.

❷ You can buy some over-the-counter medicine for that problem.

(A) But I haven't seen the doctor.

(B) Good. Where's the drugstore?

(C) I don't know where the counter is.

III 請利用下列詞句寫一篇簡短的對話：

a long-term lease	a security deposit	the utilities
prescription	medical clinic	feel a little sick

＊解答請見 254 頁

Section Three

洽談生意
Doing Business

While You Were Away

To: Juana Estevez
From: Mr. Mel Barnes
Taken by: Melanie
Date: 11/13
Time: 11:00 a.m.

Message:

Mr. Barnes called this morning to say he is looking forward to meeting you on Nov. 15. He says he wants to make sure this date is a good time to meet with you. He said he would call you back later today.

您不在的時候

留言：

伯恩思先生今天早上來電說他很期待十一月十五日與您會面。他說他想確認這個日期是否方便跟您碰面。他說今天晚一點會再打給您。

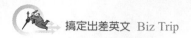

1 Biz 必通句型 Need-to-Know Phrases

1.1 ▸▸ 找某人及接聽電話　　　　　　　track 38
Asking for Someone and Answering the Phone

❶ **May I speak with (name)?**
我可以跟（名字）說話嗎？
例 May I speak with Jacob, please?
　　我可以跟雅各說話嗎？麻煩你。

❷ **Is (name) in?**
（名字）在嗎？
例 Is Ms. Thompson in right now?
　　湯普森小姐現在在嗎？

❸ **I'd like to speak to (name).**
我想跟（名字）說話。
例 I'd like to speak to Derrick Walters.
　　我想跟德立克‧瓦特思說話。

❹ **This is (name) speaking.**
我是（名字）。
例 This is Sam speaking.
　　我是山姆。

❺ How may I (help/assist) you?

有什麼我可以效勞的？

例 This is Carol speaking. How may I help you today?

我是凱若。有什麼我可以效勞的？

❻ What can I do for you (day section)?

（時段）我能為您做什麼？

例 What can I do for you this afternoon?

今天下午我能為您做什麼？

❼ Whom would you like to speak to?

您想跟哪位說話？

例 Hello. Whom would you like to speak to?

您好。您想跟哪位說話？

❽ May I ask who's calling, please?

請問您是哪位？

例 Excuse me. May I ask who's calling, please?

對不起，請問您是哪位？

1.2 ▶▶ 電話轉接、記下留言和留話
Transferring Calls, Taking and Leaving Messages

❶ **Would you like to <u>hold</u> or call back later?**
您想稍待還是晚一點再撥過來？
例 Would you like to hold or call back later, Mr. Smith?
您想稍待還是晚一點再來電，史密斯先生？

❷ **Please wait a moment.**
請等一會。
例 Excuse me—please wait a moment.
對不起——請等一下。

❸ **I'll (transfer/connect) you to (name).**
我會幫您（轉／接）（名字）。
例 I'll transfer you to Bob Jones in just a minute.
我馬上幫您轉包柏・瓊斯。

❹ **I'll put you through to (name).**
我幫您接（名字）。
例 I'll put you through to Mrs. Kennedy now.
我現在就幫您接甘迺迪太太。

 Word **L**ist

hold [hold] v.（不掛上電話）稍待

❺ Would you like to leave a message for (name)?

您要不要留言給（名字）嗎？

例 I'm sorry. He is busy now. Would you like to leave a message for Mr. Tate?

抱歉，他現在很忙。您要不要留言給泰特先生？

❻ May I take a message for (name)?

我能不能幫（名字）記下留言？

例 May I take a message for Tanya?

我能不能幫譚雅記下留言？

❼ I'll give (name) your message.

我會把您的留言交給（名字）。

例 Thank you for calling. I'll give Frank your message when he arrives.

謝謝您的來電。法蘭克到的時候，我會把您的留言交給他。

❽ Can you repeat that, please?

能不能麻煩您再說一遍？

例 I'm sorry, can you repeat that please? I didn't hear what you said.

抱歉，能不能麻煩您再說一遍？我沒聽到您剛說的話。

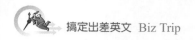
2 實戰會話 Show Time

2.1 ▸ Telephone Tag I

 track 39

Mel telephones Prime Supply, Inc., looking for Juana Estevez. Mel wants to confirm his <u>upcoming</u> meeting with her.

Secretary: Good morning, Prime Supply, Inc. How may I help you?

Mel: May I speak with Juana Estevez, please?

Secretary: May I ask who's calling, please?

Mel: This is Mel Barnes speaking.

Secretary: Please wait a moment.

About 20 seconds later.

Secretary: I'm sorry, Ms. Estevez is out of the office right now. Would you like to leave a message for her?

Mel: Could you please tell her that I want to confirm our meeting on the 15th?

Secretary: I'm sorry, I can't hear you.

Mel: Please tell her I want to confirm our meeting. I'm staying at the Ponderosa Hotel, room 317.

Secretary: Yes, Mr. Barnes. I will give Ms. Estevez your message.

Mel: OK, thanks.

Secretary: You're welcome. Thank you for calling, Mr. Barnes.

After receiving the message, Juana calls the Ponderosa Hotel.

Clerk: Ponderosa Madrid Hotel. What can I do for you?

Juana: I'd like to speak to Mel Barnes.

Clerk: Excuse me, we have a bad <u>connection</u>. Who would you like to speak to?

Juana: Barnes, Mel Barnes. He's in room 317.

Clerk: I'll transfer you to his room.

A few moments later.

Clerk: I'm afraid Mr. Barnes is not answering the phone. May I take a message for him?

Juana: Yes. Please tell him to call Juana Estevez.

Clerk: Can you repeat that, please?

Juana: Ask him to call Juana Estevez. He has my number.

譯文 打數通電話互相都找不到人（一）

梅爾打電話給全盛供應股份有限公司，要找華娜‧耶思塔維茲。梅爾想跟對方確認不久之後的會面。

秘書：　　早安，這裡是全盛供應公司。有什麼我可以效勞的？

梅爾：　　我可以跟華娜‧耶思塔維茲說話嗎？麻煩妳。

秘書：　　請問您是哪位？

梅爾：　　我是梅爾‧伯恩思。

秘書：　　請稍候。

大約二十秒過後。

秘書：　　抱歉，耶思塔維茲女士現在不在辦公室。您要不要留話給她？

梅爾：　　可不可以請妳跟她說我想要確認我們十五號的會面？

秘書：　　抱歉，我聽不到您說話。

梅爾：　　麻煩妳跟她講，我想確認我們的會面。我住在龐德羅沙飯店，317 號房。

秘書：　　好的，伯恩思先生。我會把您的留言交給耶思塔維茲女士。

梅爾：　　好，謝謝。

秘書：　　不客氣。謝謝您的來電，伯恩思先生。

收到留言後，華娜致電龐德羅沙飯店。

旅館人員：龐德羅沙馬德里飯店。能為您做什麼嗎？

華娜：　　我想跟梅爾‧伯恩思說話。

旅館人員：對不起，電話訊號不清楚。您想跟哪位說話？

華娜：　　伯恩思，梅爾‧伯恩思。他住 317 房。

旅館人員：我幫您轉到他的房間。

過了一會。

旅館人員：伯恩思先生的電話恐怕沒人接聽。我能不能幫他記下留言？

華娜：　　好。麻煩他撥電話給華娜‧耶思塔維茲。

旅館人員：能不能請您再說一遍？

華娜：　　要他打電話給華娜‧耶思塔維茲。他有我的號碼。

Word List

telephone tag　來回打數通電話連絡，但互相都找不到人（tag 是捉迷藏的意思）

upcoming [`ʌp͵kʌmɪŋ] *adj.* 即將來臨的

connection [kə`nɛkʃən] *n.* 連結；聯絡

2.2 ▸▸ Telephone Tag II

A little later, Mel gets the message from the hotel clerk and calls Juana back.

Mel: Hello, is Juana in?

Woman: What? Who's this?

Mel: This is Mel Barnes.

Woman: I'm afraid you have the wrong number.

Mel: I'm sorry. Goodbye.

Mel dials the correct number.

Secretary: Prime Supply. Melanie speaking.

Mel: Juana Estevez, please. This is Barnes speaking.

Secretary: Mr. Barnes, I'll put you through to Ms. Estevez.

Juana: Hello, Mel. How was your flight?

Mel: Not bad. However, I had an accident with my rental car.

Juana: That's too bad! I hope you weren't hurt.

Mel: No, it wasn't a serious accident. Some guy <u>rear-ended</u> me, that's all.

Juana: I'm sorry, I'm not sure what you mean by "rear-ended." What does that mean?

Mel: Rear-ended? Oh, that just means someone hit my car from behind with his car. You've never heard that <u>expression</u> before?

Juana: No, I haven't. There are a few <u>idioms</u> I don't know in English. Maybe I should teach you some Spanish phrases some time.

Mel: Sounds good. Hey, I just want to make sure that November 15 is still good for our meeting date. Are you still free at that time?

Juana: Yes, of course. I hope also after our meeting you will let me buy you dinner.

Mel: That would be very kind, Juana. Thank you very much. Well, I should let you go now. It was nice talking to you, Juana.

Juana: Yes, you too. I think it's time I said goodbye as well. Thanks for calling, Mel.

Mel: My pleasure. See you soon. Bye-bye.

譯文 打數通電話互相都找不到人（二）

不久之後，梅爾從飯店人員那裡接到留言，並回電給華娜。

梅爾：喂，華娜在嗎？

女人：什麼？你是誰？

梅爾：我是梅爾‧伯恩思。

女人：你恐怕打錯電話了。

梅爾：對不起。再見。

梅爾撥正確號碼。

秘書：全盛供應。我是馬蓮妮。

梅爾：麻煩找華娜‧耶思塔維茲。我是伯恩思。

秘書：伯恩思先生，我幫您接耶思塔維茲女士。

華娜：哈囉，梅爾。你這趟飛行如何？

梅爾：還不壞。不過，我開出租車時發生了意外。

華娜：真糟糕！希望你沒受傷。

梅爾：沒有，不算嚴重的意外。有個傢伙從後面撞我，如此而已。

華娜：對不起，我不太懂你說的「從後面撞」。那是什麼意思？

梅爾：從後面撞？噢，就是說某人開車從後面撞了我的車。妳以前沒聽過這個
　　　說法嗎？

華娜：沒有，我沒聽過。有些英文慣用語我不知道。也許什麼時候我來教教你
　　　西班牙用語。

梅爾：聽起來很棒。嘿，我只是想確定一下十一月十五號我們的會面日期沒問
　　　題。妳那個時候還是有空嗎？

華娜：是啊，那當然。我也希望我們會面之後，你會讓我請你吃頓晚餐。

梅爾：華娜，妳實在太客氣了。非常感謝。嗯，現在我該讓妳去忙了。和妳談
　　　話真愉快，華娜。

華娜：是啊，跟你聊得也很愉快。我想我也該跟你說再見了。謝謝來電，梅
　　　爾。

梅爾：我的榮幸。不久見，掰掰。

Ｗord List

rear-end [ˋrɪrˋɛnd] *v.* 從後面撞　　　　　　idiom [ˋɪdɪəm] *n.* 慣用語；成語

expression [ɪkˋsprɛʃən] *n.* 措辭；說法

3 | Biz 加分句型 Nice-to-Know Phrases

3.1 ▸▸ 處理問題 Handling Problems

 track 40

---

❶ I'm sorry; I can't hear you.

抱歉，我聽不到你說話。

例 I'm sorry; I can't hear you. Could you speak up? Could you repeat that?

抱歉，我聽不到你說話。你能不能說大聲點？你能不能再說一次？

---

❷ We have a bad connection. I didn't hear what you just said.

電話訊號不清楚。我沒聽到你剛說的。

例 Pardon me? We have a bad connection. I didn't hear what you just said.

對不起，你說什麼？電話訊號不清楚。我沒聽到你剛說的。

---

❸ I'm not sure what you mean by "(words you don't understand)."

我不確定你說「（你不懂的英文字）」是什麼意思。

例 I'm not sure what you mean by "<u>exceptional</u> <u>circumstances</u>."

我不確定你說「特殊情況」是什麼意思。

---

❹ I'm afraid you (have/dialled) the wrong number.

你恐怕（打錯／撥錯）號碼了。

例 I'm afraid you have the wrong number. There is no David Sykes here.

你恐怕打錯號碼了。這裡沒有大衛·賽克斯這個人。

Ⓦord List

exceptional [ɪkˋsɛpʃən(l)] *adj.* 例外的；特殊的

circumstance [ˋsɝkəmˌstæns] *n.* 情況

3.2 ▸ 道別 Saying Goodbye

❶ It was nice talking to you, (name).
和你談話真愉快，（名字）。
例 It was nice talking to you, Kathy.
和妳談話真愉快，凱西。

❷ Thanks for calling, (name).
謝謝你的來電，（名字）。
例 Thanks for calling, Tom. Goodbye.
謝謝你的來電，湯姆。再見。

❸ Well, I think it's time I said goodbye.
嗯，我想該跟你道別了。
例 Well, Jack, I think it's time I said goodbye. Talk to you later.
嗯，傑克，我想該跟你道別了。以後再聊。

❹ I should let you go now.
我該讓你去忙了。
例 I should let you go now, Laura. Take care.
蘿拉，我該讓妳去忙了。保重了。

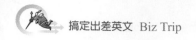

4 Biz 加分詞彙 Nice-to-Know Words & Phrases

 track 41

❶ **area code** [ˋɛrɪə ˏkod] *n.*（電話的）區碼

❷ **busy signal** [ˋbɪzɪ ˋsɪgnḷ] *n.* 佔線信號

❸ **call waiting** [ˋkɔl ˋwetɪŋ] *n.* 來電插撥

❹ **collect call** [kəˋlɛkt ˋkɔl] *n.* 對方付費電話

❺ **dial tone** [ˋdaɪəl ˏton] *n.* 撥號音

❻ **disconnected** [ˏdɪskəˋnɛktɪd] *adj.* 斷線的

❼ **extension number** [ɪkˋstɛnʃən ˏnʌmbɚ] *n.* 分機號碼

❽ **go ahead** 你說吧／請說

❾ **operator** [ˋɑpəˏretɚ] *n.* 接線生

❿ **out of order** 故障

⓫ **small talk** [ˋsmɔl ˏtɔk] *n.* 閒聊

⓬ **telephone receiver/handset** [ˋtɛləˏfon rɪˏsivɚ/ˋhændˏsɛt]
   n. 電話聽筒

⓭ **the line's dead** 電話線路不通

⓮ **the line's busy/engaged** [ɪnˋgedʒd] 電話忙線中

⓯ **tied up** [ˋtaɪd ˋʌp] 忙碌中

:::::::: **小心陷阱** ::::::::

☹ 錯誤用法：

May I ask **who are you**?

請問你哪位？

☺ 正確用法：

May I ask **who's calling**?

請問你哪位？

:::::::: **Biz 一點通** ::::::::

There are many techniques of telephone <u>etiquette</u>. In English, a key one is being familiar with the typical polite language used in business calls. Westerners <u>employ</u> certain polite English on the phone, especially when making requests or giving bad news. Learn to mimic what you hear. Expressions such as "I'm sorry," "I'm afraid," "Excuse me," and "unfortunately" are used frequently. Another type of polite phone English is structural. For example, asking if it is convenient for someone to talk. "Is now a good time to talk?" "Can you talk right now?" and "Are you busy now?" are worth learning. Also, when taking or leaving messages, make sure that all the necessary details—names, times, and dates—are included. And always remember to repeat phone numbers, especially when you leave them. Use this pattern: "The number is 2314-2525, extension 575. That's 2314-2525 extension 575."

電話禮儀的技巧非常多。在英文裡面，一個關鍵的技巧就是要熟悉商務電話中常用的禮貌用語。西方人在電話中常使用某些禮貌用語，尤其是在請求或是通知壞消息的時候。像「抱歉」、「我恐怕……」、「對不起」以及「真遺憾」等都是經常使用的話語。另一類禮貌的電話英語表現在句構上。例如，問某人是否方便談話：「現在方便說話嗎？」、「你現在可以說話嗎？」、「你現在在忙嗎？」等都值得學起來。還有，當你在記下訊息或是留下訊息給別人的時候，一定要確定所有必要的細節——名字、時間和日期——都包含在內。最後，一定要記得複述電話號碼，尤其是你留電話號碼給對方的時候。你可以使用這個句型：「號碼是 2314-2525，分機 575。是 2314-2525 分機 575。」

Ⓦord List

....

etiquette [ˈɛtɪkɛt] *n.* 禮儀；禮節　　　　　employ [ɪmˈplɔɪ] *v.* 使用

5 實戰演練 Practice Exercises

I 請為下列三句話選出最適合本章的中文譯義。

❶ I'll put you through.

(A) 我將為您轉接。

(B) 我將替您留言。

(C) 我將幫您撥通。

❷ Would you like to hold?

(A) 您想掛斷嗎？

(B) 您想稍待嗎？

(C) 您想重打嗎？

❸ I'm sorry, you have the wrong number.

(A) 抱歉，你打錯號碼了。

(B) 抱歉，你拿錯尺寸了。

(C) 抱歉，你說錯數目了。

II 你會如何回應下面這兩句話？

❶ We have a bad connection.

(A) Did I say something wrong?

(B) I'll call you back right away.

(C) I'm sorry—I'll help you.

❷ I should let you go now.

(A) Thank you for holding.

(B) OK, talk to you later.

(C) Sure, where do you want to go?

III 請利用下列詞句寫一篇簡短的對話：

How may I help you?	May I speak with...?
Would you like to hold?	I'll put you through
It was nice talking to you	is on another line

＊解答請見 255 頁

International Consumer Electronics Trade Show—Madrid Nov. 10th to 15th

Visit the 16th annual Madrid Electronics Super Show this week. You'll find all types of great electronics at this huge event. More than one thousand exhibitors in three big halls—all within walking distance of each other. Don't miss this great event!

國際日用電器商展——馬德里
十一月十日到十五日

歡迎參加本週舉行的第十六屆馬德里年度電器超級商展。在本次盛大的活動中,您將會看到各種最棒的電器。三個展覽大廳裡共有超過一千名的廠商參展——每個攤位都在步行範圍之內。千萬別錯過這場盛會!

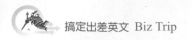

1 Biz 必通句型 Need-to-Know Phrases

1.1 ▸▸ 在商展參觀
Being a Visitor at a Trade Show

track 42

❶ Where is the (ticket/check-in) counter?

（售票／報到）處在哪裡？

例 Pardon me. Where is the ticket counter, please?

對不起，請問售票處在哪裡？

❷ How much is the admission fee to (event)?

（活動）的門票要多少錢？

例 How much is the admission fee to the Computer Trade <u>Exhibition</u>?

電腦商展的門票要多少錢？

❸ I've already <u>pre-registered</u> for (event).

我已經預先報名參加（活動）了。

例 I've already pre-registered for the Paris Cycle Show.

我已經預先報名參加巴黎自行車展了。

❹ Where can I pick up my <u>badge</u> for (event)?

我可以在哪裡拿到參加（活動）的識別證？

例 Excuse me, where can I pick up my badge for the Detroit Auto Show?

對不起，請問我可以在哪裡拿到參加底特律汽車展的識別證？

Ⓦord List

exhibition [ˌɛksəˈbɪʃən] *n.* 展覽

pre-register [ˌpriˈrɛdʒɪstə] *v.* 事先報名；事先註冊

badge [bædʒ] *n.* 徽章；證章

❺ Let's check out the exhibition booth (showing/ displaying) (product).
咱們去瞧瞧（展出／展示）（商品）的展場攤位。

例 Hey, Ben, let's check out the exhibition booth showing PDAs.
嘿，班，咱們去瞧瞧展示 PDA 的展場攤位。

❻ (That/those) (product) (doesn't/don't) (excite/ interest) me.
（那件／那些）（商品）（不）（勾起／引起）我的興趣。

例 Those power tools don't excite me.
那些電動工具勾不起我的興趣。

例 That laptop doesn't interest me.
那台筆記型電腦引不起我的興趣。

❼ I'm going to visit the (product/company) (<u>kiosk</u>/booth).
我要去看看（商品／公司）的（小攤位／攤位）

例 I'm going to visit the French perfume kiosk.
我要去看看法國香水的小攤位。

例 Let's visit the Dynamix booth.
我們去看看戴奈米克斯公司的攤位。

❽ What does this (function/feature) do?
這個（功能／特性）是做什麼用的？

例 What does this function do?
這個功能是做什麼用的？

ord List

2.2 ▸▸ 在商展參展 Acting as a Participant in a Trade Show

---

❶ **May I show you a(n) (adj.) product?**

我拿一個（形容詞）的產品給您看看好嗎？

例 May I show you an exciting product?

我拿一個非常有趣的產品給您看看好嗎？

---

❷ **Have you seen our (adj.) (product)?**

您看過我們的（形容詞）（產品）嗎？

例 Have you seen our wonderful exercise equipment?

您看過我們的神奇運動器材嗎？

---

❸ **Would you like a <u>demonstration</u> of (product)?**

你要不要看看（產品）的示範操作？

例 Would you like a demonstration of the Model XYZ Computer?

你要不要看看 XYZ 型號電腦的示範操作？

---

❹ **This (product) is one of our (adj.) models.**

這項（產品）是我們（形容詞）的機型之一。

例 This refrigerator is one of our best-selling models.

這台冰箱是我們最暢銷的機型之一。

Ⓦord List
....

demonstration [ˌdɛmən`streʃən] *n.* 示範

❺ **This (product) comes in (number) different (colors/ styles/sizes/models).**

這個（商品）有（數量）種不同的（顏色／樣式／尺寸／款式）。

例 This sofa comes in four different colors.

這張沙發有四種不同的顏色。

❻ **Do you have any questions about (product)?**

你對（商品）有任何疑問嗎？

例 Do you have any questions about the <u>photocopier</u>?

你對這台影印機有任何疑問嗎？

❼ **This (product) has some (adj.) <u>features</u>.**

這項（產品）有一些（形容詞）特色。

例 This TV has some <u>attractive</u> features.

這台電腦有些很吸引人的特色。

❽ **The (product) comes with (<u>accessories</u>).**

這個（商品）有附（配件）。

例 The camera comes with a <u>power cord</u>, batteries, case, and <u>strap</u>.

這台相機有附電源線、電池、相機盒以及吊帶。

ord List

....

photocopier [ˋfotəˌkɑpɪə] *n.* 影印機

feature [ˋfitʃə] *n.* 特徵；特色

attractive [əˋtræktɪv] *adj.* 吸引人的

accessory [ækˋsɛsərɪ] *n.* 配件

power cord [ˋpauəˌkord] *n.* 電源線

strap [stræp] *n.* 帶子；吊帶；吊環

2 實戰會話 Show Time

2.1 ▸▸ Going to the Trade Show

track 43

Cindy and Tony are visiting the Madrid <u>Electronics</u> Super Show.

Tony: Excuse me, where is the ticket counter?
Woman: It's over there on the left.
Tony: Thank you.

Tony finds the ticket counter.

Clerk: Hello, may I help you?
Tony: Hi, how much is the admission fee?
Clerk: It's five euros each, so that will be €10.00 for the two of you.
Cindy: I've already pre-registered for the Madrid Electronics Super Show. Where can I pick up my badge?
Clerk: What is your name, please?
Cindy: Cindy Kent.
Clerk: Yes, I see your name on the list. There is a special table inside the building marked "Pre-registration Pickup." You can't miss it.

Tony pays the admission fee and enters with Cindy. Cindy finds the pre-registration table and picks up her badge.

Tony: Let's check out the exhibition booth selling the videogames.
Cindy: Tony, I'm sorry. Those videogames don't interest me. I'm going to look at that kiosk displaying MP3 players and other recording devices.
Tony: OK, see you later.
Exhibitor: Hello. May I show you a really fun product—one of our new videogames? Have you seen the new game called "PowerBoy?" Would you like a demonstration?
Tony: Sure. I'm also interested in your game <u>consoles</u> as well.
Exhibitor: Wonderful. Here is our console named "The Machine." This game console is one of our most popular models. It comes in three different colors: black, blue, and green.
Tony: It looks like a good product.

Tony <u>accidentally</u> drops the videogame.

Tony:　　　Hey, it's not working. Why doesn't it work?

Exhibitor:　I think you broke it. (<u>awkward</u> silence) But don't worry. It's only a display model.

譯文　參觀商展

辛蒂和東尼去參觀馬德里的超級電器展。

東尼：　　對不起，請問售票處在哪裡？

女人：　　在那邊左側。

東尼：　　謝謝。

東尼找到售票櫃臺。

服務員：您好，我可以幫什麼忙嗎？

東尼：　　嗨，門票要多少錢？

服務員：一個人五歐元，所以你們兩位一共是十歐元。

辛蒂：　　我已經預先報名參觀馬德里超級電器展了。我可以在哪裡拿識別證呢？

服務員：請問您叫什麼名字？

辛蒂：　　辛蒂‧肯特。

服務員：是的，我看到單子上有您的名字。大樓裡面有張特別的桌子，上頭標有「預先報名領取處」。您一定不會錯過的。

東尼付了入場費後和辛蒂一起進去。辛蒂找到預先報名桌並拿到她的識別證。

東尼：　　我們去看看賣電玩的攤子。

辛蒂：　　東尼，對不起，我對那些電玩沒什麼興趣。我要去看那個展示 MP3 以及其他錄音器材的攤位。

東尼：　　好，待會見。

展示員：您好。我拿個很好玩的產品──我們的電玩新品之一給您看看好嗎？您看過叫做「強力男孩」的新遊戲嗎？要不要我示範操作一下呢？

東尼：　　好啊。我對你們的操控機也有興趣。

展示員：太好了。這是我們的操控機，就叫做「機器」。這台操控機是我們最搶手的款型之一。有三種不同的顏色：黑色、藍色和綠色。

東尼：　　看起來像是件不錯的產品。

東尼不小心把電玩弄掉了。

東尼：　　嘿，不能用了。為什麼不能用呢？

展示員：我想你把它摔壞了（尷尬的沈默）……不過別擔心，那只是展示用的樣品。

Word **L**ist

electronics [ɪlɛk`trɑnɪks] *n.* 電器；電子學

console [`kɑnsol] *n.* 操縱台（電玩）操控台

accidentally [ˌæksə`dɛntlɪ] *adv.* 意外地

awkward [`ɔkwəd] *adj.* 尷尬的

2.2 ▸▸ Talking to <u>Exhibitors</u>

Meanwhile, Cindy is talking to an exhibitor at the kiosk that displays a large <u>selection</u> of MP3 players.

Exhibitor: Hi. Do you have any questions about any of the MP3 players?

Cindy: Yes. Can you tell me a little bit about this model? What does this <u>button</u> do?

Exhibitor: This MP3 player has some excellent features. By pressing that button, you can record voice and sound with an <u>external</u> microphone.

Cindy: That is a good feature, actually.

Exhibitor: And it comes with a microphone, batteries, and a case.

Cindy: I like this model. I'm interested in importing this MP3 player. Do you have a <u>business card</u>?

Exhibitor: Here's my business card.

Cindy: Thanks.

Exhibitor: Would you like to place an order right now?

Cindy: I'd like to think it over for a bit before placing an order. Could you mail me a few samples?

Exhibitor: Perhaps. I <u>look forward to</u> talking to you in the future.

Meanwhile, Tony has left the videogame exhibition booth and sees Cindy by the MP3 kiosk.

Tony: Hey, Cindy. I want to attend a <u>seminar</u> on the future of consumer electronics. According to the exhibit <u>directory</u>, the seminar is on the second floor.

Cindy: I'd like to listen to a speech by a marketing expert on Internet marketing instead. The speech is in another exhibition hall. It's in Hall #3, I think.

Tony: I'll meet you later back at the hotel, then.

Cindy: OK. Have a good time at the seminar, Tony.

譯文 與參展廠商商談

與此同時，辛蒂在展出各式各樣 MP3 的小攤位裡和一位參展廠商談話。

參展廠商：您好。對哪台 MP3 有疑問嗎？

辛蒂： 是的。你能不能多說明一下這一款？這個按鍵是做什麼的？

參展廠商：這台 MP3 有一些很棒的特殊功能。按下這個鈕後就能用外接麥克風錄音。

辛蒂： 那個功能還真不錯。

參展廠商：它還附一支麥克風、電池，和一個盒子。

辛蒂： 我喜歡這款。我有興趣進口這台 MP3。你有名片嗎？

參展廠商：這是我的名片。

辛蒂： 謝謝。

參展廠商：您要不要現在下訂單？

辛蒂： 我下單之前想先考慮一下。你能不能寄幾個樣品給我？

參展廠商：或許可以。我很期待未來能和您談談。

同一時間，東尼已經離開電玩的展覽攤，並在 MP3 的攤子看到辛蒂。

東尼： 嘿，辛蒂，我想去參加談日用電器前景的研討會。從展覽手冊看來，研討會在二樓。

辛蒂： 我倒是想去聽一位行銷專家談網路行銷。那場演講在另一個展覽廳，我想是三號廳。

東尼： 那我們晚一點回旅館見。

辛蒂： 好。祝你在那場研討會愉快，東尼。

Word List

exhibitor [ɪgˋzɪbɪtə] *n.* 展示者；參展者

selection [səˋlɛkʃən] *n.* 選擇；精選品

button [ˋbʌtn̩] *n.* 按鈕

external [ɪkˋstɜnəl] *adj.* 外部的

business card 名片

look forward to 期待……

seminar [ˋsɛmə͵nɑr] *n.* 研討會

directory [dəˋrɛktərɪ] *n.* （使用）手冊；指南

3 Biz 加分句型 Nice-to-Know Phrases

❶ **Here's my business card.**
這是我的名片。
例 Hello, my name's Ken. Here's my business card.
你好，我叫肯恩。這是我的名片。

❷ **Would you like to place an order?**
你要不要下訂單？
例 Would you like to place an order right now? There's a discount if you do.
你要不要現在下訂單？如果現在下單的話，有折扣。

❸ **Could you (send/mail) me a sample of (product)?**
你能不能（送／寄）一份（產品）的樣品給我？
例 Could you mail me a sample of your electrical cords？
你能不能寄一份你們電線的樣品給我？

❹ **I look forward to (gerund).**
我很期待（動名詞）。
例 I look forward to talking to you in the future, Jim.
我很期待未來能和你談談，吉姆。

3.2 ▸▸ 參加商展上的活動
Attending Events at Trade Shows

❶ **I want to attend a seminar on (topic).**
我想參加（主題）的專題研討會。
例 I want to attend a seminar on customer relations.
我想參加客戶關係的專題研討會。

❷ **According to the exhibit directory, (sth.) is in (location).**
照展覽手冊來看，（某事物）在（位置）。
例 According to the exhibit directory, the workshop is in Room 116.
照展覽手冊來看，那個工作坊在 116 室。

❸ **I'd like to listen to (event) by (sb.) on (topic).**
我想要聽（某人）針對（主題）所做的（活動）。
例 I'd like to listen to a talk by George Jackson on successful selling <u>techniques</u>.
我想聽喬治‧傑克生針對成功銷售技巧所做的演講。

❹ **(Sth.) is/are in another exhibition hall.**
（某事物）在另一個展覽廳。
例 The sports equipment is in another exhibition hall.
運動器材在另一個展覽廳。

Ⓦord List

technique [tɛkˋnik] *n.* 技術；技巧

4 Biz 加分詞彙 Nice-to-Know Words & Phrases

track 45

❶ **attendee** [əˋtɛndi] *n.* 出席者／與會者

❷ **banner** [ˋbænɚ] *n.* 橫幅標語／廣告旗號

❸ **brochure** [broˋʃʊr] *n.* （廣告／簡介）小冊子

❹ **corner booth** [ˋkɔrnɚ ˏbuθ] *n.* 位於角落的攤位

❺ **floor plan** [ˋflor ˏplæn] *n.* 展場平面圖

❻ **island exhibit** [ˋaɪlənd ɪgˏzɪbɪt] *n.* 四面臨走道的展覽／陳列

❼ **multimedia display** [mʌltɪˋmidɪə dɪˏsple] *n.* 多媒體展示

❽ **power strip** [ˋpauɚ ˏstrɪp] *n.* 電源插板

❾ **registration desk** [ˏrɛdʒɪˋstreʃən ˏdɛsk] *n.* 報名、登記櫃台

❿ **rental booth** [ˋrɛntl̩ ˏbuθ] *n.* 租借的攤位

⓫ **riser** [ˋraɪzɚ] *n.* 加高的地板

⓬ **showcase** [ˋʃoˏkes] *n.* 展示櫃

⓭ **skirting** [ˋskɝtɪŋ] *n.* 壁腳板

⓮ **table top display** [ˋtebl̩ ˏtɑp dɪˏsple] *n.* 平台展示

⓯ **trade fair** [ˋtred ˏfɛr] *n.* 展銷會；商品交易會

::::::::: 小心陷阱 :::::::::

☹ 錯誤用法：

I look forward to **talk** to you in the future.

我很期待未來能和你談談。

☺ 正確用法：

I look forward to **talking** to you in the future.

我很期待未來能和你談談。

::::::::: Biz 一點通 :::::::::

Attending and participating in trade shows can be extremely useful for many businesses. If you are an exhibitor, trade shows are effective ways of allowing a large number of people to see your products in a short time. <u>Likewise</u>, if you are attending a trade show looking for suppliers, then you are able to get access to a large number of them all at once. Given the <u>expense</u> of participating in (and attending, if it is an overseas show), it's a good idea to set yourself goals and manage your time well during these events. The website called "How Stuff Works" has a useful section on trade shows: http://money.howstuffworks.com/trade-show1.htm. The website, "About.com," has tips as well at http://retail.about.com/od/merchandisingbuying/a/trade_show_tips.htm.

參觀或參與商展，對很多行業來說都會大有斬獲。如果你是參展者，商展是讓許多人在短時間內能夠看到你的產品的有效方式。同樣地，如果你為了尋求供應商而參觀商展，你也能一次接觸到很多商家。既然參與展覽（和參觀展覽，如果是在國外的商展的話）必有花費，你最好在這些活動期間，設定好你的目標並且妥善運用時間。有個叫做「事物如何奏效」的網站針對商展有個很實用的欄區：http://money.howstuffworks.com/trade-show1.htm 。另外一個叫「關於達康」的網站也提供了一些秘訣 http://retail.about.com/od/merchandisingbuying/a/trade_show_tips.htm 。

Ⓦord List

likewise [ˈlaɪkˌwaɪz] *adv.* 同樣地   expense [ɪkˈspɛns] *n.* 花費

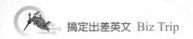

5 實戰演練 Practice Exercises

I 請為下列三句話選出最適合本章的中文譯義。

1 I've already pre-registered.

(A) 我已經預先掛號了。

(B) 我已經預先註冊了。

(C) 我已經預先報名了。

2 This product has some good features.

(A) 這項產品有一些好的特殊功能。

(B) 這項產品有一些好的特寫報導。

(C) 這項產品有一些好的賣相。

3 I want to attend a seminar.

(A) 我想主持討論會。

(B) 我這學期想旁聽。

(C) 我想參加研討會。

II 你會如何回應下面這兩句話？

1 This camera comes with batteries and a case.

(A) That's great—I need them.

(B) How much are the batteries and the case?

(C) Don't you think that's too expensive?

2 Would you like a demonstration of this product?

(A) No, I don't know how it works.

(B) Yes, it's very easy to use.

(C) No, thanks. I'm not interested.

III 請利用下列詞句寫一篇簡短的對話：

admission fee	exhibition booth	Would you like a demonstration
this product comes in	exhibition hall	here's my business card

＊解答請見 256 頁

From:	Don Ricardo, Exceptional Exports, Ltd.
To:	Daphne Chiang
Subject:	Production Facility Tour

Dear Daphne,

I was thinking, since you're coming to Madrid, and will be visiting me, why don't I give you a tour of our factory? I think it will be an informative experience for you, and I would love to show you our operations.

Best,
Don

親愛的戴芬妮：

我在想，既然妳要來馬德里，也要順道來探訪我，那麼何不讓我帶妳參觀一下我們的工廠呢？我想這麼一來會讓妳對我們公司更加了解，我也很樂意帶妳看看我們的營運狀況。

唐敬上

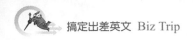

1 Biz 必通句型 Need-to-Know Phrases

1.1 ▸▸ 談談你們的營運狀況
Talking about Your Operations

track 46

❶ **(Sb.) have (number) employees.**
（某人）有（數量）個員工。
例 We have 120 employees at our company.
　　我們公司有 120 名員工。

❷ **Our company was (<u>founded</u>/established/formed/ created) in (year).**
我們的公司（創立／建立／成立／創建）於（年份）。
例 Our company was founded in 1997.
　　我們的公司創立於 1997 年。

❸ **We have (<u>branches</u>/offices/<u>subsidiaries</u>) in (number) (city/country).**
我們在（數量）個（城市／國家）都有（分公司／辦公室／子公司）。
例 We have branches in four countries: China, Canada, America, and Germany.
　　我們在四個國家：中國、加拿大、美國和德國，都有分公司。

❹ **Our products/services include (sth.).**
我們的產品／服務包括（某事物）。
例 Our products include printers, cables, and cords.
　　我們的產品包括印表機、纜線和電線。

Ｗord List

found [faʊnd] *v.* 建立；建造
branch [bræntʃ] *n.* 分公司

subsidiary [səbˋsɪdɪˌɛrɪ] *n.* 子公司

❺ We <u>specialize</u> in (sth.).

我們專做（某事物）。

例 We specialize in making leather handbags.

我們專做皮製手提包。

❻ Our (product) is/are (adj.).

我們的（產品）品質（形容詞）。

例 Our products are excellent.

我們的產品品質優良。

❼ The production capacity of (machine) is (quantity) per (hour/day/week/month/year).

這台（機器）的產能是每（小時／天／週／月／年）（數量）。

例 The production capacity of this machine is 1,000 per day.

這台機器的產能是每天一千個。

❽ This (area/room) is where we (do sth.).

這一（區／間）是我們（做某事）的地方。

例 This area is where we do <u>quality control</u>.

這一區是我們執行品管的地方。

例 This room is where we clean the <u>parts</u>.

這一間是我們清理零件的地方。

ord List

specialize [ˈspɛʃəlˌaɪz] v. 專門從事   parts [parts] n. 零件

quality control 品管

1.2 ▸▸ 帶人參觀你們的設備
Giving Someone a Tour of Your Facility

❶ Would you like to see our (company/factory/office/warehouse)?
你想不想看一下我們的（公司／工廠／辦公室／倉庫）？
例 Ted, would you like to see our company tomorrow afternoon?
泰德，明天下午你想不想看一下我們的公司？

❷ Are you interested in taking a tour of our (facility/operation/building/showroom)?
你有沒有興趣來參觀一下我們的（設施／營運狀況／大樓／展示室）？
例 Melinda, are you interested in taking a tour of our operation some time?
馬琳達，妳有沒有興趣什麼時候來參觀一下我們的營運狀況？

❸ Do you have time to see our (company/factory/warehouse/office)?
你有沒有時間來看一下我們的（公司／工廠／倉庫／辦公室）？
例 Do you have time today to see our warehouse?
你今天有沒有時間來看一下我們的倉庫？

❹ It would be my pleasure to give (sb.) a tour of our (facility/operation/building/showroom).
我很榮幸能帶（某人）參觀我們的（設施／運作狀況／辦公大樓／陳列室）。
例 It would be my pleasure to give you a tour of our Taipei facility.
我很榮幸能帶你參觀我們台北的設施。

Ⓦord List

warehouse [ˈwɛrˌhaʊs] *n.* 倉庫

❺ Please (come this way / follow me).

請（往這邊走／跟我來）。

例 Please follow me. I'd like to show you our production area.

請跟我來。我想讓你看看我們的生產區。

❻ If you look (straight ahead / to the right/left), you will see (sth.).

如果你（向前／向右／向左）看，就會看到（某事物）。

例 If you look to the left, you will see our <u>stockroom</u>.

如果你向左看，就會看到我們的貯存室。

❼ Coming up ahead (on your left/right) is the (sth.).

接下來在（你左手邊／右手邊）的是（某事物）。

例 Coming up ahead on your right is the <u>shipping</u> department.

接下來在你右手邊的是貨運部門。

❽ Is there anything you are <u>particularly</u> interested in (gerund)?

你有沒有什麼特別想（動名詞）的？

例 David, is there anything you are particularly interested in seeing today?

大衛，你今天有沒有什麼特別想看的？

ord List

stockroom [ˋstɑk͵rum] *n.* 貯藏室

shipping [ˋʃɪpɪŋ] *n.* 貨運（業）

particularly [pɚˋtɪkjələlɪ] *adv.* 特別地

2 實戰會話 Show Time

2.1 ▸ An "Exceptional" Introduction **track 47**

After arriving at Don Ricardo's company, Exceptional Exports, Daphne is greeted by Don.

Don: Daphne, thanks for coming today. How are you?

Daphne: Fine, Don. Thanks for inviting me to see your operations.

Don: My pleasure. Let me tell you about our company. We have 75 employees. Our company was established in 1990.

Daphne: Do you have branches in any other countries?

Don: Yes, we have offices in five countries: Spain, England, France, the United States, and Canada. Our products include many types of office <u>supplies</u>. We also specialize in <u>fashionable</u> office <u>decorations</u>.

Daphne: You really have some nice products, Don.

Don: Thank you, Daphne. Our products are of the highest quality. Naturally, I have to charge a little more than some other exporters because of this good quality.

Daphne: I'm really pleased with how fast you can fill our orders as well.

Don: It's because of our modern equipment. The production capacity of some of our new <u>manufacturing</u> machines is 500 units per hour.

Daphne: That's really <u>impressive</u>.

Don: Now, this room is where we hold our staff meetings. Would you like to see our factory now? Are you interested in taking a tour of our warehouse, too?

Daphne: Yes, of course.

Don: Please come this way, Daphne.

Don takes Daphne to the factory.

Daphne: I didn't realize your factory was so large, Don.

Don: We make a lot office supplies here. If you look on the right, you'll see one of our production teams. Now, coming up ahead, on the left is where we <u>assemble</u> some of the supplies, such as staplers.

Daphne: It looks like you have a very efficient operation here, Don.

譯文 一場「非凡的」公司介紹

在抵達唐‧里卡多的公司非凡外銷後，戴芬妮受到唐的親自迎接。

唐： 戴芬妮，謝謝妳今天光臨。妳好嗎？

戴芬妮：唐。謝謝你邀請我來看你們的營運狀況。

唐： 我的榮幸。讓我跟妳介紹一下我們公司。我們有七十五名員工。我們的公司建立於 1990 年。

戴芬妮：你們在其他國家有分公司嗎？

唐： 有的。我們在五個國家有辦公室：西班牙、英國、法國、美國和加拿大。我們的產品包括各式各樣的辦公室用品。我們也專做時尚的辦公室裝潢。

戴芬妮：你們真的有些不錯的產品，唐。

唐： 謝謝妳，戴芬妮。我們的產品品質一流。當然我在收費上就必須比其他的出口商高一點。

戴芬妮：我也很滿意我們下單的時候你很快就能供貨。

唐： 那是因為我們新穎的器材。我們一些新的製造機器每小時的產能高達 500 件。

戴芬妮：真了不起。

唐： 吶，這間是我們員工開會的地方。妳現在想看看我們的工廠嗎？有沒有興趣也看一下我們的倉庫？

戴芬妮：好，當然。

唐： 請往這邊走，戴芬妮。

唐帶戴芬妮去工廠。

戴芬妮：我之前不知道你們的工廠規模有這麼大，唐。

唐： 我們在這裡製造很多辦公室用品。如果妳往右邊看，會看到我們的生產小組之一。吶，接下來在妳左手邊的就是我們組合一些用品的地方，比方像釘書機。

戴芬妮：看來你們的運作非常有效率，唐。

Word List

supply [sə`plaɪ] *n.* 生活用品

fashionable [`fæʃənəbl] *adj.* 時尚的

decoration [ˌdɛkə`reʃən] *n.* 裝潢；佈置

manufacturing [ˌmænjə`fæktʃərɪŋ] *adj.* 製造的

impressive [ɪm`prɛsɪv] *adj.* 令人印象深刻的

assemble [ə`sɛmbl] *v.* 組裝

2.2 ▶▶ The Tour Continues

Don: Is there anything you are particularly interested in seeing, Daphne?

Daphne: No, not really. You're doing a fine job of being a tour guide.

Don: It would be my pleasure to give you a tour of our warehouse, now.

Daphne: Great. Lead the way, Don.

Don and Daphne enter the warehouse.

Don: I'd like to introduce our warehouse manager to you. Martin is in charge of warehouse operations.

Daphne: Hello, Martin. It's nice to meet you.

Don: Martin has worked for our company for 25 years.

Daphne: Wow, that's a long time. Well, it was nice meeting you, Martin.

Don: Daphne, I want to introduce you to someone else. This is Kathy Lawford. She is our vice-president.

Daphne: Hello, Kathy. It's very nice to meet you. You really have a good <u>setup</u> here. I have really been impressed by what Don has shown me.

Kathy: Thank you. Yes, we're quite proud of our operation. I'm glad you're enjoying the tour. I hope you enjoy your time in Madrid.

Daphne: Thank you, Kathy.

Don: Daphne, do you have time to visit our showroom? I want to show you some new products we're exporting. I really think you'll like them.

Daphne: I'd love to.

Don shows Daphne the products in the showroom for about a half hour.

Don: That ends the tour of our company. Thanks for taking the time to come on the tour. I hope you enjoyed it. Do you have any questions about anything you've seen, Daphne?

Daphne: When will the new products be ready for export?

Don: Actually, you can order anything you saw right now!

譯文 繼續參觀

唐： 妳有什麼特別想看的嗎，戴芬妮？

戴芬妮：沒有，沒有什麼特別想看的了。你是個非常稱職的導覽員。

唐： 現在，我很榮幸帶妳參觀我們的倉庫。

戴芬妮：好極了。請帶路，唐。

唐和戴芬妮進入倉庫。

唐： 我想跟妳介紹我們的倉儲經理。馬丁負責倉庫的運作。

戴芬妮：你好，馬丁。很高興認識你。

唐： 馬丁已經在我們公司服務二十五年了。

戴芬妮：哇，好長一段時間。嗯，很高興認識你，馬丁。

唐： 戴芬妮，我想跟妳介紹另外一個人。這是凱西‧勞佛。她是我們的副
總經理。

戴芬妮：妳好，凱西。真高興認識妳。妳們這邊的體制真是完善。在唐帶我參
觀了各種設施之後，我真的非常佩服。

凱西： 謝謝妳。是的，我們對自己公司的運作相當自豪。我很高興妳對這趟
參訪感到滿意。希望妳在馬德里的期間愉快。

戴芬妮：謝謝妳，凱西。

唐： 戴芬妮，妳有時間看看我們的商品陳列室嗎？我想讓妳看看我們要出
口的一些新產品。我真的覺得妳會喜歡。

戴芬妮：樂意之至。

唐花了大約半個鐘頭向戴芬妮介紹陳列室裡的產品。

唐： 我們公司的導覽就到此為止了。謝謝妳撥時間過來參觀。我希望妳感
到滿意。妳對看過的東西有任何疑問嗎，戴芬妮？

戴芬妮：新產品要什麼時候才能出口呢？

唐： 事實上妳所看到的任何一件東西現在都能下訂單！

Word List

setup [`sɛt.ʌp] *n.* 體制；組織；結構

3 Biz 加分句型 Nice-to-Know Phrases

3.1 ▸▸ 介紹職員 Introducing Staff

 track 48

❶ I'd like to introduce (sb.) to you.

我想跟你介紹（某人）。

例 Tim, I'd like to introduce Sam to you.

提姆，我想跟你介紹山姆。

❷ (Sb.) is in charge of / responsible for (sth.).

（某人）管理／負責（某事物）。

例 Veronica is <u>in charge of</u> the marketing department.

維若妮卡管理行銷部門。

❸ (Sb.) has worked for our company for (number) years.

（某人）已經為我們公司服務（數字）年。

例 Carl has worked for our company for seven years.

卡爾已經在我們公司服務七年了。

❹ This is (sb.). (Sb.) is in (department).

這位是（某人）。（某人）是在（部門）。

例 This is Peggy. Peggy is in sales.

這是佩琪。佩琪在業務部。

 Word List

in charge of 管理；掌管

3.2 ▸▸ 結束導覽 Concluding the Tour

❶ That ends the tour of our (company/factory/warehouse/ office).

我們（公司／工廠／倉庫／辦公室）的參觀就到此結束。

例 Well, that ends the tour of our factory today.

那麼，今天我們公司的參觀就到此結束。

❷ (Sb.) hope (sb.) enjoyed the tour.

（某人）希望（某人）對導覽感到滿意。

例 I hope you enjoyed the tour, Frank.

我希望你對這場導覽感到滿意，法蘭克。

例 Our boss hopes your team enjoyed the tour.

我們老闆希望你們團隊對這場導覽感到滿意。

❸ Thanks for taking the time to come on the tour.

謝謝你撥時間前來參觀。

例 Thanks for taking the time to come on the tour of our facility, Mike.

謝謝你撥時間前來參觀我們的設備，麥克。

❹ Do you have any questions about what you've seen?

你對看過的東西有任何疑問嗎？

例 Robert, do you have any questions about what you've seen on the tour?

羅伯特，你對於參觀時所看到的東西有任何疑問嗎？

4 Biz 加分詞彙 Nice-to-Know Words & Phrases

 track 49

① assembly line [ə`sɛmblɪ ˌlaɪn] *n.* 組裝線

② automation [ˌɔtə`meʃən] *n.* 自動操作；自動化

③ container [kən`tɛnɚ] *n.* 貨櫃

④ crate [kret] *n.* 條板箱

⑤ foreman [`formən] *n.* 工頭；領班

⑥ forklift [`fɔrkˌlɪft] *n.* 叉架起貨機；堆高機

⑦ high-tech [`haɪ `tɛk] *adj.* 高科技的

⑧ inventory [`ɪnvənˌtorɪ] *n.* 存貨；存貨盤點

⑨ machinery [mə`ʃinərɪ] *n.* （集合詞）機械

⑩ plant [plænt] *n.* 工廠

⑪ production line [prə`dʌkʃən ˌlaɪn] *n.* 生產線

⑫ robotic equipment [ro`batɪk ɪ`kwɪpmənt] *n.* 自動化設備

⑬ shift [ʃɪft] *n.* 輪班；輪值

⑭ state-of-the-art [`stet əv ðɪ`art] *adj.* 最先進的

⑮ cutting-edge [`kʌtɪŋˌɛdʒ] *adj.* 尖端的

::::::::: 小心陷阱 :::::::::

☹ 錯誤用法：

Is there anything you are particularly **interested to see** today?
你今天有沒有什麼特別想看的？

☺ 正確用法：

Is there anything you are particularly **interested in seeing** today?
你今天有沒有什麼特別想看的？

::::::::: Biz 一點通 :::::::::

Offering <u>prospective</u> clients a tour of your company or factory can be an effective way to <u>convince</u> them to become a customer of yours. If you are in a competitive market, showing how efficient and well-run your operation is may just be the thing that decides a contract in your favor. Of course, you'll want to do everything you can to make a good impression on the person or people you are providing the tour for. For some tips about the effectiveness of offering factory tours and how to make them <u>memorable</u>, visit the website below: http://www.businessweek.com/smallbiz/content/jan2007 /sb20070118_992411.htm.

邀請潛在的客戶參觀你的公司或工廠，可以有效地說服他們成為你的客戶。如果你身處競爭激烈的市場，展現你公司的營運效率和管理績效，可能就是幫你獲得一份契約的關鍵。當然，你會想盡全力使參訪者留下好印象。想知道有效提供工廠導覽並使你的導覽讓人印象深刻的訣竅，可以上下面這網站：http://www.businessweek.com/smallbiz/content/jan2007/sb20070118_992411.htm。

 ord List

prospective [prə`spɛktɪv] *adj.* 預期的；未來的
convince [kən`vɪns] *v.* 說服
memorable [`mɛmərəb!] *adj.* 難忘的

187

5 實戰演練 Practice Exercises

I 請為下列三句話選出最適合本章的中文譯義。

❶ We specialize in flat screen monitors.

(A) 我們專做平面螢幕的顯示器。

(B) 我們只限平面螢幕的顯示器。

(C) 我們特別喜歡平面螢幕的顯示器。

❷ The production capacity of this machine is....

(A) 這台機器的馬力是……。

(B) 這台機器的容量是……。

(C) 這台機器的產能是……。

❸ George is responsible for the warehouse.

(A) 倉庫是喬治造成的。

(B) 喬治負責倉庫。

(C) 喬治要為倉庫負責。

II 你會如何回答下面這兩句話？

❶ Is there anything you are particularly interested in seeing?

(A) No, I didn't see that.

(B) Yes, I saw that.

(C) Yes, the showroom.

❷ Thanks for taking the time to come on the tour.

(A) I'm sorry I don't have time right now.

(B) My pleasure. It was interesting.

(C) I can come next week.

III 請利用下列詞句寫一篇簡短的對話：

our company was established	our products include	take a tour
I hope you enjoyed the tour	coming up ahead	come this way

＊解答請見 257 頁

第13章 討論合作計畫
Discussing a Partnership

From:	Daphne Chiang
To:	Don Ricardo
Subject:	Thank you very much

Dear Don,

I'm writing to say, "Thanks again," for the great tour you gave me yesterday. I must say that I am indeed very impressed by the quality and professionalism of your operations. I'm wondering if I can meet with you again to discuss a business proposal that I think you might be interested in.

Yours truly,
Daphne

親愛的唐：

我來信是想向你再道謝一次，感謝你昨天精彩的導覽。我一定要告訴你，我對你們公司營運的品質與專業，印象非常深刻。我在想能不能再跟你碰面討論一個我認為你可能會感興趣的企劃案。

戴芬妮敬上

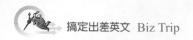
1 Biz 必通句型 Need-to-Know Phrases

1.1 ▸▸ 商談合夥計畫 Discussing a Partnership **track 50**

❶ (Sb.) would like to do business with (sb.).
（某人）想跟（某人）談生意。
例 I'd like to do business with you <u>concerning</u> this product.
我想跟你談關於這項產品的生意。

❷ I hope we can come to an <u>agreement</u> on (sth.).
我希望我們能針對（某事物）達成協議。
例 I hope we can come to an agreement on this matter.
我希望我們能針對這件事達成協議。

❸ I have a business proposal to (do sth.).
我有個企劃案，打算（做某事）。
例 I have a business proposal to import <u>handicrafts</u> from Indonesia.
我有個企劃案，打算從印尼進口手工藝品。

❹ Let's form a partnership to (do sth.).
咱們合夥（做某事）。
例 Let's form a partnership to manufacture furniture.
咱們合夥製造家具。

ord List

concerning [kənˋsɝnɪŋ] *prep.* 關於
agreement [əˋgrimənt] *n.* 協定；協議
handicraft [ˋhændɪ͵kræft] *n.* 手工藝品

190

❺ We should <u>cooperate</u> on a <u>joint venture</u> to (do sth.).

我們應該合作（做某事）的合資事業。

📓 We should cooperate on a join venture to develop software for retail stores.

我們應該合作發展零售店軟體的合資事業。

❻ I would like to develop a <u>strategic</u> partnership with (sb.) to (do sth.).

我想跟（某人）一起開發策略性的合夥關係，以便（做某事）。

📓 I would like to develop a strategic partnership with you to import machinery.

我想跟你一起開發策略性的合夥關係，以便進口機械。

❼ We can <u>leverage</u> our (skills/knowledge/<u>capital</u>) to (do sth.).

我們可以好好利用我們的（技術／知識／資本）來（做某事）。

📓 We can leverage our skills to create a new type of customer service.

我們可以好好利用我們的技術來創造新類型的客戶服務。

❽ This is a <u>mutually</u> beneficial proposal to (do sth.).

這是一個（做某事）能讓雙方互蒙其利的企劃案。

📓 This is a mutually beneficial proposal to produce low-priced electronic goods.

這是一個生產低價電器商品能讓雙方互蒙其利的企劃案。

Ⓦord List
....

cooperate [koˋɑpəˌret] v. 合作

joint venture [ˋdʒɔɪnt ˋvɛtʃə] n. 合資企業

strategic [strəˋtidʒɪk] adj. 策略的

capital [ˋkæpɪtl] n. 資本

leverage [ˋlɛvərɪdʒ] v. 利用（影響力、勢力）

mutually [ˋmjutʃʊəlɪ] adv. 互相

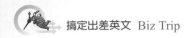

1.2 ▸▸ 建立合夥關係的架構
Establishing the Structure of a Partnership

❶ **(Sb.) will <u>draft</u> an agreement on (sth.).**
（某人）將針對（某事物）草擬一份協定。
例 I will draft an agreement on this proposal.
我會針對這項提案草擬一份協定。

❷ **(Sb.) will have a contract <u>drawn up</u> on (sth.).**
（某人）會針對（某事物）擬好一份契約。
例 I will have a contract drawn up on our decision.
我會針對我們的決議擬好一份契約。

❸ **This contract provides (sb.) with a <u>minority stake</u> in (sth.).**
這份契約提供（某人）（某事物）的小部份股份。
例 This contract provides you with a minority stake in the company.
這份契約提供你公司的小部份股份。

❹ **This agreement gives (sb.) a <u>majority</u> holding in (sth.).**
這個協定會使得（某人）擁有（某事物）大半的股份。
例 This agreement gives you a majority holding in the business.
這個協定使得你擁有公司大半的股份。

Ｗord List

draft [dræft] v. 草擬
draw up 起草；擬定
minority [maɪˋnɔrətɪ] n. 少數

stake [stek] n. 股份
majority [məˋdʒɔrətɪ] n. 多數

❺ (Sb.) has a (percentage) <u>interest</u> in (company).

（某人）持有（公司）（百分比）的股份。

例 Frank has a 25 percent interest in Titan Industries.

法蘭克持有泰坦工業百分之二十五的股份。

❻ We can set up a subsidiary to (do sth.).

我們可以成立一家子公司來（做某事）。

例 We can set up a subsidiary to sell the product in Taiwan.

我們可以在台灣成立一家子公司來銷售這項產品。

❼ The company will be <u>incorporated</u> on (date).

這家公司將在（日期）成為股份有限公司。

例 The company will be incorporated on April 20.

這家公司將在四月二十日成為股份有限公司。

❽ We need to register (sth.) as a corporation.

我們需要將（某事物）登記為公司行號。

例 We need to register ABC Company as a corporation.

我們得將 ABC 公司登記為公司行號。

Ⓦord List

interest [ˋɪntrɪst] *n.* 股份；利益

incorporate [ɪnˋkɔrpəˌret] *v.* 組成股份有限公司

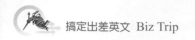

2 實戰會話 Show Time

2.1 ▸▸ Making a Proposal

 track 51

Following the tour of Don's operations, Daphne asks Don to meet with her about a business proposal she has.

Daphne: Don, I'd like to do business with you.

Don: Do business? You already import my products. What else do you have in mind?

Daphne: I hope we can come to an agreement on a proposal I have. I have a proposal to establish another company.

Don: Really? That sounds interesting. Please tell me more.

Daphne: Let's form a partnership to develop a retail chain of <u>stationery</u> stores.

Don: Stationery stores? But Daphne, there are already a lot of stationery stores.

Daphne: I've got a new idea. We should cooperate on a joint venture to create a whole new <u>concept</u> in stationery stores. I would like to develop a strategic partnership with you to make a chain of shops where people want to visit and have coffee—a bit like Starbucks.

Don: Hmm. So, people would come and stay a while and use our stationery products?

Daphne: Right. We can leverage our skills and capital to make this project a big success.

Don: Well, it sounds like it is a mutually beneficial proposal.

Daphne: If you are interested, I will draft an agreement on my proposal.

Don: Yes, I'm quite interested. I'd be interested to see the terms of the contract.

Daphne: Great. I will have a contract drawn up tomorrow.

譯文　提出企劃案

參觀過唐的公司營運後，戴芬妮請唐跟她會面商談她的一個企劃案。

戴芬妮：唐，我想跟你做生意。

唐：　　做生意？妳目前就在進口我的產品。妳還有什麼別的想法？

戴芬妮：我希望我們能針對我的提案達成協定。我提議成立另外一家公司。

唐：　　真的嗎？聽來挺有意思的。請再多告訴我一些。

戴芬妮：咱們合夥開發零售連鎖文具店。

唐：　　文具店？可是戴芬妮，文具店已經很多了。

戴芬妮：我有個新點子。我們應該合資創造全新概念的文具店。我想要跟你發展一種策略合夥關係，開發可以讓客人進店裡來看看並且點杯咖啡的連鎖店──有點像星巴克。

唐：　　嗯。也就是說，客人會進來坐一會兒並使用我們的文具產品？

戴芬妮：沒錯。我們可以好好利用我們的技術和資金，讓這個計畫非常成功。

唐：　　嗯，聽起來像是個雙方能互蒙其利的企劃案。

戴芬妮：如果你有興趣，我會針對我的提案草擬一份協定。

唐：　　有，我蠻有興趣的。我會有興趣看看契約上列出的條件。

戴芬妮：好極了，我明天就會擬好一份契約。

Ｗord List

stationery [ˈsteʃənˌɛrɪ] *n.* 文具
concept [ˈkɑnsɛpt] *n.* 概念

2.2 ▸▸ Discussing the Partnership Details

The next day, Daphne and Don continue their discussion about a partnership, getting into more details about the <u>specifics</u> of the proposal.

Daphne: This contract provides you with a minority stake in the business.

Don: Yes, I see, and it gives you a majority holding in the company.

Daphne: Yes, and there's one other investor who has a 20 percent interest.

Don: We could set up the company as a subsidiary of my company. It might make the process easier.

Daphne: I think I would rather keep it separate. We need to register this new company as its own corporation. The company will be incorporated within two months, if that's fine with you.

Don: I just want to check a few things. What is the return on investment that you expect for the company? How are you <u>raising</u> capital?

Daphne: Actually that's all explained in the documents I just gave you. Within three years of opening the business, we expect our average annual <u>ROI</u> to be around 18 to 20 percent. Regarding capital for the company, some of it will come from me and the other investor. Plus we have some <u>venture capital</u> as well.

Don: It sounds good. I'd like to see a copy of the <u>business plan</u>.

Daphne: Of course. I will get it to you as soon as I get back home.

Don: As you probably know, this needs to be <u>approved</u> by our <u>board of directors</u>. The agreement will have to be <u>voted</u> on.

Daphne: Naturally. I understand that the deal still needs to be <u>finalized</u>.

Don: Great. As long as you realize this agreement is <u>contingent</u> on approval from the majority of the board members.

譯 文 討論合夥的細節

隔天，戴芬妮和唐繼續談合夥的事，他們深入討論更多此企劃案的具體細節。

戴芬妮：這份契約提供你雙方合作事業的小部份股份。

唐：　　是，我知道，而這契約使得妳擁有公司大半的股份。

戴芬妮：對。另外一位投資者擁有百分之二十的股份。

唐：　　我們可以把這公司設為我公司的子公司。這樣整個程序會比較簡單。

戴芬妮：我想我寧可分開來。我們必須以獨立的公司註冊這家新公司。這家公司兩個月內就能成為股份有限公司，如果你覺得沒問題的話。

唐：　　我只要弄清楚幾件事。妳預期公司的投資利潤會有多少呢？妳要怎麼籌資呢？

戴芬妮：事實上這些在我剛給你的文件裡都有解釋。創業的前三年內，我們預期平均每年會有百分之十八到二十左右的投資報酬率。至於公司的資金，有一些是我和另一位投資者的錢。加上我們還有一些創投資金。

唐：　　聽起來不錯。我想看看商業計畫書的副本。

戴芬妮：當然。我一回國就馬上寄給你。

唐：　　妳大概知道，這事情需要經過我們的董事會同意才行。這份協定要經過投票。

戴芬妮：當然。我知道這項交易還需要做最後的定案。

唐：　　好極了，只要妳了解這協定要看大多數董事成員是否同意才行。

Ｗ ord List

specifics [spɪˋsɪfɪks] *n.* （複數形）具體問題；細節

raise [rez] *v.* 籌款

ROI (=Return on investment) 投資利潤

venture capital [ˋvɛntʃɚ ˏkæpət!] *n.* 創投資金

business plan 商業計畫書

approve [əˋpruv] *v.* 認可

board of directors 董事會

vote [vot] *v.* 投票

finalize [ˋfaɪn!ˏaɪz] *v.* 使完結；使結束；（計劃、安排等）定案

contingent [kənˋtɪndʒənt] *adj.* 視……條件而定的

3 | Biz 加分句型 Nice-to-Know Phrases

3.1 ▸▸ 處理財務問題
Dealing with Financial Issues

 track 52

❶ **What is the return on investment (ROI)?**
投資利潤是多少？
例 I'm wondering—what is the return on investment for this business?
我在想——這個事業的投資利潤是多少？

❷ **How (are you raising / will you raise) capital?**
你要如何（籌措）資金？
例 How are you raising capital to start this company?
你要如何籌措資金來成立這家公司？

❸ **We have some (venture capital / interested investors).**
我們有些（創投資金／有意的投資者）。
例 We have some venture capital regarding this project.
關於這份企劃，我們有些創投資金可用。

❹ **(Sb.) would like to see a copy of the (business plan /
mission statement).**
（某人）想看看（商業計畫書／公司的宗旨）。
例 I'd like to see a copy of the business plan before I make any decisions.
在我下任何決定以前想先看看商業計畫書的副本。

Ⓦord List

mission statement （公司、團體等的）宗旨

3.2 ▸▸ 談論交易決策
Talking about Finalizing the Deal

❶ This needs to be approved by (sb.).
這需要經過（某人）的同意才行。
例 We can't make a final decision now—this needs to be
approved by the board of directors.
我們現在無法做出最後決定——這需要經過董事會的同意才行。

❷ (Sth.) will have to be voted on.
（某事）得經過投票。
例 As you know, the agreement will have to be voted on before
it takes effect.
你也知道，這項協議得先經過投票才能生效。

❸ The deal still needs to be finalized before (sth.).
在（某事）之前，這項交易還需要做最後的定案。
例 The deal still needs to be finalized before we can transfer the
money.
在我們匯款之前，這項交易還需要做最後的定案。

❹ This agreement is contingent on (sth.).
這項協議得視（某事）而定。
例 Of course, this agreement is contingent on our getting the
bank loan.
當然，這項協議得視我們是否拿到銀行貸款而定。

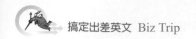
4 Biz 加分詞彙 Nice-to-Know Words & Phrases

track 53

❶ annual general meeting [ˈænjʊəl ˈdʒɛnərəl ˈmitɪŋ] *n.* (AGM) 年度大會

❷ debenture [dɪˈbɛntʃə] *n.* （公司）債券

❸ dividend [ˈdɪvəˌdɛnd] *n.* 股息；紅利

❹ equity [ˈɛkwətɪ] *n.* 普通股；股票；抵押資產的淨值

❺ indebtedness [ɪnˈdɛtɪdnɪs] *n.* 負債

❻ limited company [ˈlɪmɪtɪd ˈkʌmpənɪ] *n.* (Ltd.) 股份有限公司

❼ limited liability company [ˈlɪmɪtɪd ˌlaɪəˈbɪlətɪ ˈkʌmpənɪ] *n.* (LLC) 有限責任公司

❽ loan capital [ˈlon ˌkæpətl̩] *n.* 借款資本

❾ parent company [ˈpɛrənt ˈkʌmpənɪ] *n.* 母公司

❿ public limited company [ˈpʌblɪk ˈlɪmɪtɪd ˈkʌmpənɪ] *n.* (PLC) 公開上市的股份有限公司

⓫ share capital [ˈʃɛr ˌkæpətl̩] *n.* 發行股票而募集的資本

⓬ shareholder [ˈʃɛrˌholdə] *n.* 股東

⓭ silent partner [ˈsaɪlənt ˈpɑrtnə] *n.* 匿名股東（不過問業務的股東）

⓮ sole proprietorship [ˈsol prəˈpraɪətəˌʃɪp] *n.* 獨資經營

⓯ venture capitalist [ˈvɛntʃə ˌkæpətl̩ɪst] *n.* 創業投資人

:::::::: **小心陷阱** ::::::::

☹ 錯誤用法：

I will **sketch** an agreement on this proposal.

我會針對這項提案草擬一份協定。

☺ 正確用法：

I will **draft** an agreement on this proposal.

我會針對這項提案草擬一份協定。

:::::::: **Biz 一點通** ::::::::

Forming a partnership with someone is a big step. It can bring big <u>rewards</u>, but it can also introduce some potential problems and dangers. Experts strongly advise entering partnerships only with people you sincerely trust. They also say that even if you trust them, <u>ensure</u> you put everything in writing. <u>Stipulate</u> the all-important details so there is less chance for disagreement or argument later. There are different kinds of partnerships that offer different levels of protection to individual partners, and it's important to know the differences between them. For more information, check out this website: http://www.allbusiness.com/10794-1.html.

與某人建立合夥關係是邁進一大步。合夥關係可能讓人獲益匪淺，但也可能帶來一些潛在的問題與危機。專家們強烈建議大家只跟自己由衷信任的人合夥。專家們也認為，即使你信任對方，也要確定每件事都以白紙黑字留下書面紀錄。明文訂定所有重要的細節，以減少日後的糾紛或爭執。合夥關係有各種不同的類型，提供個別合夥人的保護程度也不盡相同，因此瞭解各種合夥關係之間有什麼差異非常重要。想要知道更多資訊，可以上這個網站：http://www.allbusiness.com/10794-1.html。

Word List

reward [rɪ`wɔrd] *n.* 報酬

ensure [ɪn`ʃʊr] *v.* 確保

stipulate [`stɪpjə,let] *v.* 規定；約定；明訂

5 實戰演練 Practice Exercises

I 請為下列三句話選出最適合本章的中文譯義。

❶ I'd like to develop a strategic partnership with you.

(A) 我想跟你一起開發策略性的合夥關係。

(B) 我想跟你一起展開合資性的策略關係。

(C) 我想跟你一起培養出一套戰略關係。

❷ This is a mutually beneficial proposal.

(A) 這份提案有兩方面的受益人。

(B) 求婚是關於雙方的權益。

(C) 這是一個讓雙方能互蒙其利的企劃案。

❸ We can set up a subsidiary.

(A) 我們可以豎立一個輔助物。

(B) 我們可以設定一個副主題。

(C) 我們可以成立一家子公司。

II 你會如何回答下面這兩句話？

❶ Will the company be incorporated next month?

(A) Yes, that's because the business was poor.

(B) Yes, that's when the company will be registered.

(C) Yes, that's when the company will be open to the public.

❷ The deal still needs to be finalized.

(A) We can do that later.

(B) Now it can't be changed.

(C) Right, it was finished last week.

III 請利用下列詞句寫一篇簡短的對話：

do business with you	a business proposal	mutually beneficial
draft an agreement	a minority stake	return on investment

＊解答請見 258 頁

Welcome!

Thanks for attending the International Importers and Exporters Association Annual Convention. You'll find a large number of interesting and informative events again this year. We have some wonderful presentations, seminars, workshops, and discussion groups on a variety of topics, including e-commerce, finding good suppliers, breaking into new markets, and many, many great topics. Enjoy the two-day event!

歡迎！

感謝參加國際進出口商會的年度大會。今年我們仍然為各位準備了非常多有趣又能增廣見聞的活動。有精彩的報告、研討會、工作坊和討論小組，主題種類眾多，包括電子商務、如何找到好的供應商、如何打進新市場，以及其他非常非常多很棒的主題。盡情享受這兩天的活動吧！

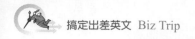
1 Biz 必通句型 Need-to-Know Phrases

1.1 ▸▸ 介紹主題及轉換議題
Introducing Topics and Transitioning

 track 54

❶ **I'd like to talk about a(n) (adj.) subject.**
我想談一個（形容詞）主題。
例 I'd like to talk about a <u>fascinating</u> subject today—the human mind.
我今天想談一個非常有趣的主題——人類的心智。

❷ **The first matter I want to discuss is (sth.).**
我想討論的第一件事就是（某事物）。
例 The first matter I want to discuss is the China market.
我想討論的第一件事就是中國市場。

❸ **I wish to begin with a(n) (adj.) fact.**
我想用一個（形容詞）事實來開場。
例 I wish to begin with an interesting fact: your heart beats more than 100,000 times a day.
我想用一個有趣的事實來開場：你的心臟每天跳動的次數超過十萬下。

❹ **To start, I want to talk about (sth.).**
首先，我想談談（某事物）。
例 To start, I want to talk about doing business in the Middle East.
首先，我想談談在中東經商的情況。

Ⓦord List
....
fascinating [ˋfæsn̩ˏetɪŋ] *adj.* 迷人的；非常有趣的

❺ The next matter I'm going to introduce is (sth.).

我要介紹的下一個議題是（某事物）。

例 The next matter I'm going to introduce is e-marketing.

我要介紹的下一個議題是網路行銷。

❻ Let's turn to the next Item, which is (sth.).

我們轉到下一個議題，那就是（某事物）。

例 Let's turn to the next item, which is how <u>elections</u> <u>tend to</u> affect the stock market.

我們轉到下一個議題，那就是選舉如何影響股市。

❼ Moving now to the next item, (sth.).

現在來看下一個議題，（某事物）。

例 Moving now to the next item, effective sales calls.

現在來看下一個議題：有效的業務拜訪。

❽ The last topic for this (discussion/seminar) is (sth.).

這次（討論／研討會）的最後一個主題是（某事物）。

例 The last topic for this discussion is building good customer relations.

這次討論會的最後一個主題是：建立良好的客戶關係。

Ｗord List

election [ɪˋlɛkʃən] *n.* 選舉

tend to 有……的傾向

1.2 ▸▸ 引出評論以及表述意見
Eliciting Comments and Stating Opinions

❶ Does anyone have any comments on (sth.)?
對於（某事物），有人有意見嗎？
例 Does anyone have any comments on Internet advertising?
對於網路廣告，有人有意見嗎？

❷ How do people feel about (sb.'s) comments?
大家對（某人）的評論有何感想？
例 How do people feel about Stephanie's comments?
大家對史蒂芬尼的評論有何感想？

❸ Who would like to talk about (sth.)?
誰想談談（某事物）？
例 Who would like to talk about last month's sales figures?
誰想談談上個月的銷售數字？

❹ Let's hear what other people think about (sth.).
我們來聽聽其他人對（某事物）有什麼看法。
例 Let's hear what other people think about the new product.
我們來聽聽其他人對這項新產品有什麼看法。

Ⓦord List
....
elicit [ɪˋlɪsɪt] v. 引出
comment [ˋkɑmɛnt] n. 評論
figure [ˋfɪgjɚ] n. 數字

❺ In my view, the (adj.) choice is to (do sth.).

依我的看法，（形容詞）選擇就是（做某事）。

例 In my view, the best choice is to open an office in Shanghai.

依我的看法，最好的選擇就是在上海設一個辦公室。

❻ From my <u>perspective</u>, (sth.) is (adj.).

從我的觀點來看，（某事物）（形容詞）。

例 From my perspective, this cell phone is wonderful.

從我的觀點來看，這款手機棒極了。

❼ To be honest, I think (sth.).

老實說，我覺得（某事物）。

例 To be honest, I think Tom is the person we should hire.

老實說，我覺得湯姆是我們該雇用的人。

❽ I tend to think that (sth.).

我傾向於認為（某事物）。

例 I tend to think that the Indian economy will continue to grow <u>steadily</u>.

我傾向於認為印度的經濟會持續穩定地成長。

ord List

....

perspective [pɚˋspɛktɪv] *n.* 看法；觀點

steadily [ˋstɛdəlɪ] *adv.* 穩定地

2 實戰會話 Show Time

2.1 ▸ Attending a Sales Seminar

One of the seminars at the convention is on improving your sales techniques. The speaker is Jeremy Pilmer, a well-known and successful salesman.

Jeremy: Hello everyone and welcome today. I'd like to talk to you about an exciting subject: how to increase your sales! The first matter I want to discuss is the qualities of a successful salesman.

I wish to begin with an amazing fact. A UCLA study suggests that about 93 percent of what is <u>communicated</u> to another person is <u>nonverbal</u>. So, your facial expressions and tone of voice are very important. One easy thing you can do is simply smile more. Your customers will like it.

The next matter I'm going to introduce is how to build <u>rapport</u> with your customers. It's important to get to know your customers and their likes and dislikes. If they like and trust you, then you are more likely to make the sale.

Let's turn to the next item, which is <u>persistence</u>. There's a common idiom that says, "Persistence pays off." This is very true. People are often unsuccessful because they give up too easily. Those who work hard and never give up are the ones who are successful <u>eventually</u>.

Moving now to the next item, setting goals. This is another key <u>trait</u> of good salespeople. They are always setting and working toward <u>identifiable</u> goals. To <u>reiterate</u>, effective salesmen and saleswomen keep setting new goals all the time.

The last item for this seminar is good listening skills. It's not enough to be a good talker—you've got to carefully listen to what your customers are saying to you. Too many salespeople don't make the effort to really listen to and consider their customers' concerns.

I'd like to <u>recap</u> what I've just talked about. It's important to smile more, build rapport, be persistent, set goals, and listen to your customers. Simple.

譯文 參加銷售研討會

會議中有個研討會的主題是改進你的銷售技巧。講者是傑若米‧皮爾曼，一個功成名就的業務員。

傑若米：哈囉大家好，歡迎各位。我想跟各位談談一個令人興奮的主題：如何提升你的銷售業績！我要討論的第一件事，就是成功業務員的特質。

我希望拿一項令人驚訝的事實來開場。根據加州大學洛杉磯分校的一項研究顯示，當我們跟別人溝通的時候，所傳達的訊息有百分之九十三是非語言的。所以，你的臉部表情以及聲音語調非常重要。有件很簡單你可以做到的事就是：多微笑。你的客戶一定會喜歡。

我想介紹的下一個議題就是：如何跟你的客戶建立融洽關係。瞭解你的客戶，並知悉他們的好惡是很重要的事情。如果他們喜歡你並且信任你，那麼你就更可能達成交易。

我們來看看下一個議題，那就是堅忍不拔。有句常見的俗語說：「堅忍不拔必有所穫」。這句話非常正確。通常人們失敗就是因為太快放棄。努力不懈、絕不放棄的那些人才是最終獲致成功的人。

現在再來談下一個議題：設定目標。這是優良業務員的另一個關鍵特質。他們總是設定具體明確的目標然後努力朝目標邁進。我重申一遍，效率高的男女業務員會不斷設立新的目標。

研討會的最後一個議題就是良好的傾聽技巧。能言善道還不夠——你必須能夠細心傾聽客戶對你說的話。有太多的業務員沒有好好傾聽、好好考慮客戶關心的事物。

我想重述我剛才講的重點。多微笑、建立融洽的關係、堅持到底、設定目標，並且傾聽客戶所說的話，這些都很重要。就是這麼簡單。

Ｗord List

communicate [kə`mjunə͵ket] *v.* 傳達；傳遞
nonverbal [͵nɑn`vɜbl] *adj.* 非語言的
rapport [ræ`port] *n.* 和諧；親善關係
persistence [pə`sɪstəns] *n.* 堅持；持久
eventually [ɪ`vɛntʃʊəlɪ] *adv.* 最後；終於

trait [tret] *n.* 特點；特性
identifiable [aɪ`dɛntə͵faɪəbl] *adj.* 可識別的
reiterate [ri`ɪtə͵ret] *v.* 重申；反覆講
recap [`ri͵kæp] *v.* 重述要點

2.2 ▸ Going to a <u>Roundtable Discussion</u>

Near the end of the two-day convention, the International Importers and Exporters Association is holding a discussion for all its members on how to improve the organization. The discussion is being led by Jason Roth.

Jason: Thanks everyone for coming to this important roundtable discussion about the future of our organization. The first matter I want to discuss is <u>membership</u>. Does anyone have any comments on increasing membership?

Harlan: In my view, the choice is clear—we need to lower the membership fee and attract new members.

Jason: How do people feel about Harlan's comments?

Simone: From my perspective, the membership fee is fine as it is. I don't think we need to change it. I think we need to offer better programs.

Jason: Who would like to talk about the programs we offer?

Daphne: To be honest, I think Simone is right.

Jason: OK, let's hear what other people think about the programs.

Sammi: I tend to think we need more programs like "Power Meetings."

Jason: Does everyone understand what "Power Meetings" means?

Simone: No, what do you mean by "Power Meetings?"

Jason: "Power Meetings" was a program we had several years ago where we invited several important government people to explain difficult <u>regulations</u>. I think "Power Meetings" was a useful program, but it wouldn't work again.

Sammi: I'm sorry, Jason, I don't follow you. Why wouldn't it work?

Jason: Well, it really wasn't very popular with most of the members. To <u>sum up</u>, the program didn't <u>generate</u> enough interest. In short, the topic was not popular with enough people.

譯文 參加圓桌討論會

為期兩天的會議接近尾聲時,國際進出口商會為所有的會員舉行一場討論會,討論如何改進該組織。討論會由傑森‧羅斯主持。

傑森： 謝謝大家前來參加這個關於我們組織前景的重要圓桌討論會。我想要討論的第一件事是會員的問題。有沒有人對增加會員人數有意見？

哈藍： 依我的看法,選擇一清二楚——我們得降低會費,吸引新會員加入。

傑森： 大家對哈藍的說法有什麼意見？

席夢： 從我的觀點來看,原本的會費沒問題,我覺得我們不需要改。我認為我們需要的是提供更好的課程。

傑森： 有沒有人想談談我們提供的課程？

戴芬妮：老實說,我覺得席蒙說的有理。

傑森： 好。我們來聽聽其他人對課程有什麼看法。

珊咪： 我傾向認為我們需要更多像「強力會議」那樣的課程。

傑森： 每個人都懂「強力會議」指的是什麼嗎？

席夢： 我不懂。你說的「強力會議」是什麼意思呢？

傑森： 「強力會議」是我們好幾年前的一個課程,我們當時邀請好幾位政府要員前來闡釋難懂的規章。我認為「強力會議」這樣的課程雖然實用,可是再舉辦就行不通了。

珊咪： 抱歉,傑森,我沒聽懂你的意思。為什麼會行不通？

傑森： 嗯,「強力會議」當初事實上並沒有受到多數會員的歡迎。總而言之,那個課程並未引起足夠的興趣。簡單來說,欣賞該主題的人數不夠多。

Word List

....

roundtable discussion 圓桌討論（指與會者不分主次,繞桌而坐）

membership [ˈmɛmbɚˌʃɪp] *n.* 會員資格；全體會員

regulation [ˌrɛgjəˈleʃən] *n.* 規則；規章

sum up 總結

generate [ˈdʒɛnəˌret] *v.* 引起；造成

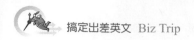

3 Biz 加分句型 Nice-to-Know Phrases

3.1 ▶▶ 闡明論點 Clarifying a Point

 track 56

---

❶ Does everyone understand what "(sth.)" means?

大家都瞭解「(某事物)」指的是什麼嗎？

例 Does everyone understand what "<u>biotech</u>" means?

　　大家都瞭解「生技」指的是什麼嗎？

---

❷ Is everything clear so far?

到目前為止每一點都清楚嗎？

例 Is everything clear so far? Are we all <u>on the same page</u>?

　　到目前為止每一點都清楚嗎？我們都有共識嗎？

---

❸ What do you mean by "(sth.)?"

你說的「(某事物)」，是什麼意思？

例 What do you mean by "the goods?"

　　你說的「貨」，是什麼意思？

---

❹ I'm sorry, I don't follow you.

抱歉，我沒聽懂你的意思。

例 I'm sorry, I don't follow you—I'm lost.

　　抱歉，我沒聽懂你的意思——我一頭霧水。

---

 ord List

....

biotech [ˋbaɪotɛk] *n.* 生物科技（為 biotechnology 的縮寫）

on the same page　瞭解、有共識

3.2 ▸▸ 總結 Summarizing

❶ To sum up, ...
總而言之，……。
例 To sum up, we need this project completed by next month.
總而言之，我們下個月之前就需要完成這項計畫。

❷ I'd like to recap what I've (talked about / presented).
我想重述我所（談到的／報告的）重點。
例 I'd like to recap what I've talked about in the meeting.
我想重述我在會議上所談到的重點。

❸ To reiterate, ...
重申一遍，……。
例 To reiterate, the customer is always right.
重申一遍，顧客永遠是對的。

❹ In short, (sth.) is (adj./clause).
簡而言之，（某事物）是（形容詞／子句）。
例 In short, the market is vast.
簡而言之，這個市場非常大。
例 In short, the timing is right for us to proceed.
簡而言之，時機恰當，我們可以著手進行。

ord List
....
vast [væst] *adj.* 廣大的

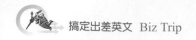
4 Biz 加分詞彙 Nice-to-Know Words & Phrases

track 57

❶ agree to disagree 異中求同

❷ articulate [ɑr`tɪkjə͵let] v. 清晰地表達

❸ contradict [͵kɑntrə`dɪkt] v. 反駁／提出論據反對（某人的說法）

❹ controversial [͵kɑntrə`vɝʃəl] topic 具爭議性的話題

❺ debate a point 針對某論點加以辯論

❻ draw a conclusion 做結論

❼ emphasize [`ɛmfə͵saɪz] a point 強調某重點

❽ facilitator [fə`sɪlə͵tetɚ] n.（討論之）引導人

❾ in a nutshell [`nʌt͵ʃɛl] 簡而言之

❿ jump to conclusions 驟下結論

⓫ reach a consensus [kən`sɛnsəs] 達成共識

⓬ resolve a dispute [rɪ`zɑlv ə dɪ`spjut] 化解某爭議

⓭ sensitive issue 敏感的議題

⓮ stimulate [`stɪmjə͵let] discussion 激起討論

⓯ switch topics 轉換話題

::::::: **小心陷阱** :::::::

☹ 錯誤用法：

From my view, the best choice is to do our best.

依我的看法，最好的選擇就是我們盡力而為。

☺ 正確用法：

In my view, the best choice is to do our best.

依我的看法，最好的選擇就是我們盡力而為。

::::::: **Biz 一點通** :::::::

Like any form of public speaking, leading a discussion or seminar can be a bit <u>nerve-wracking</u>. The good news, of course, is you're not up there by yourself giving a presentation on your own. But as a leader of the discussion or seminar, you have a responsibility to keep control of the time and the crowd. Make sure to speak clearly and loudly enough so that the audience had no problem understanding. Don't let discussions get out of hand, or allow certain individuals to <u>dominate</u> the debate. Also, you should be aware of any <u>distracting</u> habits you might have, like tapping your foot or constantly saying "uh," and try not to let them <u>interfere</u> with your leadership of the event. For a list of techniques to consider when leading a seminar or discussion, visit the following website: http://www.economics.utoronto.ca/roberts/4060/PresenterTips.htm.

就像任何形式的公開發言，帶領討論會或研討會可能會讓人有些神經緊張。當然，還好你自己不是單槍匹馬在台上做簡報。可是身為討論會或研討會的領導者，你的責任是要掌握時間和群眾。要確定你說的話夠清楚、音量夠大，觀眾都能夠聽得懂。不要讓討論失控，或讓某些人主控辯論。還有，你應該要注意自己的一些可能會讓人分心的習慣，比方像反覆踩踏地板或是常常說「呃」，不要讓這些習慣妨礙你的帶領。想知道領導研討會或討論會時該具備些什麼技巧，可以上下面這個網站：http://www.economics.utoronto.ca/roberts/4060/PresenterTips.htm。

ord List

nerve-wracking [ˈnɝvˌrækɪŋ] *adj.* 神精緊張的

dominate [ˈdɑməˌnet] *v.* 支配；控制

distracting [dɪˈstræktɪŋ] *adj.* 令人分心的

interfere [ˌɪntɚˈfɪr] *v.* 妨礙；干擾

5 實戰演練 Practice Exercises

I 請為下列三句話選出最適合本章的中文譯義。

❶ Let's turn to the next topic.

(A) 我們轉到下一個主題。

(B) 我們在下一個主題拐彎。

(C) 我們改變下一個主題。

❷ I tend to think that the data contradicts the conclusion.

(A) 我認為推論有反駁數據的傾向。

(B) 我傾向否定資料和結論之間的關連。

(C) 我傾向認為資料和結論不符。

❸ To sum up, this is a sensitive issue.

(A) 簡而言之，這是個感情的爭議。

(B) 總而言之，這是個敏感的議題。

(C) 換言之，這是個易受影響的話題。

II 你會如何回應下面這兩句話？

❶ How do people feel about Jack's comments?

(A) I think they are fair.

(B) I think Jack is nice.

(C) I think it is right.

❷ I don't follow you.

(A) You made a wrong turn.

(B) I'll explain it better.

(C) You can go now.

III 請利用下列詞句寫一篇簡短的對話：

I'd like to talk about	the next matter	let's turn to
Does anyone have any comments	I tend to think	to sum up

＊解答請見 259 頁

第 15 章 | 上台報告
Making a Presentation

A Presentation Not to Miss!

While you're visiting the International Importers and Exporters Association Annual Convention, make sure to catch a very informative presentation on the opportunities in the Indian Market. Listen to Raj Primaveetra talk about the many exciting ways to become involved in this hot, developing economy. If you think China is a great opportunity, wait until you learn about the advantages of India! Wednesday afternoon from 2:00 to 4:00. Room 5A.

千萬不能錯過的報告！

在您參加國際進出口商會年度大會的同時，一定要把握機會聽場資訊極為豐富的報告，主題是印度市場的商機。聽拉傑‧皮馬菲特拉談關於投入這個熱門開發中的經濟體，許多令人興奮的方法。如果你認為中國是個大好機會，等你了解印度的一些優勢之後就知道了！星期三下午兩點到四點，地點在 5A 室。

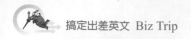

1 Biz 必通句型 Need-to-Know Phrases

1.1 ▶ 介紹並陳述你的目的
Introducing and Stating Your Purpose

 track 58

❶ **Good (morning/afternoon/evening), ladies and gentlemen.**

各位先生女士，（早／午／晚）安。

例 Good afternoon, ladies and gentlemen. My name is Ken.

各位先生女士，午安。我叫肯恩。

❷ **I'm very (adj.) to be here (time).**

我很（形容詞）（時間）來到此地。

例 I'm very honored to be here this evening.

我很榮幸今晚來到此地。

❸ **I'm <u>delighted</u> to have the opportunity to (do sth.).**

我很高興有這個機會（做某事）。

例 I'm delighted to have the opportunity to make a presentation to you.

我很高興有這個機會向你們做簡報。

❹ **I'd like to talk to you about (sth.).**

我想跟你們談談（某事物）。

例 I'd like to talk to you about the business <u>climate</u> in China.

我想跟你們談談中國的商業趨勢。

Word List

delighted [dɪˋlaɪtɪd] *adj.* 高興的

climate [ˋklaɪmɪt] *n.* 趨勢；風潮

❺ I'd like to talk about a(n) (adj.) subject: (topic).

我想談一個（形容詞）主題：（主題）。

例 I'd like to talk about an interesting subject: e-commerce.

我想談一個有趣的主題：電子商務。

❻ The purpose of my presentation is to (do sth.).

我報告的目的是要（做某事）。

例 The purpose of my presentation is to tell you about our products.

我報告的目的是要跟你們介紹我們的產品。

❼ I'm here today to (do sth.).

我今天來這裡是要（做某事）。

例 I'm here today to speak about an investment opportunity.

我今天來這裡是要談一個投資機會。

❽ My presentation will cover (sth.).

我的報告將包含（某事物）。

例 My presentation will cover five main points.

我的報告將包含五個主要重點。

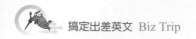

1.2 ▸▸ 強調與詳述 Emphasizing and <u>Elaborating</u>

❶ I'd like to draw your attention to (sth.).
我想請各位注意（某事物）。
例 I'd like to draw your attention to last month's sales figures.
我想請各位注意上個月的銷售數字。

❷ I want to (stress/<u>highlight</u>) (sth.).
我要（強調）（某事物）。
例 I want to stress that the India market is <u>booming</u>.
我要強調的是印度市場正蒸蒸日上。

❸ We should focus on (sth.).
我們應該把焦點集中在（某事物）上。
例 We should focus on how to improve our sales.
我們應該把焦點集中在改進銷售業績上。

❹ It's (<u>vital</u>/<u>urgent</u>) that (sth.).
（極其重要／迫切）的是，（某事物）。
例 It's vital that we become more competitive.
極其重要的是，我們變得更有競爭力。
例 It's urgent that this matter is <u>addressed</u>.
迫切的是，這個問題一定要處理。

Ｗord List

elaborate [ɪˋlæbəˌret] v. 詳細描述
highlight [ˋhaɪˌlaɪt] v. 強調
booming [ˋbumɪŋ] adj. 日趨興隆的

vital [ˋvaɪtl] adj. 極為重要的
urgent [ˋɝdʒənt] adj. 緊急的；迫切的
address [əˋdrɛs] v. 處理；辦理

❺ In other words, (sth.) is (adj./sth.).

換言之，（某事物）是（形容詞／某事物）。

例 In other words, the market is <u>saturated</u>.

換言之，市場已經飽和了。

例 In other words, customer service is our new focus.

換言之，客戶服務是我們的新重點。

❻ To elaborate, (sth.) is (sth.).

詳細地說，（某事物）是（某事物）。

例 To elaborate, marketing is where we should be focusing our efforts.

詳細地說，我們應該把努力的焦點集中在行銷上。

❼ I want to talk a little more about (sth.).

我想多談一點有關（某事物）的事。

例 I want to talk a little more about our advertising <u>campaign</u>.

我想多談一點有關我們廣告宣傳活動的事。

❽ Let's take a closer look at (sth.).

我們來仔細研究一下（某事物）。

例 Let's take a closer look at how we should <u>tackle</u> this problem.

我們來仔細研究一下該如何處理這個問題。

ord List

saturated [`sætʃə͵retɪd] *adj.* 飽和的
campaign [kæm`pen] *n.* 宣傳活動

tackle [`tæk!] *v.* 著手處理

2 實戰會話 Show Time

2.1 ▸▸ Listening to a Presentation

 track 59

Many people attending the Importers-Exporters convention have decided to go to Raj Primaveetra's presentation about India.

Raj: Good afternoon, ladies and gentleman. I'm very happy to be here today, and I'm delighted to have the opportunity to speak about the wonderful ways to make money in the Indian market. The reason I want to talk to you is to let you know about the advantages of doing business in India.

The purpose of my presentation is to excite you about and interest you in India. I'm here to let you know why you should invest in India, and how to do it. My presentation will cover investment in Indian companies, the Indian stock market, import and export opportunities, and <u>outsourcing</u>.

I'd like to draw your attention to the fact that India has seen <u>phenomenal</u> economic growth. I want to stress that this growth is expected to continue for a long time. Now, we should focus on ways to <u>maximize</u> your investments in India. It's vital that you begin looking at opportunities now.

The reason India is booming now is largely due to its very skilled labor. In other words, the labor <u>pool</u> is very deep and talented. To elaborate, the university and technical school system is very advanced. I want to talk a little more about the labor pool. Not only is this labor pool well educated, but the <u>wages</u> are far lower than in developed Western countries. This is a great advantage to companies looking to do high-tech work, yet want to keep their labor costs down.

譯文　聆聽報告

進出口商會議上有許多人決定要去聽拉傑‧皮馬菲特拉關於印度的報告。

拉傑：各位先生女士，午安。今天我很高興能來這裡，也很開心有這個機會談談在印度市場上獲利的好辦法。我之所以想跟各位談一談，原因在於要讓各位知道在印度經商的好處。

我報告的目的在於激起各位對印度的興趣。我來這裡是要讓各位知道為何該在印度投資，又該如何投資。我的報告將會包括投資印度公司、印度股市、進出口的機會以及委外承包。

我想請各位注意一個事實，那就是印度近來經濟成長驚人。我想強調的是，這個成長預計將持續很長一段時間。現在，我們應該把焦點集中在如何使各位在印度的投資達到最大效益。極其重要的是各位現在就要開始著眼商機。

印度的經濟現在之所以會蒸蒸日上，大體是因為印度擁有高技術的勞工。換句話說，勞工人力庫深遠而且人才濟濟。詳細地說，就是大學和技職學校的制度很先進。我想多談一下勞工人力庫的事。印度的勞工不止受過良好的教育，薪資也遠低於已開發的西方國家；這對有意經營高科技產業但想壓低勞工成本的公司來說是個極大的優勢。

Ｗord List

outsourcing [ˋaʊt͵sɔrsɪŋ] *n.* 委外；外包
phenomenal [fəˋnɑmən!] *adj.* 驚人的；異常的
maximize [ˋmæksə͵maɪz] *v.* 達到最大值
pool [pul] *n.* 資源的集合；需要的人員
wage [wedʒ] *n.* 薪資（常用複數 wages）

2.2 ▸▸ The Presentation Continues

Raj Primaveetra continues his presentation. Like any good presenter, he encourages the audience to ask questions and provides a good ending to his talk.

Raj: Let's take a closer look at the amazing growth in India. For the past three years, the economy has grown at more than eight percent per year. It's the second-fastest growing economy in the world, behind China.

Cindy: I have a question about the Indian stock market.

Raj: Could you please hold your questions until after the presentation? I'll answer that question later. Thank you.

Raj talks for another 30 minutes about the opportunities in India, covering several areas.

Raj: Does anyone have any questions? Please feel free to ask any questions.

Daphne: I know India and China are really growing right now. But is this really <u>sustainable</u> over a long period? I get the feeling this type of <u>incredible</u> growth can't continue forever. Isn't it possible that there could be some kind of <u>collapse</u> in the growth?

Raj: No. There are no real signs that this growth is going to slow down <u>significantly</u> in the near future anyway. Are there any more questions?

Simone: I've read that there's still a lot of <u>poverty</u> and <u>unemployment</u> in India. Couldn't these problems <u>threaten</u> the Indian economy?

Raj: It's true that poverty and unemployment are problems in India, but, generally, the <u>population</u> is becoming more <u>affluent</u>. This greater <u>prosperity</u> should definitely help the economy in the long run and enable it to keep going. I guess that's all I wanted to say about unemployment and poverty. Well, that concludes my presentation. Thank you for listening to my presentation.

譯文 繼續報告

拉傑‧皮馬菲特拉繼續報告。就像每個擅長報告的人，他鼓勵觀眾提問，並且為自己的演說做一個很好的收尾。

拉傑： 我們仔細看一下印度驚人的成長。過去三年來，印度每年經濟成長超過百分之八。是世界上成長第二快的經濟體，位居中國之後。

辛蒂： 我有一個關於印度股市的問題。

拉傑： 可不可以請妳將問題保留到報告結束之後？我稍後會回答那個問題。謝謝。

關於印度的商機，拉傑又談了三十分鐘，內容涵蓋好幾個領域。

拉傑： 有沒有人有問題？請自由發問。

戴芬妮： 我知道現在印度和中國的確在成長。可是這樣的情況真的能維持很久嗎？我總覺得，這種不可思議的成長不會永遠持續。難道在成長的過程當中不會發生什麼樣崩垮的情況嗎？

拉傑： 不會，不管怎樣，並沒有確實的跡象顯示這樣的成長在不久的未來會大幅下降。還有任何問題嗎？

席夢： 我曾經讀到過印度還是有很嚴重的貧窮以及失業問題。這些問題不會威脅到印度的經濟嗎？

拉傑： 貧窮和失業的確是印度的問題，可是大體來說，人民越來越富裕了。這般繁榮興盛，長遠來看對整體經濟一定有助益，也能推動經濟持續成長。我想關於失業和貧窮的問題我要說的就是這些了。那麼，我的報告就到此為止。謝謝各位聽我的報告。

Ⓦord List

sustainable [sə`stenəbl] *adj.* 能維持的
incredible [ɪn`krɛdəbl] *adj.* 不可思議的
collapse [kə`læps] *n.* 崩毀；瓦解
significantly [sɪg`nɪfəkəntlɪ] *adv.* 顯著地
poverty [`pɑvətɪ] *n.* 貧困

unemployment [ˌʌnɪm`plɔɪmənt] *n.* 失業
threaten [`θrɛtn] *v.* 威脅
population [ˌpɑpjə`leʃən] *n.* 居民；人口
affluent [`æfluənt] *adj.* 富裕的
prosperity [prɑs`pɛrətɪ] *n.* 繁榮興盛

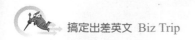
3 Biz 加分句型 Nice-to-Know Phrases

3.1 ▶ 鼓勵提問以及巧妙回答問題 **track 60**
Prompting and Fielding Questions

❶ Does anyone have any questions?

有沒有人有問題？

例 Now, does anyone have any questions about what I've said?

現在，對於我剛剛所說的有沒有人有問題？

❷ Please feel free to (ask/raise) any questions.

請自由（發／提）問。

例 Please feel free to ask any questions during my presentation.

在我報告的時候，若有任何問題，請自由發問。

❸ Could you please hold your questions until after the presentation?

可不可以請您把問題保留到報告結束之後？

例 Could you please hold your questions until after the presentation? Thank you.

可不可以請您把問題保留到報告結束之後？謝謝。

❹ I'll (answer) that question later.

我稍後再回答那個問題。

例 I'll answer that question later, if you don't mind.

我稍後再回答那個問題，如果你不介意的話。

Ⓦord List

prompt [ˋprɑmpt] v. 激起；鼓舞
field [fild] v. 巧妙地回答

3.2 ▸▸ 結束報告 Concluding Your Presentation

❶ That concludes my presentation.

我的報告到此為止。

例 That concludes my presentation for today.

我今天的報告到此為止。

❷ Thank you for listening to my presentation.

謝謝你們聆聽我的報告。

例 Thank you for listening to my presentation everyone.

謝謝你們各位聆聽我的報告。

❸ That's all I wanted to say about (sth.).

關於（某事物），我要說的就是這些了。

例 That's all I wanted to say about the <u>innovations</u> in <u>telecommunications</u>.

關於電訊傳播的創新，我要說的就是這些了。

❹ That <u>wraps up</u> my discussion on (sth.).

針對（某事物）的討論，這就是我的總結。

例 That wraps up my discussion on the new models for 2008.

針對 2008 年最新機型的討論，這就是我的總結。

Ｗord List

....

innovation [ˌɪnəˋveʃən] *n.* 創新；改革

telecommunications [ˌtɛlɪkəˌmjunəˋkeʃənz] *n.* 電訊；電訊學

wrap up 結束；完成；總結

4 Biz 加分詞彙 Nice-to-Know Words & Phrases

 track 61

❶ allude (to sth.) [ə`lud] *v.* 談及／暗指（某事）

❷ body language [`bɑdɪ ˌlæŋgwɪdʒ] *n.* 肢體語言

❸ demonstrate [`dɛmənˌstret] *v.* 示範

❹ digress [daɪ`grɛs] *v.* 離題

❺ gesture [`dʒɛstʃə] *n.* 手勢；姿勢

❻ give an anecdote [`ænɪkˌdot] 說一個軼聞／趣事

❼ illustrate [`ɪləstret] a point 闡明一個論點／要點

❽ lecture [`lɛktʃə] *n./v.* 演講；講授

❾ microphone [`maɪkrəˌfon] *n.* 麥克風

❿ overhead projector [`ovəˌhɛd prə`dʒɛktə] *n.* 高射投影機

⓫ podium [`podɪəm] *n.* 講台

⓬ power point presentation [`pauə ˌpɔɪnt ˌprizɛn`teʃn]
   n. 多媒體簡報

⓭ forecast [`forˌkæst] *n./v.* 預測

⓮ sound check [`saund ˌtʃɛk] *n.* 音效測試

⓯ visual aid [`vɪʒuəl ˌed] *n.* 視覺輔助

:::::::: **小心陷阱** ::::::::

☹ 錯誤用法：

In other **word**, the market is saturated.

換言之，市場已經飽和了。

☺ 正確用法：

In other **words**, the market is saturated.

換言之，市場已經飽和了。

:::::::: **Biz 一點通** ::::::::

Giving a presentation can be a very tense experience for many people—especially in a foreign language. There are several ways to help keep calm and feel more confident. One <u>obvious</u> way is giving yourself a lot of time to organize and practice your speech <u>in advance</u>. Having a good <u>outline</u>, understanding your facts, and knowing the language are <u>crucial</u>. The Internet hosts an <u>array</u> of websites with great tips on making successful presentations. Here are some you can visit. Toastmasters International is an organization <u>dedicated</u> to helping people improve their public speaking ability. They have ten great tips at http://www.toastmasters.org/tips.asp. For tips on giving Power Point demonstrations, see http://www.anandnatrajan.com/FAQs/powerpoint.html.

上台報告對很多人來說可能會覺得非常緊張——特別是用外語的時候。有幾種方法能幫助我們保持鎮定並覺得更有自信。一個顯而易見的辦法就是，給自己很充分的時間，事先組織並練習要講的話。列好大綱、瞭解要說明的事實，並且充分掌握要使用的語言，是至關緊要的事。針對如何成功做報告，網路上眾多網站都提供了很棒的秘訣。下面是幾個你可以瀏覽的網站。國際演講協會，這個組織致力於幫助人們改進公開演說的能力。他們在 http://www.toastmasters.org/tips.asp 列有十大演說秘訣。至於做多媒體簡報的訣竅，請見 http://www.anandnatrajan.com/FAQs/powerpoint.html 。

Ⓦord List

obvious [ˈɑbvɪəs] *adj.* 明顯的

in advance 事先

outline [ˈaʊtˌlaɪn] *n.* 大綱；概要

crucial [ˈkruʃəl] *adj.* 極重要的

array [əˈre] *n.* 一長列；一大群

dedicated [ˈdɛdəˌketɪd] *adj.* 專注的；獻身的

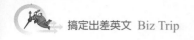

5 實戰演練 Practice Exercises

I 請為下列三句話選出最適合本章的中文譯義。

❶ I'd like to draw your attention to our new model.

(A) 我想請各位注意我們的新機型。

(B) 我想請你幫我們的新模特兒畫張圖。

(C) 我想請您照顧我們的新模型。

❷ I want to highlight that the India market is booming.

(A) 我想凸顯的是印度菜市場很受歡迎。

(B) 我想說的是印度市集中隆隆作響。

(C) 我想強調的是印度市場蒸蒸日上。

❸ Feel free to ask any questions.

(A) 請自由發問。

(B) 請隨意答題。

(C) 請任意命題。

II 你會如何回答下面這兩句話？

❶ Let's take a closer look at this product.

(A) It looks good.

(B) I can't see it—it's too far away.

(C) I'm interested in hearing more.

❷ Please hold your questions.

(A) OK. I have two questions.

(B) OK. I'll ask them later.

(C) OK. Thanks for the answer.

III 請利用下列詞句寫一篇簡短的對話：

I'm (adj.) to be here   it's vital   Does anyone have any questions?

in other words   I'm here today to   that concludes my presentation

*解答請見 260 頁

Telephone Message

From: Mel Barnes
To: Juana Estevez

Mr. Barnes called at 2:15 p.m. while you were in a meeting. He said he was calling just to remind you about the meeting you have with him at 4:00 p.m. tomorrow. He said there is no need to call him back, and that he will see you at the office tomorrow.

電話留言

伯恩斯先生下午兩點十五分來電，那時您正在開會。他說他來電只是要提醒您，明天下午四點與他的會面。他說不需要回電給他，他明天會來辦公室跟您見面。

1 Biz 必通句型 Need-to-Know Phrases

1.1 ▸▸ 出價或討價還價

Making a Proposal or <u>Counter-Proposal</u>

 track 62

---

❶ I am willing to offer you (amount of money).

我願意向你出價（錢數）。

例 I'm willing to offer you $10 million.

　　我願意向你出價一千萬美元。

---

❷ Is (offer) acceptable to you? / How does (offer) sound?

（出價）你可以接受嗎？／（出價）聽起來如何？

例 Is $100 per unit acceptable to you?

　　每件一百美元你可以接受嗎？

例 How does 12 percent sound?

　　百分之十二聽起來如何？

---

❸ What do you think about (offer)?

（出價）你覺得如何？

例 What do you think about an offer of $500 per kilogram?

　　每公斤五百美元你覺得如何？

---

❹ This is my best offer: (offer).

這是我出的最高價：（出價）。

例 This is my best offer: $35,000 per month.

　　這是我出的最高價：每個月三萬五千美元。

Ⓦord List

counter-proposal 還價

❺ What about (counter-offer) instead?

那（還價）如何？

例 What about $15 million instead?

那一千五百萬美元如何？

❻ A better proposal would be (counter-offer).

更好的出價是（還價）。

例 A better proposal would be $120 per unit.

更好的出價是每件一百二十美元。

❼ Would you consider (counter-proposal)?

你可不可以考慮（還價）？

例 Would you consider $620 per kilogram?

你可不可以考慮每公斤六百二十美元？

❽ Can you improve your offer somewhat?

你出的價能不能多少提高一些？

例 Can you improve your offer somewhat? How about $39,000 per month?

你出的價能不能多少提高一些？每個月三萬九千美元如何？

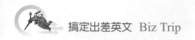

1.2 ▸▸ 接受和拒絕出價 Accepting and Rejecting Offers

❶ (Sb.'s) offer is acceptable.
（某人）出的價可以接受。
例 Sure, your offer is acceptable to me.
當然好，你出的價我可以接受。
例 Mr. Yoshihara's offer is acceptable to us.
吉原先生出的價我們可以接受。

❷ (Sb.) can agree to those terms.
（某人）能同意那些條件。
例 Yes, I can agree to those terms. We have a deal.
是的，我能同意那些條件。我們成交。

❸ We have a deal, then. / It's a deal. / Deal.
那麼我們就成交了。／那就成交。／成交。
例 It's a deal—let's sign the contract now.
那就成交——我們現在來簽約。

❹ I can go along with (offer).
我同意（出價）。
例 I can go along with $30 per unit.
我同意每件三十美元。

❺ I'm sorry, (offer) is not good enough.

抱歉，（報價）不夠令人滿意。

例 I'm sorry, $2 million is not good enough.

　　抱歉，兩百萬美元不夠令人滿意。

❻ I'm afraid I can't accept those (negative adj.) terms.

我恐怕沒辦法接受那些（負面形容詞）條件。

例 I'm afraid I can't accept those unfair terms.

　　我恐怕沒辦法接受那些不公平的條件。

❼ (Sb.) will have to do better than that.

（某人）得加價才行。

例 You will have to do better than that if you want to reach a deal.

　　如果你想達成交易，你得加價才行。

❽ (Offer) is totally unacceptable.

我們完全不能接受（報價）。

例 No, your offer of $15 per item is <u>totally</u> unacceptable.

　　不行，我們完全不能接受你出每件十五美元的價錢。

 ord List

totally [ˈtotl̩] *adv.* 完全地

2 實戰會話 Show Time

2.1 ▸▸ The Negotiation Begins track 63

Mel arrives at Juana's office and after a few minutes of small talk, two of them get into negotiations on importing some more of Juana's products.

Mel: As you know, I'm interested in increasing my orders from your company <u>substantially</u>, including importing some different lines as well. I'm willing to offer you $25 per unit on an order of one thousand.

Juana: I'm sorry, Mel, the offer is not good enough. What about $32 per unit?

Mel: Juana, I'm afraid I can't accept that. We have to keep costs down because it's a very competitive market. A better proposal would be $27.

Juana: You will have to do better than that, Mel. I still can't make much money on that kind of offer. Would you consider $30?

Mel: This is my best offer: $28.

Juana: Can you improve your offer somewhat?

Mel: No, I'm sorry. That is my final offer, Juana.

Juana: I can agree on the condition that you order at least 1,500 units.

Mel: I can't agree to your proposal unless you give me an additional 10 percent discount.

Juana: Well, if you increase your order to 2,000 units, then I will give you such a discount.

Mel: I'm sorry, I need more time to think about that quantity. I'm not in a position to make a decision on an order that large without <u>consulting</u> with my business partner. I don't want to make a <u>rash</u> decision.

Juana: Why don't you talk to your partner on the phone today, and we can meet again tomorrow?

Mel: Fine. I'll see you tomorrow.

譯文 開始協商

梅爾抵達華娜的辦公室，在閒聊幾分鐘後，兩個人針對進口更多華娜的產品開始協商。

梅爾：妳知道我有興趣大幅加訂妳們公司的產品，包括進口一些不同系列的東西。每一件我願意出價二十五美元，訂一千件。

華娜：抱歉，梅爾，你出的價不夠令人滿意。每件三十二美元如何？

梅爾：華娜，我恐怕沒辦法接受那個價錢。我們得盡量壓低成本因為市場非常競爭。比較好的出價是二十七美元。

華娜：你得要多加價才行，梅爾。你出那樣的價錢我還是沒什麼利潤。你願不願意考慮三十美元？

梅爾：這是我出的最高價：二十八美元。

華娜：你的價錢能不能再提高一些？

梅爾：不行，抱歉。這是我最後的出價，華娜。

華娜：如果你訂全少一千五百件，我就同意。

梅爾：除非妳額外給我百分之十的折扣，否則我不能同意妳提的價格。

華娜：嗯，如果你把訂貨量增加到兩千件，那我就給你這樣的折扣。

梅爾：很抱歉，那樣的量我需要多一點時間考慮。在沒跟我的合夥人商量之前，我沒有立場做這麼大筆訂單的決定。我不想草率做決定。

華娜：你何不今天跟你的合夥人通個電話，然後我們明天再碰一次面？

梅爾：好，我們明天見。

ord List

---

substantially [səb`stænʃəlɪ] *adv.* 相當大量地

consult [kən`sʌlt] *v.* 商量

rash [ræʃ] *adj.* 輕率的

2.2 ▸▸ The Negotiation Continues the Next Day

The next day, Mel comes to Juana's office again and they continue their negotiation.

Mel: I've talked it over with my business partner, and we can agree to those terms. Your offer is acceptable <u>based on</u> the conditions we've <u>specified</u>.

Juana: That's great! It's a deal then.

Mel: Let's move on then to another matter—the terms of payment. In the past, you've always given us 30 days credit in which to pay. However, with the larger orders that we are placing, what about giving us 90 days instead?

Juana: I'm afraid I can't accept those difficult terms, Mel.

Mel: OK, I understand. Perhaps 90 days is asking too much. Would you consider 60 days? That would really help us because we will be spending a lot more money on orders.

Juana: You know, Mel, 30 days really is our standard credit. Under some very <u>rare</u> <u>circumstances</u>, we've extended credit to a few customers up to 45 days. However, that's usually only in an emergency.

Mel: If 45 days is the best we can get, then we can go along with that <u>time frame</u>. That's not as good as we had hoped, but we can agree to those terms.

Juana: I suppose that 45 days would be acceptable to us as well. Sure, your offer is acceptable. I will have my secretary draw up a contract outlining all the details that we talked about and agreed to. It should be ready tomorrow morning for you to sign.

Mel: Great. I look forward to seeing you tomorrow.

譯文　次日繼續協商

隔天，梅爾再度來到華娜的辦公室，他們繼續協商。

梅爾：我跟我的合夥人討論過了。我們可以同意那些條件。根據我們已經訂明的條件，妳出的價我們可以接受。

華娜：太好了！那就成交囉。

梅爾：那麼我們來談談另一個問題——付款的條件。先前，你們一直給我們三十天的賒欠期。可是這次我們的訂量比較大，妳能不能改成給我們九十天呢？

華娜：我恐怕沒辦法接受那麼困難的條件，梅爾。

梅爾：好，我瞭解。也許九十天是要求過多了。妳可不可以考慮六十天呢？因為訂貨我們要花更多的錢，六十天對我們來說真的很有幫助。

華娜：你知道，梅爾，三十天真的是我們的標準賒欠期。在極為罕見的情況下，我們才會讓一些客戶將賒欠期延長至四十五天。不過，通常只在非常緊急的情況。

梅爾：如果四十五天是我們所能拿到的最好條件，那我們可以接受那樣的時間範圍。雖然不如我們希望的好，可是我們能同意那些條件。

華娜：我想四十五天我們也可以接受。沒問題，你的提議我們可以接受。我會要秘書擬好契約，條列我們談過以及同意的細項。明天早上契約應該就會準備好讓你簽字。

梅爾：好極了。我期待明天跟妳會面。

ord List

base on 以⋯⋯爲根據
specify [`spɛsə,faɪ] *v.* 詳細指明
rare [rɛr] *adj.* 稀少的

circumstance [`sɜkəm,stæns] *n.* 情況；情勢
time frame [`taɪm,frem] *n.* 時間範圍

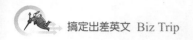

3 Biz 加分句型 Nice-to-Know Phrases

3.1 ▸▸ 有條件的接受 Accepting with Conditions **track 64**

❶ I agree on the condition that you (do sth.).
如果你（做某事），我就同意。
例 I agree on the condition that you sign a two-year contract.
如果你簽署一份兩年期的契約，我就同意。

❷ I accept your offer as long as you (do sth.).
只要你（做某事），我就接受你出的價。
例 I accept your offer as long as you shorten the delivery time.
只要你縮短送貨的時間，我就接受你出的價。

❸ I can't agree to your proposal unless you (do sth.).
除非你（做某事），不然我無法同意你的出價。
例 I can't agree to your proposal unless you give me a 10 percent discount.
除非你給我百分之十的折扣，不然我無法同意你的出價。

❹ If you (do sth.), then I will (do sth.).
如果你（做某事），那我就（做某事）。
例 If you increase your order, then I will sign the contract.
如果你增加訂貨，那我就簽約。

3.2 ▸ 要求多一些時間 Asking for More Time

❶ I need more time to (do sth.).
我需要更多時間（做某事）。
例 I'm sorry, but I need more time to get the money together for the project.
抱歉，可是我需要更多時間為這項計畫集資。

❷ (Sb.) would like to consider this proposal longer.
（某人）想要多一點的時間來考慮這項提案。
例 My manager would like to consider this proposal longer. I'll give you an answer next week.
我的經理想要多一點的時間來考慮這項提案。我下週會給你答案。

❸ I'm not in a position to make a decision.
我沒有立場做決定。
例 I'm not in a position to make a decision at this time.
此刻我沒有立場做決定。

❹ (Sb.) don't want to make a (adj.) decision.
（某人）不想（形容詞）做出決定。
例 We don't want to make a quick decision on this. I need a few days to think about it.
我們不想對此倉促做出決定。我需要幾天的時間考慮。

4 Biz 加分詞彙 Nice-to-Know Words & Phrases

 track 65

❶ trade-off [ˋtred͵ɔf] *n.* 交易；交換條件

❷ win-win situation 雙贏局面

❸ bargain [ˋbɑrgɪn] *n./v.* 討價還價

❹ bring (sth.) to the table 將（某事）提供出來

❺ compromise [ˋkɑmprə͵maɪz] *n.* 妥協

❻ confidentiality agreement [͵kɑnfə͵dɛnʃɪˋælɪtɪ ə͵grimənt]
   n. 保密協議

❼ deadlock [ˋdɛd͵lɑk] *n.* 僵局

❽ exclusive rights [ɪkˋsklusɪv ˋraɪts] *n.* 獨家代理權

❾ ink the deal 在契約上署名

❿ make a concession [kənˋsɛʃən] 讓步

⓫ minimum order [ˋmɪnəməm ˋɔrdə] *n.* 最低訂購量

⓬ quantity discount [ˋkwɑntətɪ ͵dɪskaʊnt] *n.* 量大折價

⓭ reach an impasse 陷入僵局

⓮ the bottom line 底線

⓯ warranty/guarantee [ˋwɔrəntɪ/͵gærənˋti] *n.* 擔保／保證

:::::::: **小心陷阱** ::::::::

☹ 錯誤用法：

I agree **in** the condition that you sign a two-year contract.

如果你簽署一份兩年期的契約，我就同意。

☺ 正確用法：

I agree **on** the condition that you sign a two-year contract.

如果你簽署一份兩年期的契約，我就同意。

:::::::: **Biz 一點通** ::::::::

There are several different <u>approaches</u> you can take to negotiating. Some believe that a tough, <u>confrontational</u> style is best. Others prefer a <u>give-and-take</u> attitude. Many experts say that it's important to be firm when negotiating. However, firm doesn't mean <u>inflexible</u>. If you are unwilling to compromise, it can be very difficult to conclude a negotiation. You want to also let the other party feel they are getting a good deal, especially if you hope to have a long-term business relationship with him or her. Negotiating can be a difficult, awkward process, but there are several skills you can learn to become an effective negotiator. The Web has plenty of good advice. Here are two good sites for <u>reference</u>: http://www.work911.com/articles/negotiate.htm and http://www.creativepro.com:80/story/feature/17093.html.

與人協商有好幾個不同的方法。有些人相信強悍、針鋒相對的風格是最好的。其他人則偏好互諒互讓的態度。很多專家認為，協商的時候，保持堅定的態度很重要。可是，堅定並不表示沒有彈性。如果你不願意妥協，想要搞定協商會很困難。你也要讓對方覺得達成交易對他們來說是有利的，特別是如果你想跟他或她有長遠生意往來的話。協商可能會是個棘手又尷尬的過程，可是要成為有效的協商者，有好幾種技巧可以學習。網路上有很多不錯的建議。這裡有兩個不錯的網站可供參考：http://www.work911.com/articles/negotiate.htm 以及 http://www.creativepro.com:80/story/feature/17093.html。

W ord List

approach [əˈprotʃ] *n.* 方法
confrontational [ˌkɑnfrʌnˈteʃənəl] *adj.* 對抗的
give-and-take 互諒互讓；（公平交換的）

inflexible [ɪnˈflɛksəbl] *adj.* 沒有彈性的
reference [ˈrɛfərəns] *n.* 參考；參照

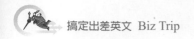
5 實戰演練 Practice Exercises

I 請為下列三句話選出最適合本章的中文譯義。

❶ This is my best offer.

(A) 這是我最好的貢獻。

(B) 這是我出的最高價。

(C) 這是我最佳的提議。

❷ I can agree to those terms.

(A) 我能接受那些期限。

(B) 我能認同那些術語。

(C) 我能同意那些條件。

❸ I agree on the condition that you sign a two-year contract.

(A) 如果你簽署一份兩年期的契約，我就同意。

(B) 我同意你簽署一份兩年期契約的狀況。

(C) 如果你以簽署一份兩年期的契約為條件，我就同意。

II 你會如何回答下面這兩句話？

❶ I can go along with that.

(A) Good, it's a deal!

(B) That's too bad.

(C) Where are you going?

❷ I can't accept those terms.

(A) What terms don't you understand?

(B) We can change the terms.

(C) Good, it's a deal!

III 請利用下列詞句寫一篇簡短的對話：

I'm willing to offer	would you consider	that's not good enough
as long as	on the condition that	it's a deal

＊解答請見 261 頁

實戰演練 Answer Keys

I 1. (B) 2. (B) 3. (C)

II 1. (B) 2. (C)

❶ 我認為還有更好的集合地點可選擇。
(A) 你說的對──那是絕佳的選擇。
(B) 你說的對──它的地理位置不佳。
(C) 我同意──那地點很理想。
❷ 它位處中心位置嗎？
(A) 對，靠近山區。
(B) 對，到那裡很困難。
(C) 對，就在市中心。

III 範例解答：

Jenny: I've changed my mind about the location for our convention. I think we should choose Vancouver instead of Tokyo.
Sam: What are the costs involved in holding it in Vancouver?
Jenny: Well, it would be cheaper than Tokyo, and more convenient. It's definitely cost-effective.
Sam: It sounds quite suitable. What are the facilities like at the hotel?
Jenny: I haven't chosen a hotel yet. I'll look into it and get back to you.

珍妮： 關於選擇我們的會議地點，我已經改變了主意。我想我們應該選溫哥華而不要選東京。
山姆： 在溫哥華舉行會議需要哪些花費呢？
珍妮： 嗯，會比東京便宜而且便利。絕對符合成本效益。
山姆： 聽起來蠻合適的。旅館的設施如何？
珍妮： 我尚未挑選旅館。我會調查一下然後向你回報。

246

ch 2 聯絡供應商與客戶

I 1. (A) 2. (B) 3. (B)

II 1. (C) 2. (A)

❶ 我那個時間走不開。
   (A) 好，我們到時候見。
   (B) 那也是條不錯的領帶。
   (C) 好吧，我們別的時間碰面。
❷ 星期三下午四點半我方便。
   (A) 那個時間我也可以。
   (B) 好，那我們改別的時間。
   (C) 那個時間我也不行。

III 範例解答：

Steve: Denise, I'd like to talk to you about a few things tomorrow. When is a good time for you?
Denise: How about at two o'clock?
Steve: I'm sorry. That won't work for me. Are you available in the morning?
Denise: Yes, the morning is convenient for me.
Steve: Great. Let's make it 10:00 a.m. then.

史蒂夫：丹尼絲，我明天想跟妳談幾件事情。妳什麼時候方便？
丹尼絲：兩點如何？
史蒂夫：很抱歉，我那個時間不行。妳早上有空嗎？
丹尼絲：有，我早上方便。
史蒂夫：好極了。那我們就約早上十點。

ch**3** 預約設備、場地和房間

I 1. (A)　2. (B)　3. (B)

II 1. (B)　2. (A)

❶ 你能不能幫我保留那個？
　　(A) 我得把它放在哪裡？
　　(B) 當然，我會為你預留的。
　　(C) 好，我可以等。
❷ 房間很寬敞嗎？
　　(A) 是的，房間很大。
　　(B) 是的，房間很乾淨。
　　(C) 是的，房間很漂亮。

III 範例解答：

Barbara:	Hello. I'd like to inquire about your hotel and convention facilities.
Hotel clerk:	Certainly. What would you like to know?
Barbara:	Do you have any vacancies from October 1 to the 7th? Also, could you tell me the room rates?
Hotel clerk:	Yes, we can accommodate you on those dates. The price for a double room is US$150 per night.
Barbara:	I'd like to book one of your convention halls as well.
Hotel clerk:	We have one that can fit two hundred-fifty people at a very reasonable price.
Barbara:	Unfortunately, that won't do. We need one for four hundred people. Is there anything else available at that time?
Hotel clerk:	Yes, you can book our larger hall that holds up to five hundred people.

芭芭拉：	你好，我想詢問一下有關你們的旅館以及會議設施。
旅館人員：	沒問題。您想知道哪些事情呢？
芭芭拉：	你們十月一號到七號有空房嗎？還有，你可不可以告訴我房間價錢？
旅館人員：	是的，那幾天我們有房間可供您使用。一間雙人房每晚美金 150 元。
芭芭拉：	我也想訂一間你們的會議廳。
旅館人員：	我們有一間能容納兩百五十個人，價錢很合理。
芭芭拉：	很可惜，那間不行。我們需要一間能容納四百人的。那個時段還有沒有什麼別的會議廳可以租用？
旅館人員：	有的，你可以訂我們大一點的會議廳，那一間可以容納得下五百人。

ch4 安排旅行事宜

I 1. (B) 2. (C) 3. (C)

II 1. (B) 2. (A)

❶ 你的護照無效。
  (A) 你說的對，我的護照遺失了。
  (B) 你說的對，我的護照過期了。
  (C) 你說的對，這護照不是我的。
❷ 你的國籍地是哪裡？
  (A) 我住在台灣。
  (B) 我要去加拿大。
  (C) 此刻，我正在參訪你的國家。

III 範例解答：

Lyle:	Hi, I'd like to book a flight to Boston. I'd like a window seat, please.
Travel agent:	Sure. You'll need to apply for a visa. What type would you like?
Lyle:	I want a multiple-entry visa.
Travel agent:	OK, you will need to go to the U.S. trade office. What will be your length of stay?
Lyle:	Three weeks in the U.S. Oh, and I have a frequent flyer card.
Travel agent:	I'll make sure that your account is credited. Thank you for your business.

萊爾：	你好，我想訂往波士頓的班機。我想要靠窗的位置，麻煩你。
旅行社人員：	好的。您得要申請簽證。您要哪種簽證？
萊爾：	我要多次入境的簽證。
旅行社人員：	好，您得去一趟美國貿易代表處。您會待多久？
萊爾：	在美國待三星期。噢，我有飛行常客卡。
旅行社人員：	我會確認記入到您的帳戶上。謝謝您的惠顧。

ch5 啟程和抵達

I 1. (C) 2. (A) 3. (C)

II 1. (A) 2. (B)

❶ 你的目的地是什麼地方？
   (A) 我要去紐約。
   (B) 我從台北來。
   (C) 我是學生。
❷ 你來訪的目的是什麼？
   (A) 我要待兩週。
   (B) 我來出差。
   (C) 我沒有東西要申報。

III 範例解答：

Clerk:　　Good morning, sir. What is your destination?
Tina:　　Hi, I'm heading to Tokyo. I have one suitcase to check in.
Clerk:　　Here is your boarding pass. Have a good flight.
At the destination airport
Customs:　Do you have anything to declare?
Tina:　　I have some duty-free items, but nothing to declare. Where is the baggage carousel?
Customs:　You can check for it on the monitors inside.

職員：　　早安，先生。您要去哪裡？
提娜：　　嗨，我要去東京。我有個行李箱要托運。
職員：　　這是您的登機證。祝您旅途愉快。
在目的地的機場
海關：　　你有什麼東西要申報嗎？
提娜：　　我有一些免稅商品，可是沒有要申報的東西。請問行李轉盤在哪裏？
海關：　　你可以在裡面的電腦螢幕上查詢。

ch6 搭計程車和其他交通工具

I 1. (B) 2. (C) 3. (C)

II 1. (C) 2. (C)

❶ 這輛計程車照表收費嗎？
(A) 是的，我每趟收美金一百元。
(B) 是的，我有執照。
(C) 是的，我每公里收美金兩元。

❷ 車資多少？
(A) 是的，這是合理的價格。
(B) 我欠你美金二十元。
(C) 美金二十元。

III 範例解答：

George: Excuse me. I'm lost. Where can I catch a taxi to downtown?
Clerk: The taxi stand is on the lower level.
George: How do I get there?
Clerk: Take that escalator over there.
George: Thanks.
To the taxi driver
George: Hi. I'd like to go downtown.
Taxi driver: OK. I charge a flat rate. The fare will be $35.

喬治：   對不起。我迷路了。請問哪裡有計程車可以搭到市中心去？
職員：   計程車招呼站在下一層。
喬治：   我要怎麼到下一層？
職員：   搭那邊的電扶梯。
喬治：   謝謝。
跟計程車司機說
喬治：   你好，我想去市中心。
計程車司機：好的。我收均一費用，車資是三十五美元。

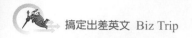

ch7 | 入住旅館

I 1. (A) 2. (B) 3. (A)

II 1. (C) 2. (C)

❶ 抱歉，我們的網路現在沒辦法連線。
   (A) 什麼時候會回升？
   (B) 什麼時候才不會下來？
   (C) 什麼時候會恢復正常？
❷ 對不起，我們現在沒有同等級的房間。
   (A) 那麼我什麼時候可以搬？
   (B) 那麼我也許應該辦理入住手續。
   (C) 那麼你能不能幫我換到好一點的房間？

III 範例解答：

Front desk: May I help you?
You:　　　Hi. This is room 420. I have some problems. My TV is not working properly, I'm having trouble hooking up to the wireless Internet, and the toilet won't stop running.
Front desk: I see. Let me contact the manager. Hold please.
You:　　　Thank you.
Manager:　This is the manager. I understand you're having some trouble with your room?
You:　　　Yes. The TV, wireless Internet, and toilet are not working properly. Also, I'm too far from the elevator. I'd like to change rooms right away if it's possible.
Manager:　Let me see what I can do.

櫃臺人員：　有什麼需要為您效勞的嗎？
你：　　　　嗨，這裡是 420 號房。我碰到了一些麻煩。我的電視無法正常使用、我沒辦法連結上無線網路，而且，馬桶的水流個不停。
櫃臺人員：　我知道了。讓我聯絡經理，請別掛斷。
你：　　　　謝謝。
經理：　　　我是飯店經理。我知道你的房間出了一些問題？
你：　　　　是的。電視、無線網路和馬桶都不能正常運作。還有，我房間離電梯太遠。如果可能的話，我希望能馬上換房。
經理：　　　讓我看看我能夠怎麼處理。

ch8 觀光與購物

I 1. (A) 2. (C) 3. (B)

II 1. (C) 2. (B)

❶ 價格可以商量嗎？
  (A) 可以，這是售價。
  (B) 可以，這是最低價了。
  (C) 可以，我們可以給你一個折扣。
❷ 這商品有瑕疵。
  (A) 那樣的話，我給你一個折扣。
  (B) 那樣的話，我退錢給你。
  (C) 那樣的話，我用信用卡來付。

III 範例解答：

In a department store

Karen: Hi. I want to see some tourist attractions. Where can I buy a guidebook? Any recommendations?

Clerk: In the book department on the fifth floor. By the way, I can recommend a great tour for you.

Karen: Thanks. Where and what time will I be picked up?

Clerk: At noon in front of your hotel.

Karen: Thank you. By the way, I bought a defective camera. Where can I get a refund or exchange?

Clerk: Go to the customer service counter.

在百貨公司裡

凱倫：　你好，我想參觀一些觀光景點。哪裡可以買到旅遊指南呢？你能推薦一下嗎？

服務員：在五樓的書籍部。對了，我可以推薦你一個很棒的行程。

凱倫：　謝謝。他們會到哪裡來接？幾點來接呢？

服務員：就在你下榻的飯店前面，中午的時候。

凱倫：　謝謝。對了，我買到一台有瑕疵的相機。我可以拿去哪裡退款或更換？

服務員：到顧客服務櫃臺。

ch9 處理特殊情況

I 1. (C) 2. (A) 3. (C)

II 1. (A) 2. (B)

❶ 最少要住三個月。
  (A) 我計劃要住超過三個月。
  (B) 那好，因為我只住一個月。
  (C) 當然，三個月夠久了。
❷ 那個毛病你可以買成藥吃。
  (A) 可是我還沒看醫生。
  (B) 好。藥房在哪呢？
  (C) 我不知道櫃台在哪裡。

III 範例解答：

Landlord: If you want to stay here, you need to sign a long-term lease and leave a security deposit.
Cynthia: Are the utilities included in the rent?
Landlord: No, they are extra.
Cynthia: OK, I'll take it. By the way, can you tell me where the nearest medical clinic is? I feel a little sick. I think I need to get a prescription.
Landlord: There is one nearby. Let me write the address down for you.

房東： 如果妳要住這裡，必須簽長期租約，然後留一份保證金。
辛西亞： 水電包不包含在房租裡面？
房東： 不包含，要另外付。
辛西亞： 好，我要租。對了，你可不可以告訴我最靠近這裡的診所在哪？我有點不舒服。我想我得去拿個處方籤。
房東： 附近就有一家。我把地址寫下來給妳。

ch10 高效率使用電話

I 1. (A) 2. (B) 3. (A)

II 1. (B) 2. (B)

❶ 電話訊號不清楚。
   (A) 我說錯話了嗎？
   (B) 我馬上再回電給你。
   (C) 抱歉——我會幫你。
❷ 我該讓你去忙了。
   (A) 謝謝你等候。
   (B) 好，以後再聊。
   (C) 當然，你想去哪？

III 範例解答：

Pauline:	Good afternoon, Pauline speaking. How may I help you?
Brandon:	May I speak with Dennis Fong?
Pauline:	He's on another line. Would you like to hold?
Brandon:	Sure, thanks.

Two minutes later.

Pauline:	I'll put you through to Dennis, now.
Dennis:	Hello, Brandon. How are you?
Brandon:	Good, thanks. How about you?

Brandon and Dennis talk for 10 minutes.

Dennis:	Thanks for calling, Brandon. It was nice talking to you.
Brandon:	You, too. Bye.

寶琳：	午安，我是寶琳。有什麼我可以效勞的？
布蘭登：	我可以跟丹尼斯・方說話嗎？
寶琳：	他正在講電話。您要不要稍待？
布蘭登：	好啊。謝謝。

兩分鐘過後。

寶琳：	我現在幫您接丹尼斯。
丹尼司：	哈囉，布蘭登。你好嗎？
布蘭登：	很好，謝謝。你呢？

布蘭登和丹尼司談了十分鐘。

丹尼司：	布蘭登，謝謝來電。和你談話真愉快。
布蘭登：	跟你聊聊也很愉快。再見。

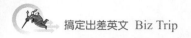

ch11 參觀及參加商展

I 1. (C) 2. (A) 3. (C)

II 1. (A) 2. (C)

❶ 這台相機附有電池和相機盒。
   (A) 太棒了——我正需要。
   (B) 電池和相機盒要多少錢？
   (C) 你不覺太貴了嗎？
❷ 您要不要看看這項產品的示範操作？
   (A) 不用，我不知道這怎麼操作。
   (B) 好，用起來很簡單。
   (C) 不用了，謝謝。我沒興趣。

III 範例解答：

Alice: How much is the admission fee to the trade show?

Peter: Not much. Only a few dollars. Let's check out that exhibition booth showing those cool cell phones.

Alice: Good idea.

Exhibitor: Hi. Here's my business card. Would you like a demonstration of any of our products? This product comes in three different styles.

Peter: No, thanks. I'm just looking. Actually, I think I'm going to check out the other exhibition hall now. Maybe I'll stop back by later.

愛麗斯： 商展的門票要多少錢？

彼得： 不多。只要幾塊錢。咱們去瞧瞧那個在展示那些酷炫手機的攤位。

愛麗斯： 好主意。

參展廠商： 你好。這是我的名片。你們要不要看我示範如何操作我們的產品？這個產品有三個不同的樣式。

彼得： 不用了，謝謝。我只是看看。事實上我現在要去瞧瞧另外一個展覽廳。也許我等一下會回來。

ch 12 帶人參觀設備

I 1. (A) 2. (C) 3. (B)

II 1. (C) 2. (B)

❶ 你有沒有什麼特別想看的？
  (A) 沒有，我沒看到那個。
  (B) 有，我看到那個了。
  (C) 有，產品陳列室。
❷ 謝謝撥時間前來參觀。
  (A) 抱歉我現在沒時間。
  (B) 是我的榮幸。很有趣。
  (C) 我可以下週過來。

III 範例解答：

Stephanie: Our company was established in 1988. Our products include jewelry, watches, and similar products.

Vince: I see. I'm fairly familiar with your line.

Stephanie: Are you interested in taking a tour of our factory?

Vince: Sure, thanks.

Stephanie: Please come this way. Coming up ahead on the left is one of our main jewelry cutting machines.

The factory tour lasts for 45 minutes.

Stephanie: I hope you enjoyed the tour.

Vince: Yes, thanks. It was quite interesting.

史蒂芬妮： 我們公司成立於 1988 年。我們的產品包括珠寶、手錶以及其他類似的相關產品。

凡斯： 我了解了。我對妳們的產品系列還算蠻熟悉的。

史蒂芬妮： 你有沒有興趣參觀一下我們的工廠？

凡斯： 當然，謝謝。

史蒂芬妮： 麻煩你往這邊。接下來在你左手邊的是我們主要的珠寶切割機之一。

工廠導覽為時四十五分鐘。

史蒂芬妮： 我希望你對這趟參觀感到滿意。

凡斯： 是的，謝謝妳。相當有意思。

ch 13 討論合作計畫

I 1. (A) 2. (C) 3. (C)

II 1. (B) 2. (A)

❶ 公司下個月會成為股份有限公司嗎？
  (A) 是的，那是因為生意不好。
  (B) 是的，那時公司會正式註冊。
  (C) 是的，那時公司就會對外開放。
❷ 這項交易還需要做最後的定案。
  (A) 我們可以晚一點再處理。
  (B) 現在不能改變了。
  (C) 對，上星期就完成了。

III 範例解答：

Hank:　Jane, I'd like to do business with you. I have a business proposal for you.
Jane:　Really? I'd like to hear it.
Hank:　It's mutually beneficial. It gives you a minority stake for only a small investment.
Jane:　What is the return on investment like?
Hank:　I think it will be about 25 percent per year.
Jane:　That sounds good.
Hank:　I can draft an agreement within a week. Let's meet again to discuss it.

漢克：　珍，我想跟妳做生意。我要向妳提個企劃案。
珍：　　真的嗎？我想聽聽看。
漢克：　這個案子雙方能互蒙其利。妳只要投資一點點就能擁有小部分股份。
珍：　　投資利潤如何？
漢克：　我想一年大約有百分之 25 的利潤。
珍：　　聽起來還不錯。
漢克：　我一週內就能草擬一份契約。我們到時再碰面討論一下。

ch14 帶領討論或研討會

I 1. (A) 2. (C) 3. (B)

II 1. (A) 2. (B)

❶ 大家對傑克的說法有什麼意見？
   (A) 我想他說的算公正。
   (B) 我覺得傑克人不錯。
   (C) 我認為它是正確的。
❷ 我沒聽懂你的意思。
   (A) 你轉錯彎了。
   (B) 我會好好解釋。
   (C) 你現在可以走了。

III 範例解答：

Dennis: Today, I'd like to talk about our sales performance last quarter. The sales performance was.... The next matter I want to talk about is ways we can improve our sales this year.... Let's turn to the next item, which is: How we can motivate our sales team?... Does anyone have any comments on this topic?

June: What about offering a trip to Hawaii to the top salesperson?

Dennis: I tend to think trips are good ideas.... OK, to sum up, we need to implement some new methods to improve sales.

丹尼司： 今天，我想談談我們在上一季的銷售業績。我們的業績……。我想談的下一件事是我們今年要如何改進我們的業務。……我們轉到下一個議題，那就是：我們要怎麼加強銷售團隊的工作動機？……針對這個主題，有沒有人想發言？

濬： 提供超級業務員一趟夏威夷度假之旅如何？

丹尼司： 我傾向認為旅遊這點子不錯。……好，總而言之，我們需要實施一些新方法，以改進業績。

ch 15 上台報告

I 1. (A) 2. (C) 3. (A)

II 1. (A) 2. (B)

❶ 我們來仔細研究一下這項產品。
   (A) 看來不錯。
   (B) 我看不到——太遠了。
   (C) 我有興趣聽更多。
❷ 請保留您的問題。
   (A) 好，我有兩個問題。
   (B) 好，我稍後再問。
   (C) 好，謝謝你的回答。

III 範例解答：

Jasmine: Hello everyone. I'm very happy to be here today. I'm here today to talk to you about the importance of setting goals. Setting goals and revising them are two of the most important things you can do. In other words, it's vital to have a plan for your life.

Does anyone have any questions? No? OK, that concludes my presentation. Thanks for listening.

潔思敏：　大家好。很高興今天來到此地。今天在這裡，我要跟各位談談設定目標的重要性。設定目標和修正目標，是各位可以做的事當中最重要的兩件。換句話說，生涯規劃極為重要。

有沒有人有問題？沒有嗎？好，那我的報告就到此為止。謝謝你們的聆聽。

ch16 協商交易

I 1. (B) 2. (C) 3. (A)

II 1. (A) 2. (B)

❶ 我可以同意那個。
   (A) 好，成交！
   (B) 那太糟了。
   (C) 你要去哪裡？
❷ 我無法接受那些條件。
   (A) 哪些條件你不懂？
   (B) 我們可以改條件。
   (C) 好，成交！

III 範例解答：

Wayne: I'm willing to offer you $100 per unit.
Jessica: I'm sorry that's not good enough. Would you consider $140 instead?
Wayne: What do you think about $120?
Jessica: I could accept $125 on the condition that you order at least 10,000 per year.
Wayne: That's acceptable as long as you reduce the delivery charge by 10 percent.
Jessica: It's a deal.

偉恩： 我願意出每件一百美元。
潔西卡： 抱歉，那不夠令人滿意。你可不可以考慮一百四十美元？
偉恩： 一百二十美元妳覺得如何？
潔西卡： 如果你每年至少訂一萬個，我就能接受一百二十五美元。
偉恩： 只要妳運費降百分之十，那就能接受。
潔西卡： 成交。

⑬ 貝塔語言出版 訂 購 單

訂購日期：_____年_____月_____日

■收件人資料

姓名：_____ □女 □男　　生日：民國____年____月____日

聯絡電話：（手機）_____　（0）_____

Email：_____

寄書地址：□□□ _____

開立發票：□二聯式　□三聯式

　　　　發票抬頭：_____　　統一編號：_____

　　　　持卡人姓名：_____　　身份證字號：_____

信用卡卡號：_____－_____－_____－_____ □□□（請填卡片背面末3碼）

信用卡有效期限：西元____年____月止

信用卡簽名：_____（需與信用卡上相同）

信用卡類別：□VISA □MASTER □聯合信用卡　發卡銀行：_____

我要訂購

A 搞定英文全系列　單本 9 折，三本以上 79 折

□ 搞定英文面試【書+1CD】定價＄220，____本

□ 搞定接待英文【書+2CD】定價＄320，____本　□ 搞定商務電話【書+2CD】定價＄320，____本

□ 搞定產品簡報【書+2CD】定價＄350，____本　□ 搞定辦公室英文【書+1MP3】定價＄320，____本

□ 搞定會議英文【書+2CD】定價＄320，____本　□ 稿定商務口說【書+2CD】定價＄350，____本

□ 搞定口說錯誤【書+2CD】定價＄320，____本　□ 搞定進階商務口說【書+1MP3】定價＄380，____本

□ 搞定談判英文【書+2CD】定價＄350，____本　□ 搞定行銷英文【書+1MP3】定價＄320，____本

任選三本以上，可額外加購：

　　　　　　　　　　　　　　　□ 出差900句典一本，特惠價＄149元

□ 辦公室900句典一本，特惠價＄149元　□ 購物900句典一本，特惠價＄149元

B 經濟學人套書　超值特惠價＄1490，____套

🛒 購書數量不足四本，需酌收運費70元，金額總計 ＄_____

■注意事項

1. 持卡人聲明已受前項告知，並同意依照信用卡使用約定，一經訂購或使用商品，均應按照所示之全部金額付款予發卡銀行。

2. 本公司保留接受訂單與否的權利。

3. 如有退貨（持卡人請自行負擔退貨運費），請連同發票一起於發票上日期起算7天之內退回（郵寄者以郵戳為憑）。

4. 請將本單填妥於上方簽名確認後，傳真或郵寄此張訂購單予本公司，我們會有專人為您服務，並儘速將貨品送至指定地點（最遲14個工作天）。

5. 當您收到商品時，請檢查送貨單、發票、商品及數量是否正確，若有任何疑問，請立即與本公司聯絡，客服部專線：（02）2314-3535，24小時傳真：（02）2312-3535，以確保您的權益。

6. 郵局劃撥帳號：1949-3777，戶名：貝塔出版有限公司，門市：台北市館前路12號11樓。

7. 請於傳真後2個工作天，週一至週五上班日9：30-17：30來電查詢。

國家圖書館出版品預行編目資料

搞定出差英文 = Biz Trip / Brian Foden 著；謝
靜雯譯. ──初版. ──臺北市：貝塔, 2007
〔民 96〕　　面；　　公分
　　ISBN 978-957-729-660-3（平裝附光碟片）
　　1. 商業英文　2. 讀本
805.18　　　　　　　　　　　　　96012940

搞定出差英文
Biz Trip

作　　者 / Brian Foden
譯　　者 / 謝靜雯
執行編輯 / 胡元媛
協力編輯 / 官芝羽

出　　版 / 貝塔出版有限公司
地　　址 / 台北市 100 館前路 12 號 11 樓
電　　話 / (02) 2314-2525
傳　　真 / (02) 2312-3535
客服專線 / (02) 2314-3535
客服信箱 / btservice@betamedia.com.tw
郵撥帳號 / 19493777
帳戶名稱 / 貝塔出版有限公司

總 經 銷 / 時報文化出版企業股份有限公司
地　　址 / 桃園縣龜山鄉萬壽路二段 351 號
電　　話 / (02) 2306-6842

出版日期 / 2008 年 12 月初版二刷
定　　價 / 320 元
ISBN : 978-957-729-660-3

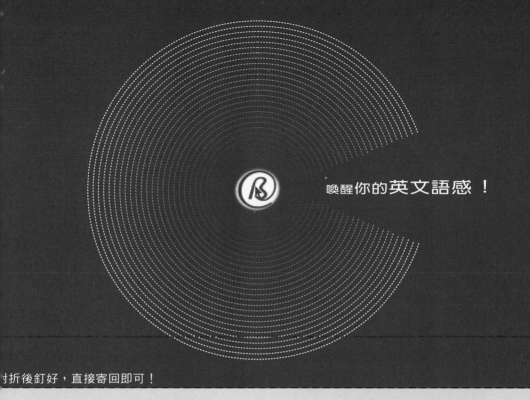

喚醒你的英文語感！

對折後釘好，直接寄回即可！

100 台北市中正區館前路12號11樓

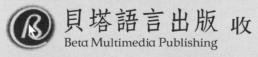

貝塔語言出版 收
Beta Multimedia Publishing

寄件者住址 ☐☐☐

謝謝您購買本書！！

貝塔語言擁有最優良之英文學習書籍，為提供您最佳的英語學習資訊，您可填妥此

表後寄回（免貼郵票）將可不定期收到本公司最新發行書訊及活動訊息！

姓名：＿＿＿＿＿＿＿＿＿＿　性別：□男 □女　生日：＿＿＿年＿＿＿月＿＿＿日

電話：(公)＿＿＿＿＿＿＿＿(宅)＿＿＿＿＿＿＿＿(手機)＿＿＿＿＿＿＿＿

電子信箱：＿＿＿＿＿＿＿＿＿＿＿＿＿＿＿＿＿＿＿＿＿＿

學歷：□高中職含以下 □專科 □大學 □研究所含以上

職業：□金融 □服務 □傳播 □製造 □資訊 □軍公教 □出版

　　　□自由 □教育 □學生 □其他

職級：□企業負責人 □高階主管 □中階主管 □職員 □專業人士

1. 您購買的書籍是？＿＿＿＿＿＿＿＿＿＿＿＿＿＿＿＿

2. 您從何處得知本產品？(可複選)

　　　□書店 □網路 □書展 □校園活動 □廣告信函 □他人推薦 □新聞報導 □其他

3. 您覺得本產品價格：

　　　□偏高 □合理 □偏低

4. 請問目前您每週花了多少時間學英語？

　　　□ 不到十分鐘 □ 十分鐘以上，但不到半小時 □ 半小時以上，但不到一小時

　　　□ 一小時以上，但不到兩小時 □ 兩個小時以上 □ 不一定

5. 通常在選擇語言學習書時，哪些因素是您會考慮的？

　　　□ 封面 □ 內容、實用性 □ 品牌 □ 媒體、朋友推薦 □ 價格□ 其他＿＿＿＿

6. 市面上您最需要的語言書種類為？

　　　□ 聽力 □ 閱讀 □ 文法 □ 口說 □ 寫作 □ 其他＿＿＿＿＿

7. 通常您會透過何種方式選購語言學習書籍？

　　　□ 書店門市 □ 網路書店 □ 郵購 □ 直接找出版社 □ 學校或公司團購

　　　□ 其他＿＿＿＿＿＿

8. 給我們的建議：＿＿＿＿＿＿＿＿＿＿＿＿＿＿＿＿＿＿＿＿＿＿

＿＿＿＿＿＿＿＿＿＿＿＿＿＿＿＿＿＿＿＿＿＿＿＿＿＿＿＿＿＿＿

Get a Feel for English !

喚醒你的英文語感！